Finding True Center

Finding True Center

A GOLF STORY ABOUT LIFE

Michael J. Gordon

iUniverse, Inc.
New York Lincoln Shanghai

Finding True Center
A GOLF STORY ABOUT LIFE

Copyright © 2004 by Michael J. Gordon

All rights reserved. No part of this book may be used or reproduced by any means, graphic, electronic, or mechanical, including photocopying, recording, taping or by any information storage retrieval system without the written permission of the publisher except in the case of brief quotations embodied in critical articles and reviews.

iUniverse books may be ordered through booksellers or by contacting:

iUniverse
2021 Pine Lake Road, Suite 100
Lincoln, NE 68512
www.iuniverse.com
1-800-Authors (1-800-288-4677)

ISBN-13: 978-0-595-31298-6 (pbk)
ISBN-13: 978-0-595-66292-0 (cloth)
ISBN-13: 978-0-595-76115-9 (ebk)
ISBN-10: 0-595-31298-5 (pbk)
ISBN-10: 0-595-66292-7 (cloth)
ISBN-10: 0-595-76115-1 (ebk)

Printed in the United States of America

Acknowledgements

Inspiration has a new accomplice in Sean Breeze. Your bravery, resolve, and quite dignity make me honored to call you friend.

Tim Murray had been my boss for quite some time before we played our first noteworthy round of golf. One cold, rainy spring morning, Tim was up for a game when all others would bow to bad weather. Although soaked from head-to-toe in forty-degree mud and muck, we managed to not only enjoy the morning, but to also discover we shared a unique interest in a side of golf many overlook—the rich world of golf literature. This shared appreciation for the games great stories and our constant book swapping helped inspire putting this story to paper. Tim is a valued sounding board, friend, and one of my absolute favorite golf buddies.

I must also express tremendous appreciation to my longtime friend, Kyle Stephens. Kyle is not only one of the smartest of our bunch, but a truly loyal and trusted soul. Were it not for his many hours of proofreading, encouragement, and drinking habits, this book and many other unmentionable yet memorable events in my life might never have happened. Bottoms up, Kyle!

Laurie Scavo I have not known long. This proves the theory that if we are fortunate enough to meet one interesting person every few years, we are indeed lucky. My appreciation for her work helping me get this book right is exceeded only by the fondness I have for her as a person and the respect I have for her many unique talents.

Greta Gilbert is amazing. No one person has invested more time, more soul, or has taught me more about writing than you have. These gifts, and the many other things you have shared with me, and all I have learned through you, will be with me all of my life.

My sweet Saint of a sister Marcia also deserves my warmest, heartfelt appreciation. Her support of my writing, willingness to critique pitiful drafts over and again, when certainly tired of doing so, means more than she can ever imagine. Without her love I would surly feel orphaned. She always serves to remind me that I am not without family, that I am not alone.

Finally, and as importantly, Darryl, Dedo, DOC, D, a man of many monikers and the greatest friend anyone could have. Somehow, the word friend seems nowhere near worthy enough to describe the miles we have traveled, the countless rounds of golf, the great times we've shared, and all you have done for me over the years. While many of our actual experiences have been fictionalized in these pages, the deep and unwavering friendship you have given could never be properly described in this or any book. I can't wait to expand our sojourn and embark upon our next great series of adventures. And by the way—you're pressed!

Chapter 1

Rounding the street corner, Nick Rose forced a swallow past the dryness in his throat. This was not a part of town he was familiar with, and he swore never to return under such a circumstance. Pausing for one final drag from his cigarette as he stood beneath a crude, hand-painted plywood sign confirming his destination, Nick considered his options. He had none. Beyond that sign humiliation lay waiting, a humiliation that just days before he never could have imagined. Late each Tuesday evening the *Mutter Mill Café* held open mike night, and Nick was scheduled fourth among seven aspiring poets allowed ten minutes to present their work. Only Nick would never need such a generous allotment of time as he had never considered, written, or read aloud a single line of poetry during the first twenty-eight years of his life. He'd never even met anyone with such dreams.

That's what made it such a brilliant bet.

World peace, ending hunger, finding a cure for cancer—when it came to concern with such weighty matters, Nick's life-long friend Easy was fond of saying, "There's not much water in Nick's end of the pool."

As Nick's name was announced to a smattering of polite applause, he dutifully approached the Café's empty stage, a wash of powder-blue stage lights instantly and without flattery sucking what little color remained from his ghostly, remote expression. He threw a quick glance toward Easy, now perched on the edge of his seat.

To Nick's way of thinking, splashing around alone in life's shallow end was perfectly normal. It had always left him unlikely to drown, as he thought Easy often did, in the arcane and absurd. Nick had feigned interest in his fair share of dinner party intellectualism over the years, from dissecting the values of post-modern Buddhism and holistic water-reading techniques, to the lesser writings of Homi Bhabha, and he considered nothing more ridiculous. Who cares if there's a there, there? And why torment oneself by scribbling such questions on sticky notes and pasting them to every flat surface in the cosmos? Fuck's fucked and that's that. A *Golf Digest* man, a Marlboro man, the only time Nick had bothered cracking a book since college he was stuck either in an airport or a television was unavailable. On those rare occasions, crime stories and tales of the early West were his books of choice, certainly not poetry.

As he silently cursed his eighteenth hole, double-bogey choke-job of that past Saturday, Nick unfolded a sheet of paper from his back pocket and inched closer to the microphone. With a shaky cadence, he reluctantly engaged his obligation. "My name is Nick Rose and my first poem is called 'Bunkered.'"

"Inside, inside I fight
Outside, I lie
Bunkered, I fight to reclaim my soul
Waves of self-affliction plunge me deeper, deeper
Hazards everywhere, wet penalties of the womb abound
What troubles me?
What guides me?
What aligns me?
What is my par?
In emerald green I find my answers
Inside, I may struggle forth

Outside, I can no longer lie
For I am my own marshal."

As Easy rose from his seat to offer a solitary, passionate ovation, the more than thirty others seated around him stared curiously ahead, as if watching a turtle lying on its back and struggling to turn over. Undaunted, yet shaking like a French soldier, Nick flipped the paper Easy had prepared and continued his scheduled reading.

"You bitch
Wicked, icy, mean
Cruel, deceptive
Unreceptive
Wry, conniving
You, without a conscience
Silently I scream
So impossible to read
Why are you doing this to me?
You, with little hesitation
Not at work
Not at home
Wicked, icy, fast and mean
You stabbed my heart
You three-putt green."

Despite the benefit of very little blood in what Nick often liked to call his alcohol system, with each verse his stage persona grew abundantly more painful than humorous to look upon. The naked self-consciousness, the total exposure of standing center stage in this grim, smoky café surrounded by beatnik, pony-tailed hipsters brought a feverish sensation to his face. As the crowd's gaze turned increasingly sour with each syllable, so grew Easy's reflection of his enjoyment for every second of Nick's indignity. Resigned to his fate and to one final verse from Easy's pen, Nick sucked back a deep breath.

> "I got an emptiness deep inside
> And I've tried
> But I can't let it go
> I'm not a man who likes to swear
> But I never cared for the sound of being alone
> I am, I said
> To no one there
> And no one heard at all
> Not even the chair
> I am, I cried
> I am, said I
> And I am lost and I can't even say why
> Leaving me lonely still."

Before the final line had fully crossed Nick's lips, a middle-aged, ascot-wearing patron with a keenly polished head rose from his chair, dismissively waved his long brown cigarette toward Nick, and shouted, "That's horseshit, sir. That's a fucking Neil Diamond song!"

Nick stood dumbfounded. Easy could hardly swallow his beer.

Quick to acknowledge a diverse range of quirky interests, Easy did not write poetry. This, he would claim, was to be his first and only writing. He had composed Nick's prose with but a single goal in mind: sheer torture.

Facing the piercing, icy, affronted stares of tomorrow's forgotten poets, beyond offended by his patently fraudulent attempt to join their club, their inner circle, Nick quickly left the stage, his thoughts flashing back to another moment of traumatic self-consciousness, back to his first public school shower after gym class the first week of sixth grade. *What in the hell is everyone looking at?*

Nick's "poetry" reading also served to underscore another simple yet overriding truth—losing a bet to Easy sucked.

Adding to the evening's considerable disgrace was Easy's flare for grinding salt, a screwdriver, whatever happened to be handy, into Nick's endless supply of open wounds. "Nick, don't play me, play the course," he would smugly drone. Or, "Nick, golf is war in disguise as a sport, and you were once again unarmed." Getting under Nick's skin with pseudo-philosophical word fare was often as wickedly pleasing for Easy as shooting 75. Worse yet, Nick had to endure Easy's chiding in the face of a losing streak nearing two long years.

"That last verse was truly inspired, Nick. You finally channeled the angst I was going for," Easy offered, enjoying a long, satisfied swig of his beer.

"Happy?" Nick asked. "Now let's get the hell out of here," he pleaded, taking a hard pull from the fresh cigarette wedged between his trembling fingers.

"What's your hurry? Relax, have a seat. The next guy could be doing some Wayne Newton. You don't want to miss that, do you? And what if somebody wants an autograph?"

"You suck."

"Come on Nickie, you of all people should know that dancing with the Devil has a price. Call it poetic justice."

"Payback's a bitch, Easy, a real bitch. This is all-out war. The gloves are off."

"Vomit three or four more clichés and I'm sold," Easy laughed.

"No, you will pay," answered Nick.

"Yeah, yeah, blah, blah, blah."

Chapter 2

At the local course where Nick and Easy played the majority of their golf, the regulars within their weekend circle had noticed a distinct up-tick of late in what they had already considered a rivalry of extremes. Once Nick and Easy's wagers began to involve the likes of rolling a golf ball from the clubhouse to the parking lot using only one's nose, or a week wearing hip-hop hairstyles, even the more moderate clubhouse elders agreed that this increased escalation had now moved well outside the intended "spirit of the game."

How Nick and Easy would allow the tone for their entire round to be defined by the random outcome of throwing a little wooden tee into the air (a ritual they used to decide who picked the bet for the day) had become a steady source of spirited discourse among their fellow golfers. But for Nick and Easy, it was simple: Golf without a serious wager was like sex without an orgasm. Be they ridiculous, severe, or austere, all bets were of great consequence and with great purpose to their design. Anyone spewing such "spirit of the game" delusions was as believable as a man saying he wears women's panties because he likes the style.

Nick and Easy saw it much, much differently indeed; each believed golf and gambling shared two unique, undeniably strong, and symbiotic bonds. First was that both golf and gambling were really nothing more than self-induced scuffles against fate. No one forced you to play or bet. Second, inherent in both activities were the razor-thin, indiscriminate, and ungoverned elements of chance. For these two simple reasons, golf and a wager actually fit quite perfectly with one another; and they fit without room in their minds for controversy, discussion, or debate.

Whenever asked how and when all of this had started between them, Nick would tell the story of how he coaxed Easy into breaking his leg the very first day they met, when they were around six-years old. That was the day Easy's family arrived in Saint Louis from Battle Creek, and moved into the cookie-cutter house next door to Nick's.

"I was up in the tree in my front yard, watching the movers unload boxes and furniture, sort of spying on the new family moving in," Nick would tell any Clubhouse Joe who asked, "when Easy saw me hiding up in the tree, walked over, looked up, and asked how I got up there. I told him I jumped over from my upstairs bedroom window like Batman. 'You can't jump that far,' he says to me. 'I do it all the time,' I tell him. 'Wanna try, or you a chicken?' It was a good five feet across and ten feet straight down. 'I'm not chicken,' he tells me.

"He missed by about two feet, dropped like a damn rock. And you should have seen his face when I slid down the rope I had stuffed up between the branches."

Once Easy's leg healed and his cast was removed, the two boys began spending sunrise past sunset together, eagerly pillaging their homes, yards, neighbors' yards, and accosting every bug and critter they could find, often ending up at one another's house to take their daily baths together. At six years old, taking baths together was not only an acceptable activity, it was a downright proper ending to a full day of youthful adventure.

Following the roof-jumping incident, bath time was among the boys' very first formal competitions. Both would allow their cheeks to nearly explode rather than pop-up first in a hold-your-breath-underwater contest, despite gray dingy water stinging their eyes and the taste of Ivory soap lining their mouths. At the time neither considered swallowing mouthful after mouthful of one another's dead skin and grime as particularly foul, and it was certainly not rank enough to force either combatant to emerge first and admit defeat. For Nick and Easy, these baths were more fun than three square meals of Capt'n Crunch.

When they discovered it was possible to sneak onto the "big course" less than a mile down the road just before sunrise, traditional activities of the day began to take a back seat to golf. Even at a young age, Easy was the more wooden, introspective, and intellectual of the two, enjoying golf's more esoteric rewards. Although Nick, too, fell in love with the cerebral aspects of the game. Nick liked the independent nature of battling against only the golf course and your opponent, unconcerned with the expectations and responsibilities of teammates. Unlike Easy's more mature and wandering thoughts, Nick's notion of finding solace in the lone-wolf aspect of golf was among the few abstractions his youth and excitable nature had allowed him to fully consider at just thirteen years of age.

Whether betting for lunch money, some imaginary championship, simple bragging rights, or to atone in some measure for the previous day's injustice, defeating one another and gaining some measure of superiority and reward was as normal for the boys as two cavemen beating each other with clubs.

When raven-haired gymnast Annette Thurman moved in across the alley, their competitions quickly became much more mainstream but no less meaningful. Annette, at the ripe old age of eleven, had not quite figured out that it was improper to be kissing boys—worse yet, two boys. In fact, they agreed later that she probably enjoyed the attention, not to mention the two dollars they'd scraped together for her affection from their neighborhood lawn mowing enterprise.

Hiding in Easy's garage, the boys would take turns giving Annette dry, grandma-style kisses while clocking activities with an egg timer, terrified that at any moment Easy's dad Pops would stomp in, discover them in mid-mug, and promptly set about beating them within an inch of never reaching their goal of hitting puberty. Such fears were well grounded, as Nick had seen Easy take more than one beating from Pops over the years. Pops was mean, pit bull mean, bloody-knuckle mean, from countless bouts as a Marine Corps boxer.

Given his experience with both options, Nick would have readily chosen a trip to the principal's office and a dozen whacks with an oak paddle that accompanied such a trip over any encounter with Pops. The thought of Pops suddenly walking in—thick purple veins popping from beneath his leathery neck at such a sight—never fully escaped Nick's brain, despite the allure and distraction of Annette's warm lips. Being caught would surely be the mother of all Hells, with Pops snarling as he closed in. "Get over here, Goofy." That's what he called Nick: Goofy. Nick owned dozens of mixed visions of how his capture would play out, each with roughly the same ending: the jolting grab of his shirt collar, a violent shaking and, finally, the back of Pops' hard hand. "What's so funny, Goofy? What's so funny?" For Easy, the face of Pops' rage was a mask he'd somehow grown accustomed to. For Nick, it never stopped short of chilling when witnessed firsthand.

Annette, on the other hand, had tapped a completely different vein of emotion within them. Regardless of what Easy would have ever admitted, Nick believed that Annette actually liked him better, and Nick took some pride in the fact that Easy would complain when he got the longer, slightly wetter kisses.

He was not known as Easy back then; rather, he was Will Edmund Easley, Jr., the Edmund taken from the revenge-driven lead character in *The Count of Monte Cristo*—a curious reflection, Nick had long thought, into the dichotomy that was Easy's dad. In addition to a vent of volcanic nasty flowing from his core, Pops was also a proud, smart, well-read man.

He'd earned the nickname Easy during their sophomore year in high school after the starting quarterback twisted a knee in the third quarter of a game and Will came in to complete nine straight passes to win the game. Everyone said he'd made it look so "easy."

Truth be told, everything had come rather easily for him, especially golf. Easy never practiced, never had a formal lesson, and yet he swung a golf club with such fluidness you'd have thought his father was Earl Woods Sinatra Presley. Whether it was golf, football, girls, or school, life seemed so clear to Easy. He was always smooth and cool, a natural at most everything except his appearance. For some reason, the just-been-chased-by-a-pack-of-dogs look suited him. This ran counter to Nick's own dapper preference. He was not one of those people who thought disheveled radiated a certain cool.

As for Nick, he'd taken golf lessons for ten years, thought no less than three hundred swing thoughts per second, and could never seem to get out of his own way whether it involved golf or girls. For Nick, maintaining a C+ average was harder than Chinese algebra.

While certainly not alpha and omega on the personality scale, it was hardly a stretch to say that the boys had grown from their bathtub days to be more different than alike. What they had not grown was apart.

Chapter 3

▼

Today was Kendra's twenty-fifth birthday, one of those dastardly milestones when, almost out of nowhere, life subtly begins to telegraph its true intent. High school is all but ancient history, the novelty and hedonism of age twenty-one has faded, the pseudo seriousness of college is gone, age thirty lies just ahead, and a world cluttered with genuine responsibility can no longer be set aside. Barring some questionable decisions or outright mistakes earlier in life, at the age of twenty-five, family, career, and financial issues begin to pile up on life's scorecard like bogeys on a blustery day.

To commemorate the event, a milestone both Nick and Easy had endured just a few years earlier, a banner with "Happy 25th Birthday" in bold block letters hung cock-eyed between the dining room and living room.

On most people, a pointed pink birthday hat would look silly. But when perched over Kendra's straight, shoulder-length dark hair it looked good. With her slender build, dark eyes, and an alluring set of full, soft, pillow lips guarding her toothpaste commercial smile, Kendra always seemed to have her choice of suitors.

After stomping his cigarette on the front porch, Nick let himself inside without the slightest thought of knocking on the front door. Knocks and polite announcements were for guests, not family.

"Happy birthday, Kendy!" Nick shouted above the chatter as he crossed the doorstep.

"Hey Nick, thanks for coming!" Kendra answered, as they met near the door to share a warm hug and a peck on the cheek.

"Welcome to the club!" Nick said, with feigned sympathy.

"Thanks. But it's not like I had a choice to join. Do you want a beer?"

"Unless you plan on this being the world's lamest party, yeah. Where's your brother?"

"I think he's in the kitchen. I'll let him know you're here."

With the guest of honor occupied, Nick scanned the room for familiar faces or, better yet, one of Kendra's cute girlfriends. Instead, he noticed Pops completely ignoring the festivities around him as he sat stiff and stern in his favorite recliner, his pug nose pointed squarely at the TV, deep wrinkles stacked above his bushy eyebrows.

Seated alone on a plain brown sofa dominating the living room next to Pops' recliner was a peculiar looking pony-tailed young man with a skinny face and round, tinted John Lennon-type glasses. A black beret, matching black T-shirt, faded jeans, and black army boots completed his odd ensemble. Nick approached this unlikely pair with equal parts caution, curiosity, and a slight, knowing grin.

"Hey Pops, how you doing?" asked Nick politely as he extended his hand.

"Get out of the way, Goofy, you're blocking the TV."

"Nice to see you, too," Nick offered in return, all the while thinking, *Nice to see you too, you scrawny, shriveled-up horse's ass.*

Choosing instead to bite his tongue, he quickly stepped around Pops' fully extended recliner and walked toward the curious looking stranger perched anxiously on the sofa's edge.

"Hi. I'm Nick Rose." Again, Nick extended his hand.

The comical looking visitor eagerly accepted his hand and shyly introduced himself.

"I'm Bob. How do you do?"

"Not bad," answered Nick, mildly surprised that such an ordinary name could belong to someone decked in such artsy garb. Niles or Alford or Bjorn or Pompey would have fit, but Bob?

"Let me guess, you're Kendra's date."

"Wow, that's pretty cool. How'd you know that?"

Nick ignored the question. "Need a beer, Bob?"

With his head and black beret bouncing with the rhythm of a wooden bobble-head doll, Bob answered, "Sure, that'd be cool."

Apparently, Nick's gesture was the first sign of warmth anyone besides Kendra had offered the party's token fish-out-of-water.

"I'll be right back. Coming through, Pops," Nick announced as he darted past Pops' recliner, careful to steer clear of the TV and Pops' line of sight.

"Get me one too, Goofy," Pops ordered.

It took Nick all of ten seconds to weave past the assorted guests and through the small old house to the kitchen, where he found Kendra holding three beers and talking with her brother who, at the moment, had his dark head stuck almost completely inside the refrigerator. In his typical unmade bed look, complete with wrinkled T-shirt and jeans missing the back pockets, Easy stood nearly two inches taller and carried a broader, more athletic build than Nick. Since Nick's unstated goal in life was to be more like Easy, the difference in their height only fed Nick's unspoken insecurity. Stuff like size mattered to Nick.

"Hey Nick, what's up?" Easy asked, as he emerged from the fridge with a beer in hand.

"Not much. I'll take one of those," Nick told Kendra as he grabbed one of beers she was holding. "Oh yeah, and my new friend Boob needs one too."

"It's Bob, and that's where I was heading," Kendra said, as she straightened her birthday hat and departed for the living room and Boob.

"That guy's a total dork," Easy suggested, while twisting the cap off his beer.

"I think that's the first time I ever felt sorry for Pops," Nick added, mildly satisfied at the prospect of Pops' misery.

"Feeling sorry for Pops is not a good use of your time," Easy answered simply.

"You know, Pops ain't looking so hot these days. He's shrinking faster than those new laptop computers. Every time I see him he looks thinner and lighter."

"Christ, all he does is sit in that chair all day, watch ESPN, and bitch about how lazy and overpaid today's athletes are. If I hear one more bitter Stan Musial anecdote I'm putting him in a home."

"If it's a good idea later, it's probably a good idea today, don't you think?" Nick suggested.

"Hey, did you get us a tee time for Saturday?" asked Easy, slugging his own beer with authority while ignoring Nick's recommendation.

"Yeah, one-thirty. But get this, Next Tuesday I've got us set up at The Saint Louis Country Club."

"The Country Club? That's major Magnus. How'd you get a time out there?" Easy asked.

"I didn't. Charlie did."

"Divot?"

"Hey, don't bitch. We're talking The Saint Louis Country Club here!"

"Yeah, but five more hours of Charlie, I'm not sure I can take it anymore. We've been playing way too much golf that prick lately. He's like Pops with a hangover."

Nick threw Easy one of those "it's not that bad" looks before warning, "And don't be late, they'll screw us on our tee time."

"Don't worry, I'll be on time," said Easy.

"Like you're always on time," Nick answered as his habitually tardy friend casually chugged his beer.

"I'll be there. But here's the bigger question, got a new bet figured out?"

"Yeah, I've got some ideas. What about you?"

"Yeah, I've got some thoughts," said Easy.
"Good," answered Nick.
"Good."

Chapter 4

Easy knew his trouble was only just beginning when that old prick Charlie untied his laces and removed the weathered golf shoe from his equally battered artificial foot.

"I hit that damn putt so perfect," Easy sighed with layered disappointment.

"I've never seen a perfect putt that completely missed the friggin' hole, so stop bitching," Charlie countered, smirking.

"I thought you'd make it for sure. Like you always do to me," Nick added.

By no small coincidence, a waitress appeared at their table, balancing two overflowing shots on her tray just as Charlie plopped his sorry-ass shoe onto the table. Even worse, her delivery featured cheap tequila. Easy hated cheap tequila.

It would have been an understatement to say that five-toed Charlie didn't care much for Easy. In fact, Easy could not think of a single person Charlie did like other than Nick, Arnold Palmer, and Linda Lovelace, the latter being two people he'd never actually met. As Nick explained it, Charlie was still extremely pissed-off that Pops had made Easy quit their championship-caliber golf team to play on their less-than-average varsity football team when golf was switched from spring to fall semester their senior year of high school.

Charlie was the high school golf coach at the time, and both he and Nick believed they would have won the state championship that year if Easy hadn't quit the team. Easy never shared this belief as deeply as Nick and Charlie did, but he certainly endured an ample load of grief in this regard. And while Nick harbored no lingering feelings about the whole episode, Charlie remained obsessed with what he unrelentingly referred to as Easy's "betrayal." From Easy's perspective, Charlie had no interest in either the truth of the matter or forgiveness, and their divergent realities fueled a dependable tension. Following a particularly contentious round of golf, Easy once told Charlie that "if Satan is indeed eternity's most evil being, you must be the bastard that buys his cigarettes."

Easy, for his part, reveled in the idea that after all this time he could still drive Charlie to seven-dollar Scotch. More than ten years had passed and Charlie still hadn't let it go. But change was lost on Charlie. As Easy saw it, Charlie's reason for hating the world and all its innocent occupants dated back to the day he lost his foot in Vietnam—the day he lost all hope of becoming a professional golfer.

It was rare for a full week to pass without Charlie's mentioning the time he beat Walter Morgan in the military's All-Service Tournament back in 1973. Morgan, also known as "The Sarge," had gone on to win the All-Service Tournament in 1975 and 1976, and later won three times on the Senior PGA Tour. Charlie, meanwhile, lost his right leg midway between the knee and ankle on a land mine two days before Christmas in 1973, just four months after beating "The Sarge" and three months before his tour of duty was to end.

Shortly after losing his temper with a particularly sensitive kid on the high school golf team, Charlie lost his job. More than a few parents complained about Charlie's style of tough-love coaching. Charlie was now Head Professional and clubhouse bartender at one of St. Louis's more nondescript municipal golf courses.

While Charlie's bizarre mental mechanics left him with few friends, his peculiar orientations had also furnished Nick and Easy with some outrageous tales—with their all-time favorite involving breakfast before a round of golf one morning at a greasy diner Charlie frequented. As the story went, Charlie just completely blew a gasket, launching into a sixty-second stream of obscenities and insults at the recently-hired, instantly-traumatized waitress who put his eggs on the same plate with his other food, ignoring his request that they be put in a separate bowl. While Charlie hemorrhaged an incoherent rant about chicken abortions, Nick and Easy watched in horror, all but certain that the cooks in the back would soon be spitting between their pancakes as they satisfied Charlie's request to segregate his eggs.

Since high school, Nick and Charlie had maintained what Easy viewed as an unhealthy mentor/protégé relationship, similar to that of the evil Darth Vader coaching an impressionable Luke Skywalker on the proper use of The Force. Yet, from Easy's perspective, that was typical of Nick, always looking for answers in the wrong places.

"This is seriously testing the limits of our friendship," Easy suggested, as Nick took the tequila shots from the server and dumped both into Charlie's waiting shoe.

"No worse than making me tee-off wearing that Victoria's Secret shit last week," Nick added, now taking a long draw from his Marlboro Light before sending a cloud of bluish smoke toward the ceiling.

"It's called a camisole, it was only one hole, and that was funny. This is just disgusting," Easy countered.

"And never once did I bitch, and I certainly never put our friendship into question, did I?" Nick responded.

"I guess it is my fate and perhaps my temperament to sign agreements with fools," Easy replied.

"Quit stalling and start drinking," Charlie demanded.

Personality differences notwithstanding, Nick and Easy were far more than garden-variety best friends; they were also blood brothers, having performed an official ceremony one summer morning when looking for cool gadgets in a trashcan of medical waste in the alley behind a neighborhood doctor's office. Having grown bored with using a syringe they'd found to inject Kool-Aid into unsuspecting worms, the boys decided to prick their fingers and mirror a blood-sharing ritual they'd seen two Indians perform on a TV western.

Outside of failing to contract some fatal disease or infection from the syringe, many other events would come to define and further cement their friendship. When both boys were only twelve, Nick's mom had died of breast cancer. To this day, the most disturbing sight Easy had ever witnessed occurred when he and Nick accidentally walked in on Nick's mom in the hospital as she was having her bandages changed, prior to her second surgery, when the tumor had returned. Neither had spoken of it since that day. Both knew what they'd seen and were too scared to talk openly about it.

This, too, was a common misery of sorts, as Easy's own mother was gone by that time. As it happened, he couldn't really say that he blamed her. Easy wasn't the only one to get the back of Pops' hand. When his mom moved away, she took Kendra with her—a trauma that still left him fiercely protective of his baby sister. Kendra returned home some months later when their mom realized she really couldn't take proper care of the girl. When he was younger, Easy often thought that while Pops may have had a temper, at least he didn't drink like his mother did. As he grew older and thought more of that period in his life, he often wondered which came first for his mother, the heavy drinking or Pops' abuse.

Forging through their tragedies together, Nick and Easy became as inseparable as dimples on a golf ball. Nick, among his many noble qualities, was exceptionally loyal, the trait that most singularly explained why he and Charlie had maintained such a close friendship well beyond their high school golf days. Charlie's providing Nick with free golf lessons and spare cigarettes, and both boys with their first twelve pack of Budweiser, also factored into Nick's loyalty.

During Easy's first year of law school, when the evidence concept of fruit from the poison tree was introduced, he immediately thought of all the illicit beer Charlie had purchased on their behalf—the beer having been the fruit and Charlie the toxic tree.

Not that Easy was thinking about any of this as he hoisted the heel of Charlie's shoe toward his lips and studied its contents.

"Down the hatch, boy," Charlie demanded.

"Screw you, Charlie," Easy answered.

Down deep, Easy's disgust at having to drink cheap tequila from Charlie's putrid shoe was more directed at himself than Nick. He consoled himself with the thought that at least there had never been a living foot inside that shoe.

To everyone's delight, except of course Easy's, and with the help of some salt and lime—training wheels as Charlie called them—Easy took his medicine. He really hated cheap tequila. Within seconds of choking back the urge to vomit, he let out a series of sneezes, six in rapid succession. Easy was allergic to hard liquor. Never a severe adverse reaction though, just a predictable sneeze-attack.

A normal person might have found it difficult to be philosophical when gagging on rotgut tequila from a soiled shoe, but Easy took the loss in stride. Serious complaining was forbidden when it came to paying off a bet. That was the single golden rule: take it like a man.

More troubling for Easy was that one stroke—a misread of a four-foot putt on the last hole for a three-putt bogey—was what ultimately left him drinking from Charlie's size-eleven FootJoy.

"But that putt was perfect, so pure," Easy announced as he wiped sneeze snot from his nose with his forearm.

"Apparently not," Nick fired back.

"Nothing sucks more than hitting the ball just the way you want, just where you want, and not being properly rewarded. But what can you do? As Ronald Firbank once said, 'The world is so disgracefully managed, one hardly knows to whom to complain.'"

"Who on God's earth is Ronald Firbank?" asked Charlie.

"I don't know. It's just something I heard once that stuck in my mind."

"That's the great thing about you, Will. When you die, no one will give a fuck," Charlie barked while avoiding all eye contact with Easy.

Charlie's comment prompted Easy to dig deep into his pocket.

"Divot, here's two dollars," Easy started, while flinging the two bills toward the center of the table. "Go buy yourself a tub of Country Crock, grease up that leg, your ass, whichever you prefer, and go fuck yourself."

"Did you just call me Divot?" Charlie snarled back.

"If the shoe fits. Oh, sorry about that. I forgot," Easy deadpanned.

"I've still got one foot I can plant up your ass if you'd care to step outside."

"Are you children done?" Nick asked, with a satisfied half-grin.

Nearly two years had passed since Easy had lost a golf bet to Nick, and while losing in general made him mad as hell, losing with such a weak score—an 81—left Easy near boiling. Losing to Nick had become unthinkable of late, but losing twenty-two dollars and the round to Charlie's 76 had Easy seriously considering the theft of a certain prosthetic leg. *No way he can beat me without that damn leg*, Easy thought.

"Thanks for the donation, girls. See you on Tuesday." Charlie crowed, as he stood, smiled, scooped the wad of money from the table, and limped toward the exit. Easy's thoughts now focused on how he hated that evil bastard Charlie, and whether or not he could feel that his shoe was wet and squishy.

Chapter 5

It felt good to win, damn good, Nick thought on the drive home following Easy's shoe shots. Countless times over the past several months he was certain he had Easy beaten only to outright choke or somehow finish with a sister-kisser tie. As thoughts of the day's victory ricocheted in and among the alcohol-saturated molecules of his brain, Nick considered the games of chance where he'd enjoyed his last success. Rock-paper-scissors and credit card roulette jumped to mind, although the most important bets were always the golf bets. (Credit card roulette was a potentially expensive game where they each gave a credit card to the server, allowing for a blind draw of the card responsible for paying the full tab.) The last golf wager Nick remembered winning involved having Easy eat from a big pinkish jar of pickled baby pigs' feet soaked in vinegar that had been sitting untouched for what must have been years next to the cash register at their favorite neighborhood tavern, Arnie's Bar & Grill.

While the bathtub may have been the genesis of the boys' competitions, it wasn't until their final game of Little League that beating each other's brains out would become the center of their gambling universe.

When asked, Easy would begrudgingly describe that last game as "no big deal, all I did was throw the ball." For Nick, it was a ball and chain he dragged around almost daily. Next to his mom's passing away, their final Little League game was without question the moment he relived most often. Not only did the memory quietly haunt him on many levels, but the entire event provided such juicy symbolism that it was difficult for him not to think about it whenever something bad would happen. As it turned out, that final game would soon come to represent the perfect microcosm of what the next three long years were about to bring.

It had begun innocently one typical summer Saturday in St. Louis. A day so muggy, so humid, so hot, that waves of heat vibrated not only above the blacktop, but seemingly around everything. A day for iced tea and slow motion, a day when people's sweat breaks into a sweat. Only one of the two baseball diamonds at Shorty Dale Field was busy on championship day, where a large crowd had gathered for the sole purpose, Nick would often say, "of making me shit-my-pants nervous."

Like most Midwestern kids of the day, baseball was Nick's favorite sport. And he was the best player on his team, Arnie's Bar & Grill. Back in 1978, it was not uncommon to have your team named after any sponsor that would pony up the required money, and local taverns routinely sponsored dozens of teams around town. While players were only supposed to wear their jerseys to the actual games, Nick proudly advertised for Arnie on many a summer day, often wearing his white cotton button-down jersey with Arnie's Bar & Grill in dark red cursive letters sewn across the front several days in a row without thought to giving it a proper washing. Even though Joe Torre was the Cardinals' third baseman and loyalties should have fallen with the local hero, Nick chose instead to wear number five, Brooks Robinson's number, a tribute to the best third baseman ever in Nick's view.

Team rosters were decided at tryouts each year. The fact that Easy and Nick lived next door to one another had no bearing on which team they played for within their district. Coaches alone made those decisions. Easy was the star player for the perennial powerhouse, the West Side Jaycees. Some believed that a Little League Mafia existed in west St. Louis at the time, and that the Godfather was a member of the West Side Jaycees. Year after year, they would dominate the league with kids who looked old enough to have two ex-wives. At least that's how they appeared in the young eyes of all the other teams. While it was not much of a surprise to find Easy and the Jaycees again in the finals, it was the first trip to the championship game for Nick and Arnie's Bar & Grill.

Walking from behind the dugout fence, grabbing his 26-inch wooden bat as he shuffled toward the on-deck circle along third base, Nick carried the expression of a wounded deer caught in a hunter's crosshairs. Taking serious practice swings, hoping against hope that the kid ahead of him would get the game winning hit and his moment under the microscope would never happen, Nick watched closely as a pitch came toward the plate. He would get no such reprieve.

"Ball four, take your base," shouted the umpire.

With the bases loaded, his third-base coach, a round, stumpy man with a face like a happy catcher's mitt, signaled Nick over for the standard pep talk.

"Okay son, this is why we practiced all summer. Now, don't be afraid to take a walk: it's as good as a hit. But if you get a good pitch, swing away. I think Will's getting tired, okay?"

Nearly paralyzed, all Nick could muster was a weak, "Okay, Coach."

Stepping into the batter's box and tapping home plate with his suddenly heavy bat, Nick squinted toward the pitcher's mound at Easy, standing tall, a man amongst boys, composed as always behind the hornet-like yellow and black colors of the West Side Jaycees. Staring one another down in a manner reminiscent of their bathtub contests many years before, Easy threw Nick the blankest of looks. Following a spit into his Bob Gibson autographed glove, Easy hardened his look as he threw to the plate.

"Strike!" bellowed the umpire, as Nick stood completely frozen.

The catcher quickly fired the ball back to Easy. Snatching it from mid-air, Easy turned his back to Nick, removed his cap, and ran his fingers through his dark brown hair. Slowly replacing his sweaty yellow cap, he turned back to home plate, gave the ball a good rubbing, and looked to the catcher for his next pitch.

Nick still mentions the look on Easy's face at that moment. He called it the "Little League look." It was a look unlike any Nick had ever seen before, or since: conflicted, uncomfortable, yet determined. Following a quick nod to the catcher, Easy dug in and fired his second pitch. Nick decided to swing, albeit much too late.

"Strike two!"

This rather weak effort caught the full attention of Nick's coach, as he decided it was time for part two of the standard pep talk.

"Time out!" he shouted, waving his hat and hitching his pants up near the base of his substantial belly. All the kids joked that Arnie must have been giving the coaches free beer since they all had the bowling-ball belly hanging over their belts.

Meeting his coach halfway between home plate and third base, Nick listened intently as he received fresh instructions, not once making eye contact.

"This is for all the marbles, son. Let's be a hitter up there. You can do it! Just take a deep breath and put some wood on the ball. Let's go!"

Following a firm pat on the ass, Nick returned to the batter's box, tapped home plate, and sucked back a big, deep breath. Without hesitation, Easy smoked a fastball straight down the middle. With eyes as big as golf holes, Nick swung as hard as a twelve-year-old could swing. As Nick's helmet flew off, the ball popped hard into the catcher's mitt.

"Strike three! You're out!"

Those four words still echoed in Nick's mind.

"Strike three! You're out!" Game over.

Immediately, Nick's shoulders fell and his thin frame folded in half over home plate. It was as if he'd been punched in the stomach. Despite the celebration triggered by his strikeout, all Nick could see was his red plastic batting helmet spinning helplessly in the powdery dirt surrounding home plate. As a mob of kids from the West Side Jaycees dashed to the pitcher's mound to embrace their star pitcher, Nick remained hunched over home plate for quite some time, frozen, afraid to look up at all of those he had surely disappointed.

Little League tradition required the combatants to line up, walk across the field, and shake every hand of those against whom they had just competed. And Arnie's Bar & Grill and the West Side Jaycees were no exception to this worthy tradition. As Easy and Nick shook hands for what may have been the first time in their lives, Easy leaned over to Nick and muttered "Sorry." It was a moment they somehow knew they would never forget.

On the ride home, Nick sat in the back seat of Pops' musty Ford Galaxy with Easy, Easy's trophy, and Easy's sister Kendra as Pops set about systematically sucking every ounce of accomplishment from the day. At some age, amidst a barrage of arbitrary parent/child conflicts, it's not uncommon to begin questioning one's gene pool, and Easy was fast approaching that time, if not already doing so.

"You almost blew it, Son. How in God's name could you walk those kids? All you had to do was throw it over the plate. They can't hit." How Pops could totally disregard the fact that both boys had made it to the championship game, and that his son, his namesake, was the winning pitcher, was more than Nick's tender young brain could process. Pops grumbled on.

Nick's face turned quizzical as he sat thinking, *"Hey dick-face, I'm one of those kids!"*

"I was getting tired," Easy explained.

"Tired! Twelve-year-old kids don't get tired. What the hell is wrong with you?" Pops barked back.

Having heard enough of Pops' bullshit, Nick turned up the end of his nose with his index finger and began to imitate the pug-nose face of William, Sr. Try as they did to hold back, to muffle their collective giggles as Nick did his best Pops impression, the rear-view mirror quickly betrayed them. Familiar with Pops' wrath, Kendra and Easy quickly straightened up and shut up. Nick, however, didn't really care.

"What's so funny back there?" Pops demanded to know.

"What's so funny back there?" Nick mocked in his lowest adult sounding voice.

Catching Nick's impression in the mirror, Pops was none too happy.

"That's why you lost, Nick. You never take anything seriously. You need to toughen up and stop acting like a goof or you're gonna get your ass kicked the rest of your life, boy."

Little Kendra could sense the bad feeling in the air and tried to change the subject. "Nick, Nick…do you want to come over and play later so I can make you a cake in my Easy Bake Oven and we can act like we're drinking wine and you can act like you're my boyfriend?"

Completely uninterested having just struck out with bases loaded, single-handedly losing the championship game, Nick turned his face to the side and chose instead to stare out the window before mumbling to Kendra, "That's little kid stuff."

"So?" she replied innocently.

Upon pulling into the driveway, Nick immediately slid from the car, across the yard, and toward the porch steps of his almost identical house next door. Looking back over his shoulder, he spotted Easy, standing on his front porch proudly holding his trophy. They waved to one another, and with only his dejection to hold, Nick carried himself inside.

Once through the front door, Nick immediately spotted his father slumped to one side in his favorite chair, snoring as the TV blared. Nick's dad had a union meeting that afternoon and couldn't make it to the game; at least that's what he'd said. He never went to any of Nick's games, a snub that had always left Nick feeling a bit embarrassed, almost ashamed. For Nick, it seemed like he was the only kid who didn't have a parent, a brother, or someone at the game. Now, empty beer bottles littered the table at his father's side, coarsely explaining his true priority that afternoon. Dragging himself upstairs, Nick couldn't decide which was worse, having someone like Pops ruining the moment, or not having anyone to share the moment with.

As had become a grim and recurring exercise in recent weeks, Nick decided to look in on his mom, to see if she was awake. Pill bottles and other weird objects that no one had ever bothered to explain littered her nightstand. She was out cold.

Deep down, he was almost happy that his misery of the day would not be discussed or open for display.

As it would go, Nick's mother passed away just a few months later. The pills, weird stuff, and constant sleeping, he learned later, were the accessories of her cancer.

Chapter 6

▼

"If he ain't here in two minutes we're gonna start without him," growled Charlie, pacing about the tee box.

"He'll be here," Nick sighed, considering his warning to Easy just two days before.

"Why are you always late?" was a question Nick had asked Easy hundreds of times over the years. Easy had been late to everything from graduation day to his first sexual experience. Both boys had nearly missed out on free tickets to a Cardinals and Royals World Series game because Easy hadn't quite finished the omni-important task of sifting out all of the sugar-coated raisins from a full box of Raisin Bran he'd mysteriously dumped on the kitchen table. Even worse, claiming any measure of responsibility was completely out of the question for Easy. Something or someone else was always to blame: a jack-knifed condom truck, defective batteries in a faulty alarm clock, witness to a bank robbery. Rather than admit apathy or that he didn't own a watch—a reasonable excuse for a self-proclaimed renaissance man—Easy preferred to intentionally annoy Nick with the ridiculous. More than any single trait, Easy's glib disrespect for punctuality was a constant, predictable source of frustration for Nick.

The Country Club, as it's known locally, was founded in 1892, prompting the United States Golf Association to list it as one of the first one hundred clubs established in the United States. Local opinion held it to be the best course the St. Louis area had to offer, although some claimed that the newer, Bellerive Country Club held a higher "official" ranking in the monthly golf rags that chronicled such things.

"Did you know they played a U.S. Open here in 1947?" Nick asked Charlie.

"I know they played something here once," Charlie answered.

"Yeah, some guy named Lew Worsham beat Sam Snead in a playoff. Snead missed like a two-foot putt on the last hole."

"Snead was never a great putter. Cost him several Opens. It's all putting on Tour, Nick," Charlie added, chewing a golf tee.

Nick had always admired Charlie's past standing as one of St. Louis's most accomplished players. Every round with Charlie was story time, time for obscure facts, and to hear colorful tales as only Charlie could tell them. Charlie seemed to know some older fellow at every course they played and was on a first-name basis with most all of the top local players, including many former pros. He had played competitive golf for over thirty years in some form and would talk openly and endlessly of a player's tendencies, of a course's pedigree, or of how legends like Byron Nelson, Gene Sarazan, Ben Hogan, and Sam Snead had faced many of the same decisions and shots they would soon face.

But on this day, it was Nick, Charlie, Easy, and the unknown fourth player—not Snead, Sarazan, Hogan, or Worsham. And it was a near-perfect day for golf—hot and sunny, with bright, clear skies and not a single puff of wind. It was also an amazing golf course, with narrow fairways gliding over hilly terrain and smallish to medium-sized greens that rolled in multiple, mind-bending directions, deftly designed to disguise their trickery. But the best part was the immaculate condition of the course, conditions so pristine that municipal players like Nick and Easy felt uncomfortable taking a divot from such sacred, well-tended turf.

Joining Nick on the tee box was the unknown fourth player, a Black gentleman in khakis and a royal blue polo shirt that appeared to be somewhat smaller than when originally purchased—or its owner considerably larger. There was also a noticeable paunch around his belly determined to accentuate either option.

His name was Thomas Brown, a good-natured, family-first, thirty-six-year-old father of two, and a top-notch developer at the software company where Nick worked as a sales representative. Due to Nick's recent hiring and with Thomas' having taken Nick under his wing to a degree, having steered Nick clear of some long-standing internal rivalries and their sordid politics, the two colleagues had quickly become fast friends in Nick's new corporate world. Nick quickly learned to appreciate that Thomas had little interest in ambition's seedy underbelly. Thomas had passed up the opportunity to be lead developer on several high-profile projects, confessing a preference to harmony over stress despite his considerable talent and aptitude.

Standing next to Thomas on the tee box was the crusty spectacle of Charlie, decked in an obnoxious red and white flowered Hawaiian style shirt complimented with Ray Ban sunglasses, cutting a profile favoring Jack Nicholson more than Jack Nicklaus.

Nick, as usual, was pleated and pressed, prepared at least to look good if playing well wasn't in the cards.

"The little bastard had better not be over there warming up while we're over here with our thumbs up our ass," snarled Charlie.

"He never warms up. A few putts and that's about it," Nick said with Easy unavailable to defend himself.

"Is he any good?" asked Thomas.

"He thinks he is," Charlie grumbled.

"I'm gonna go ahead and hit. We can't wait all day." That said, Thomas placed his ball on the tee, stood directly behind it, and stared down the fairway. After no more than a second or two, he moved around and formally addressed the ball. Following a few quick glances down the fairway and a series of waggles and jiggles, Thomas put a confident but jerky swing on the ball as if he'd done this with some regularity. His shot flew nicely down the middle of the fairway before leaking a bit toward the right side.

"Just follow me, boys!" Thomas offered, proudly.

"Hurry up, dip-shit," Nick announced, as Thomas and Charlie turned to find Easy scurrying along a narrow walkway toward the first tee box.

"Sorry I'm late," Easy called, all the while tucking his wrinkled shirt into his semi-wrinkled pants and jogging cheerfully toward the threesome.

"No problem. Thomas, this is Will Easley," Nick said, politely.

"Hi, Thomas. Nice to meet you," Easy said, shaking Thomas' hand as he set his clubs to the ground.

"Let's go, boy. You got all day to make nice," Charlie barked in his best snarl.

"Has everyone hit?" asked Easy.

"Just me, straight down the middle," Thomas replied.

With formal introductions behind them, Nick threw a tee in the air to decide who would pick the bet for the day. It landed pointing toward his left toe.

"What's the bet?" Easy asked.

Nick had decided long before the tee toss that a change from their recent history of shoe drinking, women's clothes, or a month of wearing Elvis sideburns would offer more appropriate reverence to the venue.

"Let's keep this civilized. We don't get to play a good course like this that often, and I'd like to enjoy it. So no silly shit, just cash. How about ten bucks a hole?"

"Ten bucks a hole," whined Easy. "What's so civilized about ten bucks a hole? That's a little rich for a starving law student."

"I thought you were a teacher. When did you become a fucking lawyer?" Charlie asked, generously blending his contempt with mild surprise.

"I'm still teaching, but I'm going to law school at night," Easy answered, without any hope of approval.

"Christ, just what the world needs, another jerk-off lawyer. Look, Ms. Reno, I've only got one foot and a piss-ant job and I'm in for ten bucks, so don't act like a cheap skirt."

"Yeah, but since a pair of socks lasts you twice as long as the rest of us, you should have plenty of extra cash," Easy wryly announced to the foursome.

"Ten a hole is too rich for me. I've got a wife and kids to feed," added Thomas.

Charlie, more than mildly fed up with something as simple as a golf bet creating such delay and controversy, took charge.

"You can play for a buck a hole if that's okay with the boys here. Everyone else is in for ten. Now let's just play some golf, can we?"

"Fine with me. Let's go."

"Then someone needs to hit the damn ball. Nick, hit the ball," Charlie snarled.

Without further delay, Nick pulled his slightly offset, stiff-shafted titanium driver from his bag and quickly assumed a tall stance directly behind the three-dollar ball freshly planted into the ground. With his feet together, he made a few slow practice swings.

"You swing real pretty at the ground. Now have a try at the ball," Easy said while sliding his glove onto his hand.

"Can you just shut up?" Nick shot back, as he swung at air.

After tapping his club firmly on the ground, Nick moved in behind the ball and stared down the fairway. With a slow back swing, he accelerated on the way through, blasting his ball well past Thomas's earlier effort.

"Magnus shot, Nick."

"Thanks," was Nick's modest yet satisfied reply to Easy's compliment, spoken while bending over to pick his tee from the grass.

Charlie, employing his driver as a cane, leaned over and teed up his ball. Without wasting time or motion, and with a smooth half-swing owning to near perfect balance, Charlie launched his ball down the middle of the fairway just short of Nick's shot, but easily past Thomas's poke.

Casually shaking his head, Easy murmured to Nick, "One-legged prick can still get it out there, can't he?"

Nick nodded in agreement, as Easy teed his ball and threw a quick glance down the fairway. Armed with a well used hand-me-down wooden driver Nick had given Easy when he started buying his clubs from a defense contractor, Easy blistered his ball down the middle of the fairway with a swing so smooth it looked like most players' practice swing. "Nothing to it," he muttered to himself.

All four walked in near lockstep from the first tee toward two waiting golf carts, Nick, and a fresh cigarette leading the way.

Predictably, Easy would have no part of riding in the same cart with Charlie. He'd made that clear to Nick when told of the foursome, saying he'd rather eat runny roach shit than ride with Charlie all day. With a keen interest in keeping matters as simple and civil as possible, Nick hopped into one cart with Charlie, while Easy rode shotgun beside Thomas in the other. Once settled in the cart, Nick took a long draw from his cigarette and leaned over to subtly question his cantankerous mentor.

"Are you and Easy gonna go at it like this all day?"

"The boy acts like he's still in high school, like a spoiled little smart-ass," Charlie scowled.

"So, that's a yes," Nick said, while tilting his head to one side.

"He's a smart-ass pretty boy. Other than that, I'm sure he's a fine human being," offered Charlie with a dismissive shrug.

"He didn't want to quit the golf team. You know that. Pops made him play football," Nick explained.

"Doesn't it bother you that he cost us the state championship?" asked Charlie with a cold, serious stare.

"Not anymore."

"Doesn't it bother you that he's still kicking your ass on a regular basis?"

Nick took his eyes from the cart path and looked at Charlie. "I don't think so!" The cart veered to the right, grazing the curb.

Charlie immediately pounced on Nick's denial. "Bullshit, you've beaten him maybe twice in two years! And now you're taking up for him. You're soft as a marshmallow. You're his lily-white marshmallow bitch. And he's no better." Charlie suddenly switched to a Scottish accent. "Where I'm from, they would say his soul lacks depth. He fancies himself a thoughtful man, yet at heart, he's without conviction. Yup, and you're his bloody, wig-wearing little marshmallow!"

"Charlie, first of all, you're not Scottish. In fact, you've never even been to Scotland. And second, you're starting to piss me off."

"Then act like it. We've been working hard for five months, kick his ass!" implored Charlie, his dark glasses unable to mask his stern expression.

Nick flicked his cigarette and shook his head in denial as they motored down the fairway to the spot where four golf balls and Thomas and Easy stood waiting.

Old was the only appropriate description for the clubhouse at the prestigious Saint Louis Country Club. The air was old, the furniture old, the carpet old, the money was old money, and the majority that comprised the membership of the reputable club was old. Any item not actually measured in geologic time was probably purchased with its oldness in mind.

Nick surveyed the setting. "Half these people look like they're embalmed. We had the whole course to ourselves, did you notice that?"

Easy had a different take. "It's stately, Nick. Grand. And I think they look distinguished."

"If you think near death is distinguished, then they're distinguished all right."

Easy laughed. "It reminds me of a by-gone era. A golf time capsule."

"I can see that, like most of the members were gone 'cause they went to buy some Depends," Nick suggested, with a straight face.

Thomas and Charlie, having consumed their share of post-round beverages and banter, were set to abandon the table, a table where everything sat empty: empty beer pitchers, several empty beer mugs, an empty plastic popcorn basket, and a dirty ashtray. Nick, with the customary cigarette dangling from his lips, rose from his chair. Easy decided to forgo any formal farewells and remained seated, his legs crossed, the beer in his right hand the complete focus of his attention.

Nick graciously made it around the tight semi-circle to shake hands with Thomas and Charlie. "Thanks for setting this up, Charlie. It was fun," Nick said, offering Charlie a firm handshake.

"My pleasure, boys," replied Charlie, as he leaned in toward Nick's ear. "Nice playing today, Nick. It's good to see you show some balls."

Charlie then turned his attention to Easy. "Hey, Ms. Reno, sorry you didn't win any of your money back."

"If you ever need a lawyer, Charlie, which is sure to happen, look me up so I can laugh in your face in person," Easy said without expression.

"Thanks guys," added Thomas. "I finally got to play with the big boys and it only cost me three dollars. I'm happier than Mike Tyson at a beauty pageant. And don't forget, Nick, I get all the details come Monday," Thomas added, hitching up his pants and waving as he and Charlie departed.

"See you guys later," Nick called out, "And drive safe."

"What's he mean by that, all the details come Monday?" asked Easy.

After a hearty slug of beer and hit from his cigarette, Nick explained Thomas's request. "I always tell him the shit we do, the parties, golf, the vacations. I think he gets a bit of a kick out of us. Says he lives vicariously through us single guys. We do manage to have some fun occasionally."

Easy looked around the room. "Well, speaking of fun, do we get another beer here at the Wrinkle Room or go somewhere else? You're the big winner, you make the call."

"Let's go shoot some pool. I feel lucky today!" Nick said, peeling a ten-dollar bill from the folded wad of money he'd pulled from his pocket.

"Then let's go, Mr. Lucky."

Nick threw the bill toward the center of the table as they exited.

It wouldn't have taken a Betty Ford graduate to recognize that Nick and Easy were soon deep under the influence of a half dozen pitchers of beer and at least four shots of tequila as they stumbled around the pool table like pirates. Knocking the cue ball into a side pocket, Nick flung his pool stick onto the table, grabbed his beer and cigarette, and, raising them to shoulder level, pronounced, "Cheers to me. It's a Nick Three-peat!" As their waitress walked by, Nick politely called for two more tequila shots. "Good tequila," he shouted.

As he leaned back in his chair, sucked a long draw from his cigarette, and pointed his chin toward the ceiling to exhale, Nick noticed his cigarette had cracked and snuffed it into the black plastic ashtray.

Eager to discuss anything but his daylong series of defeats, Easy changed the subject. "What's going on with work? Got any trips coming up?" he asked.

"Yeah, I'm going to D.C. in two weeks," replied Nick, lighting a fresh cigarette.

"No shit! When?"

Nick though for a second. "The twenty-second through the twenty-sixth. I'm doing this platform integration bid for the Department of Energy."

"No shit, I'll be in D.C. from the twenty-eighth to the first for a teacher's conference," Easy added. The waitress arrived with two more shots and two more limes. By virtue of the men's earlier efforts, a saltshaker sat ready. Nick licked and salted the web between his index finger and thumb.

"Let's set up our trip so we can play some golf while we're out there!" Nick suggested as he threw back his tequila, slammed the shot glass on the table, and made the wincing, contorted face that only tequila can create.

"Are you sure you want to do that?" Easy asked as he mirrored the required tequila ritual, followed immediately by a series of weak sneezes.

Prepared in advance for the impending salvo of saliva, Nick shielded himself with the promotional piece from the center of the table normally used to hype greasy snacks and weak, fruity drinks. He snapped his fingers to a sudden thought, "Hell yeah, I'll expense the whole thing, say I'm golfing with the D.O.E. boys."

"That's not what I'm talking about, Nickie. I'm asking if you're sure about going half way across the county to get your ass kicked."

"That was the old days, Junior," Nick shot back.

Easy perked up like a dog hearing an unexpected noise and with a serious look, he leaned in toward Nick. "Don't call me Junior. And you seem to be forgetting—I kicked your ass in Chicago last year, in Tulsa at T-bone's wedding, and in Missouri almost every week since Little League, and I ain't just talking about golf. In fact, I've beaten you so often for so long at so many things, losing once in a while would be a refreshing change." Easy pointed to his temple, "See, I've got your number, Nick, got you psyched out. And don't think for a second that this little two-round winning streak you're on changes anything."

"That's bullshit! And you know what else? I'm getting sick of you treating me like your little bitch."

Interrupting what he knew was just a preamble to Nick's oncoming rant, Easy said, "I see what's going on here. Is that you talking or did Charlie put that in your head today? I know what a hard-on that twisted old bastard gets pushing my buttons."

"That's exactly the bullshit I'm talking about, Junior. Sometimes your smug, cocky shit gets real tiring."

Going for the kill, Easy used his best baby voice: "Looks like I hurt your feelings. Did I hurt your feelings? I'm sorry Nickie."

"Okay dip-shit, that's it."

Nick simmered inside. Charlie's admonishment from earlier that day was now echoing loud in his head. *I am a fucking marshmallow. Charlie's right*, he thought. "Alright, Will, here's what we're gonna do. We're gonna settle this once and for all." Nick paused for effect. "But only if you're ready to quit hiding behind that Little League shit and make a man's bet."

Easy, pretending to be completely unaffected by the comment, leaned back stoically in his chair and folded his arms across his chest. "Challenging my manhood, huh? Bring it on, what'ya got?"

Nick put a light to a fresh cigarette, took a long draw, and sent the smoke blowing toward the swirling ceiling fan. Having an immediate epiphany, Nick pointed at Easy, a cigarette between his fingers. "Okay, here's the bet, asshole," Nick announced, as he gathered his thoughts. "The bet starts in D.C., we play head-to-head, me and you, in every state in the country, all fifty. Whoever wins the most states is the winner, the best golfer, period, end of story!"

Easy unfolded his arms, grabbed his beer, took a big long drink, and thoughtfully considered Nick's challenge.

Nick, still fighting the marshmallow demons, dug his grave a little deeper. "And I'll even give you a head start. Since you brought it up, you can have Illinois and Oklahoma, I'm not gonna need 'em."

Easy, still pondering this considerable proposition was quickly becoming seduced by visions of walking fairways and greens from North Carolina's wooded Pinehurst, to Florida's diabolical Sawgrass, to California's mystic Pebble Beach. "Okay, Charlie Junior, that's a Magnus bet. You're on."

Nick extended his hand to seal the deal. Easy eagerly accepted, adding, "All fucking fifty, including Alaska and Hawaii."

Their clinch grew firm, neither wanting to end the handshake out of some juvenile fear that it might display some sign of weakness.

"Although it won't take fifty," said Easy, finally releasing Nick's painful grip in order to grab his beer. He raised the beer toward Nick, who hoisted his own glass, as they toasted the birth of their grandest wager yet.

Nick couldn't resist capping his challenge by getting in the final word: "Let's start tomorrow, for Missouri, unless, of course, you're a pussy."

Easy's brow furrowed as they again clanged their beers together and stared each other down like two Mexican prizefighters before round one of a Tijuana alley brawl.

Chapter 7

▼

Game on. It occurred to Nick that an occasion as important as the first official state of their bold new wager might merit at a least shower, or perhaps a comb through his hair, but Easy didn't seem affected by any such notion. Instead, he had arrived looking as if he'd gone no further than the closet floor to select clothes for the day.

Nick, consistently in contrast, was dapper as usual: pressed shirt, pleated pants, and clean spikes. Leaning firmly on his prized new Ping putter, Nick knew what was coming as Easy studied a short putt for the win.

"Christ Easy, I didn't take that long reading my first issue of *Playboy*."

"I'd expect not."

Easy surveyed what appeared to be a routine four-foot putt—uphill, with little or no break. Without further delay, Easy threw two quick glances at the hole, drew back his putter, rapped the ball firmly, and idly watched as it fell straight into the center of the cup. A big grin washed across his face.

"That would make it Easy, three states, Nick, zero," Easy announced.

"Nice job. Let me buy you a beer," Nick said with a hint of dejection in his voice.

"That'd be nice. I didn't realize how much of a thirst one acquires when winning a whole state," Easy lamented without the faintest scrap of sympathy.

Inside at their clubhouse table, Nick bit at his cigarette while marking their scorecard with a short green pencil.

"At five bucks a hole, I owe you twenty bucks."

"Keep it. I've got my eye on the bigger prize," Easy said, without looking up from his own scorecard.

"You know, I was thinking, we could probably do four states in D.C." Nick counted on his fingers as he called them out; "Maryland, Virginia, Delaware, and Pennsylvania are all within an hour. If we do this right, we could be up to seven states by the end of the month."

Easy, still staring down at his scorecard, was oblivious to the geography lesson.

"Hey Junior, are you listening to a word I'm saying here?"

"What's that?"

Nick feigned an apologetic tone: "Didn't mean to bother you."

"I was just replaying a few shots in my head," Easy offered.

"Let me save you some time. You won, okay," Nick said while executing a nice chokehold on the neck of his beer bottle.

"No," Easy commented, "I mean I was visualizing it, the round, seeing the shots."

"I don't buy that visualization shit."

"You should ask the great and all powerful Charlie about it. It works," Easy said. "True story, Nick, I read a story once about this Vietnam POW who once spent four years in captivity, a lot of it in solitary confinement. All he thought about was getting home to play his favorite course. I mean, he knew that course like the back of his hand, had played it probably a thousand times before. Anyway, I don't know whether it was out of boredom or for motivation or what, but he played that same course over and over and over in his head for four years. Keep in mind now, he never shot better than 80 before he was captured. Know what he shot when he finally got to play that course again for the first time in over five years?"

Nick thought for second. "After four years, I don't know, an 85, 90?"

Easy's response took on an almost lecturing tone. "Sixty-eight! Twelve shots better than his best score. That's how powerful the human mind can be."

Nick was unimpressed. "Well, thank you, Obi Wan."

Easy shook his head. "Hey, if you want to go through life thinking like a simpleton, that's your problem, not mine." But Nick had stopped listening and instead was looking through his wallet.

"Can you spot me twenty for the tab? I don't have any cash with me."

"Yeah, what else is new," Easy muttered as he reached for his wallet.

"So, what do think about the bet?" Nick asked.

"What do I think?" Easy pondered the question for a second. "I think I should have it wrapped up in about thirty-five states, or less."

"Visualize this my friend: no way," Nick announced in his most defiant tone. "No fucking way!"

Only the presence of a golf calendar saved the walls in Nick's office from resembling a branch office at the Bureau of Motor Vehicles. The skyline behind him featuring St. Louis's famous arch compensated nicely and naturally for his lack of interest in extraneous corporate decor. Scanning his cluttered desk, Nick acted as if he was going through a mental checklist when Thomas Brown walked into his office carrying a laptop computer. Thomas was still sporting the borrowed-a-shirt-from-my-little-brother look. Only this time he'd chosen a red polo to compliment his brown Dockers.

"She's all ready to go!" Thomas declared as he placed Nick's laptop on an empty corner of the desk.

"Were you able to make all the changes they wanted?" Nick asked.

"Does Mike Tyson sweat at a spelling bee?" Thomas joked.

"That's Magnus, Thomas, I appreciate how hard you worked on this," Nick said thankfully, keenly aware that more than a week's work lay behind the delivery.

"If the D.O.E. don't like this, they can kiss my A.S.S," Thomas added with authority. "When's your presentation?"

"Tomorrow, two o'clock," Nick replied.

"When do you get back?"

"Sunday night. Will has a conference on Monday so we're gonna hang out for the weekend and play golf."

"Man, you two play a lot of golf," Thomas said with envy.

"Yeah, and we're fixin' to play a lot more. We made this bet. We're gonna play every state in the country, head-to-head, and whoever wins the most states gets bragging rights for eternity. It's the ultimate bet," Nick explained.

"No shit! When did this happen?" Thomas asked, all the while thinking that a journey of this magnitude would surely provide a steady new source of tawdry stories.

"That night after we played The Country Club," Nick explained as he took the laptop from the desk's edge and stuffed it into a black leather case. "We were just shooting some pool and having a few drinks when we got to bullshitting about our schedules and realized we were going to be in D.C around the same time. You know how it gets, next thing I know we're shooting tequila and I'm challenging him to a cross country tournament."

Thomas couldn't decide which of many questions dancing in his head to ask first. "So, is this the first match?"

Nick continued packing. "No, Will's ahead three states to zero, but we're gonna do four states this week. And don't ask how I've already lost three."

"How do you decide which state you're gonna play?"

Nick scanned his desk one final time, checking to ensure he was avoiding one of the deadly sins of sales—leaving behind something central to his upcoming presentation. "Whoever wins the last state gets to pick the next state. Hell, we were up drinking until three o'clock making up all kinds of rules." Nick began counting on his fingers again. "We're gonna finish all fifty in three years, ties count as ties, you get two weeks notice on travel, and you get two challenges each."

"What does two challenges mean?" Thomas asked.

"It's something Will learned in law school. When lawyers are picking a jury, they can kick a certain number of people off as jurors without reason. Well, we each get two chances to back out if we can't make it to a state. After that you either show up and play or forfeit the state, excluding birth, death, and marriage."

"That sounds like a hell of a lot of fun. Good thing you're both single," Thomas added, as thoughts of how his wife would never allow such a selfish excursion crossed his mind.

"Oh yeah, and no matter who we're dating or what the circumstances, we do at least fifteen states a year—that's nonnegotiable," Nick added, checking his watch. "Shit, I've got to get going."

Chapter 8

Aided by two cheap, limp hotel pillows to prop his head, Nick was determined to kill time and keep his frustration with Easy's constant slowness at bay by surfing over the limited selection of channels offered on the hotel TV. Their room, a Red Roof Inn walk-up special at fifty-six dollars a night, was the best deal they could find late at night in Laurel, Maryland, without a reservation. Outside of tee times, it was a rare occurrence when an actual itinerary or a detailed set of reservations was ever made. Both men preferred the flexibility of flying by the seat of their pants.

"Let's go, slow ass! Our tee time is in less than an hour," Nick barked.

"Give me five minutes," Easy shouted from behind the partially closed bathroom door.

Making another quick lap through the channels, Nick stopped when something caught his eye. He immediately hit the volume button. "Easy, check this out! Magnus is on." Toothbrush in hand, Easy darted out of the bathroom and stationed himself between the two double beds. He stared intensely at the TV.

"That guy's a stud," was Easy's only comment.

With a manufactured air of drama, the TV screen panned among a collection of extremely muscular men and other abnormal onlookers, all surrounding another hulk of a man sporting short, tight blond hair as he occupied center stage of a large outdoor platform. With each of his massive arms extended at shoulder level, and an "I'm having a serious bowel movement" look on his face; this Adonis of a man was straining to hold up two large and obviously heavy cast-iron swords, one in each hand. A clock ticking in the corner of the TV screen showed an elapsed time of nearly three minutes. A British announcer, whispering so as not to disturb or distract from this unusual effort, provided a running commentary.

"Defending champion Magnus Ver Magnusson needs only to hold on for twenty more seconds to retain his fourth straight title as World's Strongest Man. This is unprecedented. Look at that face, displaying all the pain and determination of a true champion. Only ten more seconds for Magnus. It looks like he is going to make it with ease. There it is, yes; Magnus has done it once again. Simply tremendous!" shouted the announcer as Magnus tossed the two swords aside and thrust his bulging arms into the air.

"That guy is Magnus, baby! Now let's go!" Nick said impatiently.

After seeing this program for the very first time some years earlier, and countless times since, Nick and Easy had immediately converted "Magnus" from a noun to an adjective and quickly adopted it as their own personal catch phrase to describe any effort they deemed as uncommonly strong or generally just cool. Since Magnus was a four-time winner of the World's Strongest Man competition, no one person better represented the traits both admired. Moreover, they decided, "Magnus" had a ring to it and was fun to say.

Getting a tee time for two at a new course, in a new state, was often at best a total crapshoot. Not only were they certain to be paired with two total strangers, but the greater possibility was that this pair was either related, close friends, or worse yet, married. Both Nick and Easy shared a mutual aversion to the possibility of spending five hours listening to a know-it-all husband confuse his marginally interested wife with conflicting on-course lessons, rules, swing tips, and tirades.

Anyone who had played much golf under these conditions was well aware that these newfound "hook-ups" for the day would come from all walks of life and would certainly have attitudes as unique as their swings. And what was deemed passable social behavior with one's regular foursome would quickly become a question for fate to decide given the random nature of these new pairings. But of all possible considerations, attitude was the single most important ingredient in determining how these temporary new pairings would play out. Attitude alone defined if the day ahead was going to be a good experience or one that made people wish that they had never left the couch, their ice-cold beer, or the comfort of their dominant hand in their pants.

Much like their use of the word Magnus, the boys took great pleasure in first categorizing these new partners, and when appropriate, then taking pot shots at them as they played their round. Among the growing list of peculiar personalities and patently offensive types were:

> "Divot." The quintessential moron both on and off the golf course. A partner only the deeply desperate would spend five hours with given a choice. Slow, grumpy, and often spends thirty minutes looking in the weeds for a worthless 20-year old Dunlop golf ball. Typically chatters non-stop about every single shot, often yelling tired phrases like "I got hosed" or "fuck me naked" with every miscue. As if people usually wear clothes during sex.

> "Lance." A.k.a., Lance Armstrong. This player miraculously pulls off the incredible shot hole after hole long after being given-up for dead. This is actually a supreme compliment to an opposing player. When on the wrong end of a bet, however, being "Lanced" too often during a round is extremely annoying and demoralizing.

> "O.J." This type blames everyone but himself for a sorry shot—the cart girl, a gust of wind, bad yardage, mud on the ball, someone talking during his swing, people standing too close, the Asian stock market, the real killers. Sucking the fun from a round of golf with the zeal of ten Draculas appears to be their life's calling.

"Betty." The total drunk. Looks and acts like he's been in and out of Betty Ford more than Gerald Ford. Always with a six-pack hidden in his golf bag and always with an overused quip handy. "I need another can of swing lube," or "Where's the cart winch, I'm out of aiming fluid." As the booze kicks in, up goes the decibel level and with it come more tired clichés.

"Tagger." This guy is too cool. He's played all the great courses and drones on endlessly about them, whether asked or not. The Tagger has no less than 532 bag tags from every course he's ever played hanging and clanging from his golf bag like unearned trophies. This type can't stop offering everyone swing tips and lessons, but he can't back up the assertion of knowledge with a game that allows them to crack 80.

Leaning on his club in the middle of the fairway, Easy stood waiting for one-half of the day's hook-up, Hank, to play his shot. This elderly, over-served gentleman sported a toupee that couldn't have looked worse if it had had a chinstrap. At that moment, it felt to Easy like Hank was taking longer and longer between shots, with his current effort seeming just short of forever before he finally skulled a miserable shot that barely left the grass—typical of his shots this day.

Easy, distracted, and bitterly annoyed at having to wait all day behind another "Betty," finally launched his ball toward the green only to have it fade weakly into the front bunker. Old Hank couldn't have picked a worse time to ask for swing advice.

"You play pretty well, son. Any tips you can give me?"

Easy couldn't resist repeating an old golf quote he'd once read, "Other than lessons for the rest of your life, yeah I've got a tip: take two months off and then quit all together." Easy turned away quickly, uninterested in Hank's reaction, and walked steadfastly toward the cart where Nick and his beer sat waiting.

"I'm putting. Where did you go?" Nick couldn't wait to ask.

"I'm in the bunker. So, unless you five-putt, it looks like you win Maryland."

"Maryland—I love Maryland. I can't think of a finer state in the union to kick your ass in than Maryland," Nick said, not suppressing his smile.

"Nick, a man that studieth revenge keeps his own wounds green," Easy replied tersely, pissed-off with the entire day.

"What the hell does that mean?" Nick asked.

"It means, if revenge is your ultimate motive, then your wounds will never heal."

Nick pondered the appropriate response for a moment. "Then why didn't you just say that? Or, do I need to put a friggin' wound on your head to get you to stop talking like some goofy Swedish literary Divot? Besides, you're way off base."

Easy quickly countered. "I'm sorry. I didn't know you were an authority on anything Swedish or literary."

"Ah, go blow yourself."

"That's pithy, Nick."

"Then it's okay to tell you to kiss my pithy ass." They drove off in silence toward the green.

Despite what some could have characterized as a cutting exchange between the two, an exchange that in some cultures would have ended with someone receiving a cracked skull or a swift kick to the genital jewel box, a genuine strain on their friendship wasn't possible from such a minor offense. There was simply too much history. They understood each other much too well. Besides, banter of this type was more common than missing a fairway.

Nick would not five-putt and took Maryland by three strokes. With his win in Maryland, a one-stoke victory in Virginia (80-79) and a two-stroke claim in Delaware (84-82), he trailed by only one state after playing seven. Easy, however, found his game in Pennsylvania and won easily with a 78 to Nick's 83, adding to his wins in Oklahoma, Missouri, and Illinois.

Still, Nick had beaten his life long nemesis five times in the last month, a feat he hadn't managed to accomplish in the past three years total. *This should put a grin on old Charlie,* Nick thought to himself behind a smirk as he walked off the final green following four days of battle.

Easy interrupted Nick's moment of celebration with a healthy shot of reality. "Nick, I'm glad you're planning to make this interesting, but think about this for a second. I don't normally shoot in the mid-eighties, so you're gonna need to raise your game if you're serious about winning. This past week was a gift."

Nick, of course, had already realized this fact. Yet, not for a second was he going to let Easy's Pops-like comment to taint his other accomplishments of the week. For the first time, he actually believed he could win, and Easy's admonishment had just confirmed that maybe, subconsciously, Easy might be thinking the same thing.

With Easy's pious lecture a distant memory, Nick had a little extra bounce in his step as he made his way through a canyon of cubicles toward his small office. The fact that he at least had a window and real walls crossed his mind as he peeked into each passing cube.

Not ten seconds after Nick threw his computer case on his desk, Thomas entered Nick's office, a mischievous grin framing his face.

"Well, who won? Give me the details!" Thomas asked with sophomoric anticipation.

"Three to one." Nick paused for effect. "I won three and he got one. It's four states to three."

"Which states?" asked Thomas.

"I won Delaware, Maryland and Virginia, and he got Pennsylvania."

"Alright, you're in the game!" Thomas declared. "Hey, how'd it go at D.O.E.?"

Before Nick could answer the question, his phone rang. "Nick Rose." There was a brief pause. "What's up, Easy? Ah man, how's he doing?" Nick listened intently. "When did it happen?"

It was obvious to Thomas that something was wrong, that something had happened. Nick's next question confirmed his suspicion.

"What hospital?" he asked. "Sure, I'll drop by after work. Let me know if you need anything else. Hang in there, man." Nick hung up the phone and took a deep breath.

"What's up?" Thomas asked with concern.

"Will's dad had a heart attack," Nick said sadly. The answer seemed to take Thomas aback.

"How's he doing?"

"Not real good."

"How's Will, is he all right?"

Nick didn't really know how to answer. "It's hard to tell, they don't get along too well. Pops is an ornery dude, the stereotypical over-zealous parent. He sounded okay, I guess. But he never shows much emotion."

"That's too bad." Trying to change the subject to something more positive, Thomas repeated his question, "How'd it go at the D.O.E.? Did everything run all right?"

"Yeah, but five other companies also had bids in," Nick said with little interest now in work. Still, Thomas pressed on.

"Did you show them the Internet interface we put in?"

"Yeah, but I'm telling you, we've got some tough competition."

Thomas was undaunted. "Do you need me to go with you next time? I've got a suit and tie."

Nick shook his head. "Why does everybody want to be a salesman?"

Chapter 9

▼

Desperate to pass time and distract from the unpleasant reality of Pops' condition, Easy sat alone in the corner of the hospital room reading Nietzsche and waiting for Kendra and Nick. He had only looked at his father twice since he'd arrived, and both times Will Sr. looked at peace, despite the tangled array of equipment monitoring his every condition. The entrance of a young, sneaky-cute blond nurse with bright, haunting blue eyes broke the solitude of his vigil. He noticed the name CASSIE on her gold nametag.

"Hi, I'm Cassie. How are you?"

Easy leapt quickly to his feet, placed the book in his seat behind him, and extended his hand. "Good, thanks! I'm Will Easley."

"Well, since you have the same name, I'm going to assume that's your father," Cassie said with a serene smile.

"It is. And since you're dressed like a nurse, I'm gonna guess that you're...a nurse."

"Yeah, I work the three to midnight shift. Is everyone in the family so perceptive?" she added, grabbing Pops' medical chart hanging at the foot of the bed.

Easy took instantly to her sassy disposition. "The nurse that was in earlier said the first night is the most important. Is that true?" Easy asked, feeling immediately at ease with her sense of humor.

"How a patient responds the first twenty-four hours is extremely important. It's a good thing you brought a book; it could be a long night. If you don't mind me asking, what are you reading?" Easy studied her expression as he held up his book, allowing her to see the title. "Nietzsche, huh? He's a little preachy for my tastes," she said matter-of-factly.

"Yeah, he does get a little long-winded," Easy admitted.

"You might want to try some Voltaire; he's more fun, with a bit of a dark side."

"Sounds interesting," Easy thought. *How does this girl know so much about philosophy?*

A sudden movement at the door caught their attention. Kendra walked in quickly and looked blankly over at Pops lying motionless in the bed. She threw herself into her brother's arms. They shared a long hug.

"How's he doing?" she asked, her voice projecting a slight quiver.

"He's still critical," Easy answered, carefully controlling the tenor of his voice, conscious of the need to put on a strong front for Kendra's sake.

"Has he gotten any better?" Kendra asked, searching for good news.

"I don't know. Cassie, do you know when the doctor is coming by again?"

Cassie took a second to shake Kendra's hand and introduce herself. She explained that the doctor would check in every half hour while she looked down at Pops' chart and began to make notes. The room fell silent, making Nick's unintentionally hard knock seem to resound through the corridors.

"I didn't think I'd ever find you guys." Nick immediately walked toward Kendra and gave her a lingering, heart-felt hug. He also gave Cassie a thorough inspection.

"I'll leave you folks alone. But I'm right down the hall if you need anything," Cassie said, returning Pops' chart to the end of the bed.

"Thanks, it was nice to meet you," Easy said warmly, waving lamely as Cassie walked from the room.

Nick studied her exit. "Whoa! Not bad at all!" he said, without a touch of shame.

"Nick, you're a pig," Kendra said, shaking her head.

"Is she married?" Nick asked.

"No ring—and she reads philosophy," Easy added approvingly.

"Then you can have her."

Nick finally dared to look over at Pops. "So, how's he doing?" he asked.

"Still critical. But if he can make it through the night, they say he's got a good chance. But, they said it was a pretty bad one," Easy reluctantly admitted.

"He'll be all right. He's a tough old bird," Nick offered. Tears began to well up in Kendra's eyes.

"First Mom and now this," she said, referring to events just a year earlier when they'd received word from Oregon that their mother had died in a car crash. They would later learn she was drunk—twice the legal limit drunk.

"If life were fair, Elvis would be alive and all the impersonators would be dead," Easy said without an ounce of sympathy, as he had decided long ago that their mother had abandoned the family and was unworthy flowery sentiment. Their mother's passing was the only point on which Kendra and Easy had ever had a serious disagreement. Easy begrudgingly attended their mother's funeral, but only to provide emotional support for Kendra. He knew this was going to be hard on her as well.

Having spent most of the day and well into the night at his father's bedside, Easy decided he needed a break. Slowly he made his way through the still and eerie corridor, past dozens of darkened rooms made even spookier by the countless other patients within them no doubt clinging to life. When he reached the nurse station, he found

Cassie absorbed in paperwork. He watched her for a moment before interrupting.

"Cassie, is there somewhere I could get a cup of coffee?" he asked politely.

"There's vending machines in cafeteria, but I can get you a cup from the employee lounge if you don't tell anyone. The hospital is dreadfully close to falling below a twenty-five percent profit margin and they're watching coffee pretty closely." She set her paperwork aside and looked directly at him. "So, how you holding up?"

Easy thought for a second before replying, "Not bad, considering."

"If you don't mind me asking, are you two very close?"

"No, I don't mind," Easy replied. "But to be honest, he's always been a tough man to get along with. In fact, he's probably the most stubborn, narrow-minded person I've ever known."

Cassie offered a measured response. "That's a trait of a lot of strong people."

"I just hope I never end up like that," Easy said, looking down at his hands and picking at his fingernails.

With family and friends gathered at the grave of William Easley, Sr., to pay their final respects, Nick did his best to console a crying Kendra as she placed a solitary flower on the casket.

For Nick's final tribute, and for reasons he didn't really understand, he took his thumb, turned up his nose, and made a subtle mocking face toward the casket suspended just above ground. An unexpected sadness filled his body. He searched without success for its source. *What's behind this sadness? Is it for Kendra, for Easy, for death, for Pops' place within his own history?* "See you later, Pops," he whispered, tears beginning to fill his eyes as well.

Easy followed Kendra and Nick, placing a flower on the casket. Several feet away, Nick stopped to watch Easy's reaction, to ponder what he must have been thinking and feeling in this moment of ultimate finality. The minister placed a comforting hand on Easy's shoulder as

Easy bowed his head and slowly and quietly moved his lips. Nick wondered, was it a prayer? One final good-bye? A tribute? Or was he cursing the old man? Nick thought it odd that he himself had cried, but Easy had yet to shed a tear.

As they were led away from the casket, cemetery workers began preparations to lower Pops to his final resting place. Walking slowly, Easy was surprised to notice Cassie lurking in the back among the many mourners. Easy shook a few hands and accepted several warm hugs from Pops' old cronies before stopping to acknowledge Cassie's unexpected presence.

"Thanks for coming by," Easy said softly.

"This is not something I normally do, but I wanted to tell you again how sorry I am."

"I appreciate that, I really do," Easy said.

"Well, I really should be going. My shift starts in an hour." After a long pause, Cassie offered a half wave and turned to walk away. Easy's mind flooded with uncertainty about what to do next. He called to Cassie.

"Hey, ah Cassie, ah, this is kind of awkward, but, would you like to get a cup of coffee sometime?"

Cassie was somewhat surprised but happy for the invitation. "Yeah, I'd like that. I'm in the book under Cassiopeia Young. Give me a call when things settle down for you."

"Cassiopeia, the Queen," Easy said with surprise.

"Yeah, my parents were hippies," she said nonchalantly.

"Okay, well, I'll give you a call in a couple days. And thanks again for coming," Easy said, as Cassie leaned forward and gave him a measured hug.

"It's been one weird day," Easy told Nick later over a beer. "Pops was a royal pain in the ass most of the time, but he was also a decent and moral man, and he took good care of us. It's hard to explain. He was the only dad I ever had, but he was never the dad I always wanted him to be."

Nick offered his perspective. "Easy, we get to choose our friends, our jobs, our wives, and sometimes our foursome, but we don't get to choose our family. Forget about that shit. Just think of the good times. Life is too short to dwell on things you can't change."

"Thanks, Nick, you're right. Life is too short."

"I do have one question I've been dying to ask. What's up with that little nurse?" Nick asked with a smirk.

"I don't know, but we're meeting for coffee," Easy offered with a sly grin.

"Leave it to you to pick up a chick at a funeral," Nick said accusingly.

"I didn't do a thing,"

"Yeah, right."

Over the next several days, Easy would think a lot about Pops. Holding tight to Nick's advice, whenever sour memories bristled to mind he tried to replace them with thoughts of better times, although it wasn't always easy. For Will Easley, Jr., Pops' death was nearly as confusing and complicated as his life had been. For the first time, Easy began to question his own mortality, to reconsider his internal thought processes. If confronted with the same choices, would heredity deliver him to the same decisions? Without ever realizing it until his passing, Easy now began to understand that Pops' status as the dominant example in his life was the reason for his interest in philosophy. He craved outside perspective, balance to his upbringing, choices beyond those Pops had ever offered.

Chapter 10

▼

Squealing the fat tires of his Jeep Wrangler as he turned a sharp corner, Easy was once again late. A check of his dashboard clock confirmed that he was just past acceptable late (15 minutes) and would likely be rude late (more than twenty minutes).

Meanwhile, Cassie was seated quite comfortably in the cafe section of the bookstore casually thumbing through a magazine, the type she'd never subscribe to, *Modern Woman*. An empty seat sat available across from her at an old wooden library-style table. Out of the corner of her eye, a figure moving quickly in her direction drew her attention.

"Sorry I'm late. Have you been waiting long?" Easy said as he approached Cassie, He immediately noticed the contrast between her nurse's uniform and her current look and decided that the Southern Illinois Saluki sweatshirt and her medium-length messy blond hair made her look younger than twenty-seven.

"To be honest, I was just getting ready to leave. I didn't think you were going to show," she said.

"I'm really sorry." Easy's response conveyed more panic than apology. "Please don't go."

"Are you sure you want to be here, Will? 'Cause sometimes people feel some weird obligation because we help take care of their families. It's okay, really."

"Cassie, I do appreciate that, but that's not why I'm here," Easy answered, slowly placing his hand on her shoulder and lightly squeezing it. "Let's start over. I'm gonna get a cup of coffee, need anything?"

"Green tea would be great. Thanks."

"I'll be right back—don't go anywhere." Easy walked away as quickly as he'd arrived, hoping he hadn't blown this first impression. Her smile told him she was forgiving.

Normally Easy hated first dates, preferring to get to know someone in casual situations before thinking romance, before sequestering himself for hours with someone he hardly knew while forming initial impressions, evaluating general chemistry and ultimately deciding if the all important second date was desired. The bookstore was safe and logical. And to his way of thinking, safety in numbers belonged in the early dating process just as clearly as excessive attention to hygiene. But something about Cassie was different. The normal first-date anxiety felt out of place with her.

In less than an hour, they had agreed to escape the distraction of others. In less than an hour, both wanted to abandon all standard-dating protocols; both felt comfortable enough to elevate this first-date thing to a more private setting, to be totally on their own, to work without a net. Easy hadn't blown it.

At over 1,700 acres, Greensfelder Park was St. Louis County's largest park. Lying at the extreme, outermost foothills of the gently rolling Ozark mountain range, the park was quiet, tranquil; it was a good place, Easy thought, to get to know someone. As he looked around at the massive trees, shaded trails, and spectacular views, more than once he fantasized about the possible placement of golf holes throughout the park's more scenic areas. Cassie, he discovered, was reminded of horseback riding and an elementary school hayride at the park many years before. And what started as a simple meet-and-greet for coffee with little or no expectations on his part had turned quite naturally and effortlessly into the perfect nine-hour first date.

"So how much more law school do you have left?" Cassie asked.

"About a year and a half," Easy said, while considering that aspect of his future.

"What do you want to do once you're finished?"

"I don't know. Law school was Pops' idea." Easy paused to reflect upon the discussions that led to his enrollment. "Pops used to say, 'Anybody can be a damn school teacher.' I don't even know if I want to finish now."

"You've got to do what makes you happy," she said without hesitation.

"That was never much of an option with Pops. He made us do what made him happy. What made you get into nursing?"

Having thought about this many times before, Cassie offered her standard, yet honest response. "I don't know exactly. Somehow I just always knew I'd be a nurse. It was never something I had to decide. I just did it."

"God, I wish I knew what I was meant to do," Easy said.

"If only it were that simple, Will. Some people wander their whole lives, while others gravitate naturally to what they're meant to do. I don't think it's really our choice which type we are."

The crunchy footsteps and heavy breathing of a jogger growing louder from behind prompted both to move toward the edge of the gravel path just as the fit young man dashed past. Easy used their close proximity to change the subject to matters of much more immediate interest.

"Are you free on Sunday? I'd like to get together again if you're free, I mean, if you want to."

"I knew something was up with you two," Nick offered over a beer. "I haven't heard a peep out of you in two weeks. Hell, if it weren't for this trip, it would've probably been another month before you called me back."

Easy swigged his own beer, deciding he couldn't really deny the allegation, even though Nick expected him to. "Oh yeah? When did you become so in tune to the human condition?"

"About four beers and a poetry reading ago."

"Glad to know I could help in your latent evolution," Easy laughed.

"That's where we disagree, Junior. I've decided any form of evolution is a curse."

"So, you still think life is one giant Mensa meeting and it's okay to be Jethro Clampett?"

"Is something wrong with keeping things simple?"

"Not at all. Welcome to Pinehurst, Jethro."

By virtue of having won the last state, Nick had earned control of course choice and travel dates, and he'd immediately picked Pinehurst, North Carolina, as their first non-working, golf-only trip. Both had long agreed that the U.S. could lay claim to only two true golfing Meccas, with Pebble Beach, California, being the second. Much like St. Andrews, the Scottish birthplace of golf, it was common practice, almost a calling, for certified golf addicts to set pilgrimage for at least one of these historic and hallowed grounds, and Nick and Easy were no different. Besides, Nick had something up his sleeve concerning Pebble Beach that would need to wait.

The patrons crowding the neighborhood watering hole that first night were divided almost equally between locals and well-informed out-of-towners. Many, they surmised, were there for identical reasons, visiting Pinehurst for the first time to fulfill their long-standing fantasy.

Instantly standing out among the typical Friday evening bar crowd of weekend golfers and gray-haired locals, a drop-dead gorgeous, shiny-haired brunette strolled in. A starched white button-down shirt and extremely painted-on blue jeans added nicely to her already considerable allure. Nick and Easy exchanged a pleasantly stunned look as she sauntered past. As if almost rehearsed, they turned to one another and offered the same alcohol enhanced conclusion.

"Outstanding!" Easy declared.

"Man, that's got to be the nicest ass in North Carolina." Following a pause, Nick couldn't resist a slight dig at Easy's expense: "Too bad you've got a girlfriend."

"Yeah, but I'm not dead," Easy declared, studying her walk like a tricky green. Nick quickly jumped from his barstool and began tucking his shirt back into his jeans.

"Where you going?" Easy asked.

"To the bathroom. Then I'm gonna show you how it's done with little Miss North Carolina there," Nick announced, a six-beer confidence fueling his manufactured cockiness.

"Hold up, hotshot. I got ten bucks that says I get further than you do."

"You've got a girlfriend, remember." Nick reminded him again.

"Let's just do it for the sport of it. Nothing's gonna happen. A guy can't let himself get rusty," Easy countered.

Nick found this amusing. "Ten bucks, huh? Why not."

He decided to take immediate advantage of already being out of his seat and walked slowly toward the slender brunette, now seated alone at a table near the restroom door. He offered a lingering stare in her direction. It went completely unnoticed. Not wanting to appear awkward and blow his chance at making a good first impression, Nick clumsily continued past and ducked into the restroom where he decided to regroup and consider a more thoughtful introduction.

With Nick temporarily removed from the picture, Easy measured his opening. Walking slowly, but with disarming confidence, he approached her table, extended his hand, and offered a greeting that quickly brought a broad smile to her fresh, narrow face. They shook hands.

Primping before the restroom mirror as if simply moving a hair or two could mean the difference between failure and success, Nick rehearsed several opening gambits. Without due appreciation for how completely unimportant the arrangement or part of his hair was to successfully wooing the prized brunette, he dried his hands with a paper towel and plotted his next move, unaware that just outside the door, Easy's preemptive strike was quickly making trivial any strategy Nick decided upon.

Emerging from the bathroom to find Easy sitting at the table with their ten-dollar bet, Nick stood dumbfounded, sporting a look normally reserved for the last kid picked when choosing sides for a game of dodge-ball.

"Nick, this is Janelle," Easy offered, acting as if he'd known her forever. They shook hands as Nick threw a quick glare in Easy's direction.

"Nice to meet you, Janelle."

"Nice to meet you, Nick," Janelle answered in a polite, thick, very southern twang.

"Janelle is home for the weekend from Wake Forest," Easy explained, intent on showing what substantial progress he'd made in the short time Nick labored in the restroom checking his teeth, nose hair, and generally offending the mirror with an assortment of contorted faces.

"And my parents are driving me plain nuts. I just had to get out of that house before somebody got strangled," she said quickly.

"Sounds like you need a shot, Janelle," Nick offered, resorting to the tried and true alcohol-based strategy.

"I would absolutely love a shot! Do you guys like tequila? I love tequila. That's my favorite."

"Perfect," Nick thought to himself. "Junior, be a sport and run up to the bar and get us some tequila shots," Nick said slyly, looking to get Janelle alone for a moment.

"Sure! Janelle, any preference?" Easy asked politely, intent on playing it a bit more laid-back. *Poor Nick*, Easy thought to himself. *Like she's not gonna see right through this shark attack.*

"Cuervo if they've got it, unless they have Patron. Patron's even better," she added.

"Coming right up!" Before making his way to the bar, Easy leaned over and whispered something in Janelle's ear that brought another short, loud laugh and a corresponding scowl from Nick.

"Your friend is really funny," she said, as Easy walked away.

"I don't really know the guy that well," Nick answered. "In fact, we just met on this trip. He's actually a friend of a friend from back home, but my buddy had to get foot surgery and left me stuck with the reservations and with this guy."

Janelle was sympathetic. "Are you still having a good time?"

"Yeah, he's been cool. But to be honest," Nick leaned in closely, glanced around once and lowered his voice, "I think he might be gay. I mean, he's said some things." For Nick, Easy's prompt return to the table was well timed, as he was certain Janelle was about to ask him to explain his bogus allegation and he hadn't thought that far ahead.

"Cuervo Gold was the best they had," Easy offered apologetically as he set three shots down on the table. After downing the shots, Easy launched into his rapid-fire sneeze attack, took a quick breath, sneezed again, took another short breath, and repeated the exact motion four to five times within a half-minute.

"Are you okay?" Janelle asked, startled.

"Yeah, I'm fine. I'm kind of allergic to hard liquor."

"That is so cute."

Easy sensed an opening. "Janelle, would you like to dance?"

"Sure, but can we do another shot first? I've got some catchin' up to do."

"Absolutely. Nick, your turn to buy," Easy demanded, pointing toward the bar.

Nick gave Janelle a small wink. "Be right back," he said with confidence, knowing he had Easy at a slight disadvantage since Janelle wasn't likely to ask him point blank about his sexual preference. At least not in the next five minutes.

"Have you ever been to North Carolina before?" Janelle asked politely.

"First time, but everything is really beautiful here," Easy said in his best flirting tone.

"So, you're having a good time?" she added.

"It could be better. Nick's girlfriend is coming into town tomorrow and we had to cancel our last two rounds." This surprised Janelle.

"He's got a girlfriend?"

"I mean, fiancée. He just got engaged. I keep forgetting," Easy claimed with such complete sincerity, he knew that it bordered on sinister.

Nick returned with three more shots. After taking his seat, the three clanked their shot glasses together above the center of the table and downed the sneaky smooth, golden liquid. Once again, Easy started to sneeze. Quivering slightly through the shoulders and smacking her red lips together, Janelle turned toward Easy, "Your name's Will, right?"

"It is."

"What about that dance, Will?"

"I'd love to dance."

As they removed themselves from the table, Janelle took Easy's hand and led him through the bar toward a small, crowded dance floor. Easy looked back at Nick with a satisfied smile as he and Janelle made their way to what Easy was quickly becoming convinced would be the day's final payoff.

Halfway through their first dance, Janelle leaned over and began shouting above the music toward Easy.

"Can I ask you a question?" she said. Without giving Easy much chance to respond, she continued, "Are you gay? I had to ask 'cause we don't get many gays coming down here to play golf. Now it's okay if you are 'cause I got gay friends at school, but you don't seem like you're gay, the way you dance and all."

Easy's first reaction was surprise, followed immediately by the realization that he would have probably been mad as hell had he not appreciated the sheer genius of Nick's move. "Gay? No! What makes you say that?" he asked, now certain of the only possible source.

"Because Nick said you might be, but he wasn't exactly for sure. I mean, you don't look like it to me, but I guess you never know," Janelle explained without prejudice. Suddenly, Easy seized Janelle's slender hand and dragged her back to the table where Nick, reasonably confident now of what was coming his way, chugged his beer between smirks.

Easy immediately leaned over the table and into Nick's face, "Gay huh? Outside asshole! Let's go!" Easy demanded.

Nick stood up and turned toward Janelle, "We'll be right back."

Easy pointed to Janelle, "Yeah, don't go anywhere. We'll be right back." They each grabbed their beers and darted toward the patio door.

Striding several steps ahead, Easy quickly exited the side patio door and abruptly stopped, wheeled around, and shouted at Nick, "What is your problem?"

"My problem? You're the one who threw the cock-block when I went to take a piss. You always do that shit, Junior!"

"Sometimes, Nick, you act like a complete psycho," Easy said bluntly.

Nick was no longer able to remain calm. "This ain't about me. You've spent a lifetime trying to one-up me and this is where it stops, Junior."

"Don't call me Junior," warned Easy.

Nick pointed to Easy's chest. "Starting right now, I'm dedicating the rest of my life to kicking your ass. Let's go, right now."

"Are you saying you want to fight me? You've got to be kidding! Nick. This is a new low."

Nick was defiant. "Hell no, I ain't talking about fighting. If we walk back in looking like Ned Beatty from *Deliverance*, neither one of us gets laid. I'm talking about Strongest Man gets the girl."

Easy was puzzled. "Strongest Man? What the hell are you talking about?"

"That's right, Strongest Man!" Nick declared.

With this ambiguous declaration, Nick immediately began searching around the parking lot, looking for something that would facilitate his challenge. Easy, his hands resting on his hips, watched Nick wander the parking lot in a state of drunken disorientation. Finally, leaning against the foundation in the back corner of the old pub near the property's back fence, Nick spotted an old tire. As if getting caught taking this rotting tire could violate some local statute, Nick scanned the area to make sure the coast was clear. Feeling safe, he grabbed the weathered tire from the corner and hauled it back to where Easy stood holding his beer.

"Three throws. Whoever throws it farther is the Strongest Man, and the Strongest Man gets the girl."

"This is retarded. You're retarded," said Easy, astounded by the prospect of actually having a drunken tire toss in the middle of the parking lot.

"So, you admit you cock-blocked." Nick insisted.

"It was a bet Nick, come on."

"Then let's settle this like men," Nick demanded.

"Why do you keep doing this to yourself?" Easy thought aloud.

"Okay, if you don't want to go first, then I'll go first. This is for Little League!" Nick took the tire and started swinging it back and forth. With a muffled grunt, he let loose and sent the tire flying.

Realizing he had no choice but to indulge Nick at this point, Easy walked over and placed an empty beer can to mark the spot where the tire had landed. "Have at it, Junior!" Nick slurred.

Easy walked back to the unofficial starting line and turned toward Nick. "You must love humiliation."

"Shut up and throw the tire!"

Begrudgingly, Easy took the tire in one hand and started swaying it back and forth. After three swings, he heaved it about fifteen feet, just short of Nick's toss.

"That's not even worth marking. Is that all you got?" Nick said as he picked up the tire and zigzagged back to where Easy was standing.

"And this is for stealing Paulette Rigger in tenth grade. Remember that?" Nick added, as he wound up, let loose a deep grunt, and flung the tire just past the beer can marking his earlier toss.

Easy methodically moved the beer can up to the new benchmark and returned with the tire. "Okay, Nick, this is for wasting my time with your silly-ass games." Easy again wound up and heaved the tire high in the air, watching as it fell short of the mark.

"You're not getting laid with that weak shit," Nick said as he retrieved the tire.

Easy slugged his beer and wiped the sweat building on his forehead with his forearm. Nick zeroed in on the beer can standing upright in the parking lot and started his wind-up. "And this is for Pops, for calling me a fucking goof for twenty years and for training you to be a fucking Nazi."

Tire in hand, Nick's mind flashed back to Magnus Ver Magnusson. What would Magnus do? How would Magnus attack this challenge? As the tire spun airborne, Nick, having nearly fallen down, staggered to regain his balance. Nick thrust his arms into the air as the tire sailed nearly ten feet past the can.

In virtual silence, Easy moved the can to the new mark and returned with the tire for his final throw. Drunk with concentration, he started his wind-up. "To fucking hell with you and with Pops!" Easy shouted, as he let out a deep grunt and a mighty heave that sent the tire spinning tight and flying high before finally returning to the ground a good three feet past Nick's best effort.

Stunned, Nick shook his head and murmured to himself. "That son-of-a-bitch Pops is haunting me from the grave."

Easy overheard the remark, "Not anymore Nick, not anymore. I'm sorry, I really am. Now let's get out of here before some cop with a tourist fetish decides to shackle us for the rest of his boring-ass shift."

"What about Janelle?" Nick asked.

"She's probably surrounded by now. Feel like another battle?"

"Not really."

"Me neither."

As they walked off, arm over shoulder, Nick looked back at the tire and shook his head in extended disbelief. He could almost feel the hair on the back of his neck rise, sensing Pops' wry spirit now leering down at him from the heavens, his turned-up pug nose snorting its evil approval.

Pulling up the long circular driveway that next morning, around a huge front lawn manicured so precisely it resembled a giant putting green, Nick and Easy eased their convertible rental up to the main entrance of the historic Carolina Hotel at the Pinehurst Resort. Four obsequious young men in knickers, white shirts, and plaid sweater vests bolted forward to offer assistance. One attendant opened the car door, two went for the trunk, and the fourth offered the official "Welcome to Pinehurst" greeting.

As they exited the car, a stately, almost ghostly aura presented itself around the historic building and its immaculate grounds. Easy was impressed.

"This place is Magnus!"

"Pops would turn in his grave if he knew you were spending his money on shit like this. I guarantee my dad's rolling," Nick suggested, weirdly gratified by the thought. A quick grim glance was Easy's only response.

Less than two hours later, Nick, ever dapper in his black sweater vest and pleated khaki pants, threw a white golf tee into the air to determine which of the two would hit first to start the round. Resembling a wadded up paper towel, in pants that looked like they had never met an iron and a free shirt given to him at some forgettable corporate golf outing, Easy watched the tee Nick had thrown into the air land softly atop the short grass.

"Looks like I'm first," Easy said calmly.

This place is like out of a friggin dream, was Nick's more immediate thought, feeling a sudden wave of nerves as their names were announced, formally allowing entrance onto the first tee.

Of the eight courses open to public play within the resort, the No. 2 Course at Pinehurst was easily the most famous and storied, having hosted more than a dozen major amateur and professional championships over the past seventy years. Adding to Nick's nervous energy was the busy practice green a few yards away, filled with multiple foursomes waiting their turn and listening for their name to be announced. Many had caddies, friends, and spouses on hand to watch, further adding to the frenetic atmosphere and already substantial first-swing pressure.

Despite the unnerving environment, Easy proved equal to the challenge as he planted his ball into the ground, stared down the wide, straight, first fairway, and smoothly launched a dart down the middle.

"Nice shot!" Nick offered as he teed up his ball, stood behind it for a moment, and took a few easy practice swings. With a deep breath behind him, he approached the ball, glanced once more at his target, and clobbered the ball down the middle, just left and slightly past the spot where Easy's ball had settled.

"Looks like we're gonna have a battle today!" Easy said gamely.

"It's gonna be a battle all right!" Nick answered, trying to convince himself that he could tame this beast of a course, have a great round, and ultimately claim the state.

After collecting their bags, Nick and Easy began the surreal march down the fairway toward their waiting balls. With each step, Nick's mind wandered between admiration for the towering longleaf pines framing each side of the first fairway, appreciation for the rich and colorful history of the course, and, most importantly, whether or not he would play well. Having read several reviews of the course, he knew it had tamed the world's best golfers many times over, yet he couldn't help but think of how harmless and serene it looked to his eye. Where had Donald Ross, in nearly forty years of tinkering with the layout since the first ball was hit in 1907, hidden the gremlins that had caused titans like Hogan, Snead, Palmer, and Nicklaus to scratch their heads? What was it about these perfectly groomed fairways and fiendish greens that had lent themselves so readily to the creation of such celebrated new chapters in golf's already grand legacy? The focused gaze Easy was wearing left Nick considering another pressing truth, that they, too, had a bit of history to write in whom would claim North Carolina.

With unceremonious regard to the venue, Nick stopped to light a cigarette as they walked in lockstep toward their waiting golf balls.

"So, how is Cassie taking this, you going on these trips without her?"

"She has no choice," Easy said with conviction. "Either we get to finish or she's finished."

Nick laughed. "Yeah, you talk tough!"

"She knows this is serious, Nick."

"Yeah, but here's the million-dollar question, is she any good in bed?" Nick cocked his head to one side and threw Easy a curious look, eager to hear his response.

"Have you ever heard of a nurse that was lame in the sack?" Easy then paused, measuring his next thought. "In fact, if I don't put a ring on that girl's finger, I probably won't ever get married."

Nick stopped in his tracks. "Fuck, we're never gonna finish this. You're gonna run off and get married and screw this whole thing up!"

Easy continued to walk ahead, very matter-of-fact in his response. "Oh, we're gonna finish all right. Don't worry about me!"

Nick took another puff from his cigarette as they continued walking down the first fairway. Suddenly he let go with a series of deep, hacking coughs so severe both were forced to stop.

"Jesus, I thought you were going to quit that shit!" said Easy.

"I've tried, Lord knows I've tried. I've got demons, okay, serious demons. They won't let me quit." Nick hacked again.

As always, Easy made the solution sound all too simple. "Nick, it's all in your head. Just don't think about it."

"No, Will, it's a serious addiction."

"That patch seemed to work for a while. Get back on those things," Easy suggested sincerely.

"I can't wear the patch the rest of my life," Nick countered.

"Why not?"

"Because, it's not practical. Besides, I'd probably end up rolling the damn thing and smoking it one night in some bar." Easy smiled and shook his head at the mental picture of Nick desperately putting a lighter to a rolled up patch.

With the match tied as they approached the tenth tee, shaking heads and hanging jaws had far out-paced fist pumps and smiles. "This place is insane," Easy suggested.

"Almost ridiculous," Nick countered.

"I guess you don't get to be one of the ten best in the world without good reason."

"I know it's one of the ten hardest," Nick said, while studying the yardage book.

"Donald Ross must have been seriously pissed-off when he laid this out. It's the only possible explanation. He must have caught his wife humping a caddie or something."

"Especially on eight," Nick suggested, referring to the nearly impossible 470 yard, left-bending par four.

As they played their way through one inspired hole after another, all seeming as good or better than the last, both agreed that Pinehurst No. 2 lived up to its lofty ranking among the world's best golf courses, public or private. Yet, despite the course's relentless difficulty, or perhaps because of it, this was the tightest match to date of their bet, with neither man able to manage more than a one-stroke lead.

Stationed near the front of the eighteenth green, Nick stood behind his ball studying his upcoming putt, a forty-footer that must first cross an understated mound before gently bending to a back right pin position. Easy stood to Nick's left, leaning on his putter and watching with keen interest. Nick, uncomfortable with his line, walked another circle around the hole, trying to dissect the break and speed.

"Are you gonna putt or what? I've had relationships that didn't take this long," Easy said.

"Shut the hell up. This is important." Following two quick glances toward the cup, Nick finally sent his ball rolling. He stood nearly frozen as the ball approached the cup. To his complete astonishment, it disappeared into the hole.

"Yeah, baby," he said behind clinched teeth, cutting the air with a stiff upper cut from his clinched fist.

"Looks like I need this to tie, huh?" Easy asked rhetorically, already certain of the score.

"That's right, Junior!" Nick affirmed, outwardly happy with holing his birdie putt.

Easy's expression turned rigid as he walked to a spot less than fifteen feet from the cup. Bending from the waist, he placed his ball on the green and retrieved a dime he'd used to mark the exact location of his ball. After spending a few seconds squatting behind the ball and studying the intended line, Easy moved in, glanced one final time at the hole, and without hesitation struck his old putter to the ball. Nick could only curse as the ball rolled on a perfect line straight into the heart of the cup.

"Magnus, baby, Magnus!" Easy shouted, a huge grin splashing across his face.

"You son-of-a-bitch!" Nick said, while walking over to where Easy was plucking the ball from the cup. He threw an arm around his friend.

Neither seemed to mind that there would be no clear winner, the first tie of their tournament. Both had played some of their best golf yet, and more importantly, both were satisfied that they'd withstood a surprising new pressure unlike any they had felt with their previous bets—the pressure now associated with winning a state.

Nick and Easy agreed that Pinehurst No. 2 had more than lived up to its reputation. It had proven demanding yet ultimately fair, and they had walked away feeling as if they had shown it some of their best golf. Both had shot an 81 from the blue tees, which at 6,741 yards, was a sturdy test for even the most capable low-handicappers, considering it was their first time around.

As they loaded their gear into the trunk of the rental, Nick offered his summary of the day: "If all 50 states are this much fun, we're in for a hell of a ride."

"I'd have preferred to kick your ass, but I can't say this wasn't fun."

"I think a cocktail might be in order."

Not long after, they found themselves standing below the bright green neon glow at the foot of a stairway leading down to the entrance of a bar called The Basement. One of their playing partners that day had assured them they would find plenty of cute locals in The Basement.

It didn't take long for the appropriate libations to begin flowing, and even less time to find acceptable company, as evidenced by a waitress delivering four tequila shots to the table where Nick and Easy sat with two young ladies in their mid-twenties, Cindy and Kim. Finding female companionship was surprisingly easy when you were, a) on vacation; b) friendly toward people; and c) willing to buy a lot of drinks. Under these conditions, it had taken all of twenty minutes for Nick to get a response to his flirting from the two girls and for the foursome to snag a table together.

With a cigarette smoldering between his lips, Nick handed the waitress a green American Express card and passed out the most recent round of tequila shots. Hoisting his shot in the center of the table, Nick started to offer the obligatory toast but stopped when he noticed a perplexed look on Kim's cute, suntanned face. Kim, the short blonde of the two, threw a puzzled glance toward the waitress and, more specifically, toward the credit card. She followed this peculiar look with a question, delivered in a suitable southern accent. "What kind of card was that?"

Nick looked directly at Kim. "That is an American Express Card. Don't leave home without it!"

"They make green ones?" she answered, quite pretentiously. Nick was not amused.

"Yeah they make green ones. Haven't you ever had a job, or should we be toasting to Daddy's money?" he asked, not sacrificing sarcasm.

"Let's drink to Daddy's money, I like that!" Kim answered sincerely.

Nick, buoyed by a great round of golf, was in rare form, flirting, dishing compliments, and kissing ass in every manner possible. And Kim, much like Annette Thurman many years before, appeared to enjoy his attention.

As the recently acquainted foursome threw back their shots, Nick shouted, "Duck, girls" over the house band's loud and dreadful cover of Bob Seger's "Old Time Rock and Roll." No sooner did the warning register with the girls than Easy had ripped off a series of big, juicy sneezes.

Kim gave Nick a puzzled look. "How did you know he was going to sneeze?"

Easy, having long grown tired of any lengthy explanation detailing the when's and how's and cause and effect of his sneeze attacks, said simply, "I'm allergic to tequila."

"Then why do you drink it?" Kim asked.

Easy held his shot glass in the air and, with a mildly drunken slur, declared, "In the words of John Fletcher, 'Best while you have it, use your breath. There is no drinking after death.'"

Cindy, the taller, somewhat plainer but equally attractive second blonde chimed in, "Aren't you the drunken poet."

"Yes I am! I am a drunken poet," Easy said simply, the tequila spurring his newfound identity. "Nick's even read some of my poetry on stage, haven't you, Nickie?"

"Fuck you, Junior!"

In the middle of what started as a hearty laugh, Nick began coughing, almost choking on his beer. After taking more than a moment to regain his composure, he decided the next logical step for the evening should not involve Easy or Cindy. It was time to make his move on Kim before everyone was too trashed. It was time for "divide and conquer." He followed Easy into the restroom to suggest his strategy.

The "divide and conquer" was a pick-up ploy designed to separate the multi-female support unit, to pair off and let each girl decide what happens next without undue influence from the other girl or girls who may be present. Females, Nick had observed, tended to be more spontaneous and open-minded when their behavior was not under the scrutiny of friends. It boiled down to a reputation thing that made no sense whatsoever, given that most girls always end up telling each other every blow, so to speak, of what happened when they picked up guys.

His strategy paid immediate dividends. Less than a half-hour later, a drunken Nick was humping an equally drunken Kim in a side parking lot of the celebrated Carolina Hotel. Although Nick would have liked to believe his magnetic personality and endearing charm were responsible for having this near-stranger's panties strewn on the dashboard, the credit for current events had much more to do with the tequila shots he'd bought at the bar, the time-tested "divide and conquer" strategy, and Kim's predisposition toward an ending of this sort.

The random flashing of headlights around the parking lot suddenly caught Nick's attention. His gut reflex was panic and fear that at any moment, a bright spotlight would flood the cab of Kim's sport utility vehicle and some local Barney Fife type would cart him off to jail for lewd conduct, indecent exposure, or some other equally embarrassing offense.

After staring more closely for a moment, Nick shook his head in amazement. "Crazy bastard," he muttered. Less than a crisp seven-iron from Nick's spot in the parking lot, he recognized Easy behind the wheel of the convertible, top down, with Cindy at his side. Suddenly, the bright brake lights dimmed and Easy and Cindy streaked off across the manicured front lawn of the Carolina Hotel. Following a brief fishtail through the once undisturbed grass, Easy quickly maneuvered the car back onto the circular driveway and sped off toward the exit, never actually coming too close to the main entrance and, as it would turn out, without actually doing much damage to the velvet turf.

Nick, sitting alert alongside a fully exposed Kim, watched in complete disbelief. "That was so incredibly Magnus."

"He's crazy!" Kim said directly.

Nick, eager to return to business, offered Kim a measured dose of sincerity as he resumed kissing her neck. "Speaking of crazy, I'm not leaving until tomorrow. I need to get your number."

Kim's reply slapped Nick back to near sobriety. "I don't think my husband would like that."

Nick was momentarily speechless, "Did…you ever mention you were married?" he asked sincerely.

"You never asked," she replied without a trace of guilt.

Nick shook his head, all the while thinking that this was not the sort of information he should be responsible for discovering.

Stretched out across the bed and nursing a quart of Gatorade, Nick was relieved to see Easy walk through the door of their hotel room. "Good morning, Mario." The reference to famed racecar driver Mario Andretti was not acknowledged.

"Hey," Easy said softly.

"I thought I was going to have to bail you out of jail," Nick added with relief.

"For what?" Easy said with manufactured innocence.

Nick looked him dead in the eyes, "Come on, I saw the whole thing spinning across the front lawn."

Easy acknowledged the worst. "No shit! How?" he asked with a hint of surprise and panic blended in his voice.

Nick softened his judgmental tone. "Me and super freak were doin' it in her car in the parking lot when you decided to go off-road."

Easy was astonished. "You're kidding. You saw that?"

Nick needed details. "Do they know it's you? Did they catch you?"

"No, I don't even know if they've noticed. We went straight to Cindy's house. And this morning, I took a cab back. You don't think I'm stupid enough to drive that car back here, do ya?"

Nick relaxed a bit, "I wasn't exactly sure how stupid you are. I mean, that was a pretty dumb move, Junior."

It was obvious now that no one from the front desk or, worse yet, security, had approached Nick about the incident.

"Let's get showered and get the hell out of here," Easy said, walking into the bathroom.

"Are you sure you don't want to trash the room before we check out?" Nick shouted back.

"Funny!"

"So how was she?" Nick called back, keenly interested in whether Easy had fallen off the fidelity wagon and had been unfaithful to Cassie.

"I slept on the couch." Easy yelled back before poking his head from behind the door. "I don't think she had much interest after I threw up," he added, his mouth now full of toothpaste. "Besides, I wouldn't do that to Cassie."

With a bit of honest shame, Easy went on to offer some insight into his conscience and into the events of the past evening. "We've gotta grow up, Nick."

Nick could afford only mild offense at the remark. "What do you mean, 'we'?" he asked, thoughts of his own transgression with a married woman still fresh in his mind.

Having escaped from the Carolina Hotel without prosecution and now safely on the flight home, Easy was reclining in his aisle seat, trying to get some much needed sleep, when he felt a firm tap on the shoulder. When he opened his eyes, he noticed Nick in the window seat, hunched forward and wrestling with the carry-on bag sitting at his feet. After a considerable tussle with the bag, Nick was finally able to place it in the open seat between them and unzip its top. Easy's eyes lit up as Nick pulled a leather bound folder from the bag. A gold seal across the front read, "Pinehurst Since 1895."

"Where did you get that?" Easy asked, his eyes wide.

"I stole it from the hotel room." Nick said proudly. "I thought we could make it into a traveling trophy, keep the scorecards and stuff in it. Plus, Thomas from work, he's so into this that he keeps a log and a color-coded map of our states on his computer. I was thinking, whoever wins the whole thing gets the book for a trophy. In fact, since you're still ahead, you get to keep it."

Easy took the folder and began inspecting it closely. With a small smile crossing his face, he looked over at Nick and nonchalantly offered a thought, "I'll bet they can't wait to have us back at Pinehurst!"

Nick and Easy spent most of their free time that first summer and fall chasing cheap airfares to the more remote states and road tripping to other states close to home. Thanks to an unofficial airline pilot strike, where calling in sick and wrecking havoc with flight schedules was the pilots' tactic of choice against management, the two were able to take advantage of unusually inexpensive tickets offered by the airlines to lure back disgruntled customers. With discount tickets readily available, the boys decided to cover as much ground as possible and were able to fly to Nevada, Colorado, and Georgia for less than one thousand dollars total per man.

On several occasions, namely at prominent courses like Harbor Town and Pinehurst, green fees took more from their pocket than did airfare. But to their way of thinking, the cost of a plane ticket was secondary; as they had decided their bet warranted playing the very best courses they could find. Walking up the eighteenth fairway with the red and white stripes of the Harbor Town lighthouse to guide them, or having a herd of elk meander the greens and fairways at a great Nicklaus-designed course high in the Rocky Mountains, was only fitting.

From a drunken bar bet between friends had emerged a golf junkie's dream come true, a highly personal and unique links-style adventure. And, of course, it was still the ultimate bet.

In fact, it was not at all uncommon for some "Betty," "Divot," or "Tagger" to comment with genuine envy on their wager and suggest an immediate desire to replicate the cross-country excursion.

Of all the characters Nick and Easy would be paired with that summer, their favorite was a chicken by-products executive from Little Rock, Arkansas who introduced himself as Dickey, or, to his closest friends, Big Dickey.

Everything about Big Dickey was casual, large, and loud, from his belly to his banter. Even his putter had personality. With a shaft thicker than a wooden broomstick and an oversized head that resembled an anvil, the monstrosity that was his putter sported the name "The Hog." And every time Big Dickey sank a putt with "The Hog," he would let out a loud pig-like oink, oink, oink sound. Not a Razorback "Soooweee" as might have been expected, but a solid oink, oink, oink. Dickey also had clever names for many of his shots. One putt he missed he called a Rock Hudson—looked straight but it wasn't. Or the Linda Ronstadt drive because he just "Blue Bayou."

Old Dickey asked for details about every state the boys had played. He expressed openly, while treating everyone to post-round drinks, of his building new desire to load up "The Hog" and convince his best buddy Doc to undertake a similar journey, only with considerably larger financial implications.

All together, Nick and Easy played eighteen states that first year: Illinois, Oklahoma, Missouri, Pennsylvania, Delaware, Virginia, Maryland, Indiana, Ohio, Minnesota, Kansas, North Carolina, South Carolina, Colorado, Tennessee, Nevada, Utah, and Arkansas.

The tie in Pinehurst seemed to start a trend of playing close matches and above-average golf. When it came time to set the clubs aside for the winter and refocus on oft-neglected personal matters, Nick was more than holding his own. The official tally rested at one tie, nine states in Nick's favor, and eight for Easy.

Chapter 11

It was a bitter cold night, near zero, and the heater in Easy's Jeep was unable the keep pace with the cold air leaking in and swirling about inside. Easy loved his Jeep nine months of the year, recognizing that during the winter months it might as well have been the poorest vehicle ever made in terms of keeping outside elements where they belonged—outside. Hunched over and sitting on her hands, Cassie tried in vain to keep her extremities from freezing as she and Easy approached Nick's apartment for a dinner date with Nick and his new girlfriend, Rachel.

"So, what's this one do?" Cassie asked between shivers, inquiring partly out of curiosity but also in search of relevant material to discuss later that evening.

"She's a flight attendant. Nick met her on a business trip. He acts like he really likes her," Easy said, optimistically.

"How long have they been going out?"

"About three months," answered Easy.

"Is she from here?"

"No, she's based in Chicago."

"Oh, a GUD." Cassie said with dismissive charm.

"What's a GUD?" Easy asked, thinking he'd heard them all.

"Geographically Un-Desirable." Cassie shook her head. "Long distance never works. All you get are the good times: getting together is always one big party. Since you never have to deal with any of the day-to-day crap, you don't get to know the person on terms that can make the relationship work out in the long run."

"GUD, close, near, far…he's never had much luck when it comes to relationships. I'm just happy to see him excited about someone," Easy said in defense of Nick's latest companion.

"That's too bad. He's a cute guy," Cassie admitted graciously.

"Don't let him hear you say that. His ego is big enough already."

"Ego doesn't bother me. I'm dating you, aren't I?" Cassie leaned over to Easy's cold cheek and planted a kiss.

Nick and Easy, contrary to conventional male behavior, were taking turns loading the dishwasher following dinner. Cassie, meanwhile, was sipping her wine as she surveyed Nick's kitchen. She was surprised at how well equipped and neat it was kept.

Nick's girlfriend, Rachel, a petite brunette with a model face and wide, toothy smile, was enjoying another glass of Merlot while inspecting the various Christmas decorations littering the kitchen. For no apparent reason, she plucked a ceramic cooking grandma figurine from the stovetop and gave it an odd look before returning it to its rightful place.

"So Nick, what's the next state going to be?" Cassie asked, having learned from Easy that Nick had temporary control of their travel schedule.

"Yeah, Nick," Easy was eager to discover, "where are we off to next?"

"Well, I've been saving this as sort of a surprise, but now's as good a time as any, so here's what I was thinking. I've got a convention in San Francisco in January and, well, Jack Nicklaus once said that if he had only one more round of golf to play," Nick paused for effect, "he'd play it at Pebble Beach!"

Easy jumped to his feet and immediately gave Nick a high-five. "Major Magnus!" he said, having seen the course so many times on TV and well aware of its standing as the best golf course in the world (although the subjective nature of a World's Best distinction was an ongoing debate between their golf buddies in St. Louis, as was what constitutes the panel of so-called experts making this decision). "Except, I've got school," Easy added with some hesitation.

"I'm talking Pebble Beach here!" Nick passionately argued. "Sea lions, crashing surf, the Lone Cypress Tree, 'A once in a lifetime experience, every time'—that's what their web site said. School can wait, dude."

Easy's mind was churning as he dried a wine glass with a dishtowel. "How long we talking about here?"

"Leave Wednesday night, back by Monday."

"I'd only miss two lectures, and two days of class," Easy surmised.

"Then what's the problem? Spyglass, Spanish Bay, Cannery Row—besides, if missing one Torts for Tots class ruins your legal career, it's probably a bonus for humanity," Nick insisted.

"First, don't confuse yourself with what's good for humanity. And second, I wish I could say I hate it when you're right, but I can't," Easy concluded.

"That-a-boy!" Nick added, sensing Easy's change of heart.

"Screw it, let's do it. I'm in."

"I just don't get it. I don't know why everyone likes golf so much," questioned Rachel. "Chasing a little ball all over the place seems kind of stupid, if you ask me."

Nick, Easy, and Cassie looked at Rachel as if she had just beamed into the kitchen from a spaceship.

"There's a lot more to golf than chasing a little ball around," Nick said defiantly. Rachel folded her arms across her B-cups. "Well, explain it to me then, 'cause I'd really like to know what the big deal is."

Cassie, partly in Rachel's defense but also because she'd recently developed her own thoughts on the nature of golf and its place in Nick and Easy's life, tried to lighten the mood. "I'll tell you what it is. It's a man's outlet for his feminine side."

"This ought to be good," Easy interjected sarcastically.

"I'm serious," Cassie added. "Women aren't afraid to show other women emotion. Men can't do that. Women will hug and kiss other women, tell each other how nice they look, tell them 'I love you'. The closest men ever get to dropping their emotional inhibition is on the golf course." Cassie switched to her deepest guy voice and grumbled, "'Nice shot. Beautiful. You were great today.' You throw your arms around each other, flirt with each other. It's cute," she concluded.

"That's bullshit! See?" Nick said defiantly as he threw his arm around Easy's neck and kissed him on the cheek.

Cassie continued, "You laugh now, but get a bunch of men on the golf course and they act like a bunch of women. They even talk about shopping: 'Check out my new putter. That's a nice hat! What kind of shirt is that?' I've seen you guys, I know what's going on." The foursome couldn't help but laugh.

"I think it's simpler than that," Nick explained. "It's fun, it's competition, it's tradition, and it's usually a beautiful setting with alcohol, friends, and gambling involved. What could be better? Now true, there is a social aspect to it, but I hardly think it's about getting in touch with my feminine side."

"What's your theory, Will?" Rachel asked sincerely.

"You know, I've thought a lot about this," Easy began to explain.

"This should be good!" Nick chimed in.

Ignoring Nick's sarcasm, Easy continued. "Why, all over the world, do millions of people love golf so much? All ages, cultures, and even genders have thousands of games and sports to choose among, but they pick golf. Why is that?" Easy rhetorically asked, punctuating his studious pause with a brief, deep look at his captive audience. "I believe it's that golf embodies the quest for the elusive 'Wow!' moment. I have this theory that people toil about daily, thinking mainly about and thirsting for their next great life event, that next great moment of importance or joy, when everything feels exciting, just like when we were kids. It's in these rare moments of joy and awe that we achieve a perfect life balance, when a person finds what I call his 'true center', where a simple yet tranquil state of mind is achieved despite life's constant chaos. Only in the midst of a true center moment can all negative thought and our constant daily turmoil be temporarily set aside and wonder allowed to rule."

"I think I need more wine! This is getting hard to swallow," Nick joked.

Rachel became increasingly intrigued, "That's kind of interesting."

Much to Cassie and Nick's annoyance, Easy took Rachel's remark as a green light to launch into even greater detail on his theory. "Look, they call it a round of golf, right?" he said, rotating his index finger in a circular motion, "And the earth revolves around the sun, the moon around the earth, and in the center of this are mind and body. Golf has similar relationships."

"This is kind of Zen-like," Rachel interjected. Nick rolled his eyes.

"In some ways it is," Easy said. "Okay, here's an example," he added. "You center the ball on the center of the tee. Then you try to meet the center of the club with the center of the ball in an effort to send it down the center of the fairway toward the center of a little four and a quarter inch hole. Now, to accomplish this you create an arced swing. In the center of this arc, the hands join the club. And when you find true center, that magic shot, that moment when all of these elements join in perfect harmony, it's a feeling of the purest beauty. Click, it's orgasmic. But as we get older, it all rarely comes together like that for more than a brief moment or two, if at all. Let me ask you, how many hours of our lives do we devote to chasing a ten-second orgasm? That disproportionate relationship in effort to reward doesn't discourage our orgasmic quest. It's that moment of indescribable treasured blankness that keeps us going in between all the bullshit. That's why we play golf. In fact, I'd suggest that's the lure of life."

Rachel was not to be converted. "And when during this process do you drink the blood of a virgin?" she mused.

With the top down (Nick insisted they always rent convertibles when available) and the stereo blasting the up beat hit song of the Irish pop group *The Proclaimers*, the twosome drove along the most breathtaking stretch of road either had ever seen en route to their appointment with state nineteen. The 100-mile stretch of Pacific Coast Highway from San Francisco to Monterey, showcasing its rolling coastline of farmland interspersed with serene parks and rugged, rocky shoreline spilling into the ocean, inspired both to out-sing an already blaring stereo. "I'll have Al Jolson sing I'm sittin' on top of the world," was the line in the chorus receiving their most strident, off-key attention.

In more than twenty years of friendship, Nick had never seen Easy so taken, so impressed with anyone, anything, or any other place as he was with Pebble Beach at that moment.

"Cassie would love this place," Easy suggested as they weaved along 17-Mile Drive toward The Lodge at Pebble Beach.

"It's like Pinehurst by the sea." Nick added.

"Can you smell it, Nick?"

"Smell what?"

Easy took a full breath. "The sweetness of the air. It's incredible."

Nick took a deep breath. "Think we'll see any celebrities? I hear Clint Eastwood plays here all the time."

"We're in the middle of Steinbeck country and you're worried about Clint Eastwood?"

"What movie was Steinbeck in?"

"Tell me you're joking."

Based on the presence of a spanking new shirt bought just moments before in the pro shop and a hard crease in his pants, Easy's attire demonstrated a reverence for the golf course Nick had never before seen.

Nick also grew impatient. "We've got thirty minutes to check in, hit balls, and get to first tee. You need to hurry the hell up."

"I checked out this book in the pro shop. Did you know that two amateur's designed this place?" Easy asked.

"Everyone was an amateur back in 1920, dip-shit. Let's go."

Easy stood puzzled. "Guess they were, huh?"

"Surprised you didn't know that, Mr. Steinbeck."

Considerably more nervous than usual, with dozens of golfers and tourists wandering around the first tee, Nick began covering every imaginable detail with Paul, the caddie they would share for the day. A short, slight, moustached man with a hint of an accent. Paul, Nick guessed, could be from somewhere in Latin America, or maybe Cuba.

"You a golfer, Paul?" Nick asked.

"Yes, sir."

"What do you play off?"

"About a two handicap. How 'bout you?"

"Okay, so where's the trouble on this hole?" Nick quizzed.

"Favor the left side if you want a good angle to the green, its jail in the trees on the right. But it's wide open otherwise," Paul answered, with authority.

"Did you catch that, Easy? Trouble right?"

"Yeah, I heard," acknowledged Easy.

"If I hit a good drive, say 250, what do we got left?" Nick asked.

"It plays to about 160 yards," offered Paul.

Nick, with the customary cigarette hanging from his lips, was studying a yardage book that he'd bought in the pro shop while Easy was trying on shirts. Nick stood puzzled. "If I hit it 250 yards, then 160, that's 410 yards. The book says it's only 381 yards. That doesn't add up."

Paul patiently explained his math to Nick. "It plays a little uphill, and there's a lot of wind you don't feel down here on the tee box. And second, the ground is soft so the ball won't roll five feet. Plus, the flag is in the back of the green, which is slightly elevated, so I added fifteen yards." Nick nodded his head. Paul went on to add, "Guys, you'll have a lot more fun today if you just trust me. I've been doing this for three years, and I know some tricks to this course that you just don't see the first time around."

"Okay, Paul, I'm in your hands," Nick relented.

"Good, now hit away. We've got the tee," Paul declared.

Nick threw his tee into the air to determine who would hit first. It landed pointing to Easy. "You're up," Nick said.

Paul pulled Easy's driver from his bag, removed the head cover, and stared curiously at Easy's old wooden club.

"Don't they have a K-Mart where you live?" Paul deadpanned as he handed the club to Easy.

Without comment, Easy teed his ball up, took a deep breath, and then delivered a fluid, smooth swing. The ball sailed on a line down the middle of the fairway, center cut. With this task safely behind him, Easy now felt compelled to respond to his hired hand. "When you swing as sweet as I do, you don't need all that high-tech bullshit," he said to the now mildly impressed caddie.

Paul immediately whispered to Nick, "What's he usually shoot?"

"High 70's, low 80's," Nick offered proudly.

Paul took another long look at Easy's club. "I don't think I've ever seen such a shitty club hit such a sweet shot."

"Nice shot, Easy!" Nick said, as he took his driver from Paul. After carefully placing his burning cigarette near the tee marker, Nick planted his ball into the ground and studied his target. After a moment, with his jitters now partially under control, he approached the ball, set up, and smacked a nice lazy fade just short of Easy's ball. Striking a golf poster pose, Nick relished the moment.

"Good shot," Paul offered. Nick and Easy were unaccustomed to using resort caddies, and, as they walked to the green, they quietly discussed Paul's motivation for his compliments, concluding that the frequency of compliments Paul threw out during the day was often in direct proportion to the tip he expected at round's end. They briefly joked that a new, tip-driven pet name might be necessary, although they decided to withhold final judgment for a few holes.

Nick, his priorities ever changing, stopped to grab his Marlboro, took a deep, long puff, and immediately started hacking and coughing. He survived his minor attack and they continued walking down the first fairway.

As Paul guided them through the opening inland holes, they talked of how lucky Paul must feel each day as he punched the clock and headed out to work in such a sublime setting. Both agreed that spending a summer hauling bags around Pebble would be worth the cut in pay. As they approached the fourth tee box to begin a stretch of seven straight coastal holes, the boys concluded that a single summer might not be long enough, that a full year would be more than worth the lost wages.

Perched atop a modest cliff jetting out from a small peninsula that separated two coves sat the famous par-three, seventh hole. As the surf crashed against the rocks protecting the back of the green, Nick threw several blades of grass into the air and studied the breeze from the elevated tee box. "What do you think we need here, Paul?"

"With this wind and your swing, definitely a nine-iron," Paul said with a confidence that only someone with a thousand rounds of experience could voice so quickly.

"Then I'll take a nine-iron and a beer!"

"Make that two, please!" Easy politely requested. Paul pulled two beers and an eight-iron from Nick's golf bag.

"Hey Paul, grab that camera in there and get a picture," Nick called to the young man who had also become their personal bartender and photographer.

As they waited for the green to clear, Paul snapped a picture of Nick and Easy smiling, arms draped over one another's shoulders. "Cassie will love this—showing our feminine side," laughed Nick.

"Do you guys work together or what?" Paul asked.

"No, we've been friends since we were little kids," Nick started to explain. "Except for the day you struck me out to win the Little League championship."

"That really happened?" Paul asked.

"Yup. In fact, we lived next door to each other until after high school," Easy added, knowing how it enhanced an already good story.

"That's pretty cool." Gone was the manufactured interest and tip-driven sincerity detected earlier in Paul's voice.

"And now I get my revenge," Nick declared.

"How's that?" Paul asked simply.

Nick launched into the spiel he'd delivered on at least eighteen previous occasions, maintaining an enthusiasm equal to the moment he had conceived the wager some fifteen months before. "We're having a kind of a golf tournament. We're gonna play all fifty states, head-to-head, and whoever wins the most states is the winner, and with winning comes eternal bragging rights, which is a much bigger prize than the Little League championship."

"No shit? How many states have you played?" Paul asked.

Nick turned to Easy, already satisfied with the tally he was about to hear. "Tell him, Easy!"

"We've played eighteen states so far. Nick's ahead nine states to eight with one tie."

"Have you played California yet?" Paul asked.

"That's why we're here," Easy declared.

"That makes this a lot more interesting," Paul decided, thinking immediately of all that an endeavor of this type involved. Paul next asked the second most commonly asked question the two heard when outlining the scope and status of their bet. "Either of you married?"

No, or, *hell no*. Nick couldn't decide which to use. He settled for the one word version.

"No wonder you can get away with this," Paul declared.

Following the tenth hole, Pebble Beach wound back inland in a return loop featuring some equally difficult and compelling holes, not returning ocean side until the seventeenth green.

After shared pars on seventeen, Nick insisted they head to the back left portion of the green and attempt the chip shot Tom Watson holed for birdie to preserve his two-stroke victory over Jack Nicklaus in the 1982 U.S. Open. Both Nick and Easy, based upon Paul's knowledge of the exact spot where the shot had taken place, attempted to duplicate Watson's miracle, although neither faired nearly as well as Watson.

Neither, however, had failed to rise to the challenge of Pebble Beach, perhaps the most celebrated jewel of their fifty-state crown. For the sixth time in only eighteen states, they arrived tied as they approached the final hole.

As California ebbed toward its defining moment, Nick and Easy stood at opposite sides of the par-five, eighteenth fairway studying their third shot. Paul was stationed in the middle, minding their clubs; Nick was near the surf on the left, with Easy and the famous Lodge to the right. All three enjoyed a light, crisp breeze, a cold beer, and an appreciation for the moment. "You're both around 145, 150 yards away. I think Nick is first," Paul announced.

Nick asked Paul for an eight-iron, set his beer and cigarette to the grass, then deftly hit a towering fade onto the green, settling some twenty-five feet left of the flag, which had been cut this day on the right side of the green.

Easy bettered Nick's effort and stuck it to about fifteen feet, straight behind the hole. Following two clutch shots, both guys had a little extra bounce in their steps as they headed toward the final green, but as Nick was about to learn, it was for completely different reasons. They met a hundred yards or so from the green and walked together carrying the putters Paul had provided.

Carrying one's putter to the green was an honor Paul had introduced early in the round to reward a nice approach shot. Showcasing this honor had become somewhat of a contest in itself, with Nick or Easy, whomever had hit the green, displaying the putter to the other as a testament to his prowess.

As they enjoyed the final 100-yard walk to the eighteenth green, Easy casually turned to Nick. "Now, don't let this bother you when you're putting, but Cassie and I are getting married in August."

Nick stopped in his tracks. Easy continued his slow, deliberate march toward the green. "Are you fucking serious? Stop, Will—are you bullshitting me?" Easy continued walking without reply.

"I knew this would happen, we're never gonna finish," Nick said, as Easy moved out of earshot. Nick, meanwhile, continued digesting the news with a confusing mixture of disbelief and happiness.

Easy stopped a few yards short of the green and waited for Nick to catch up. "And of course, I want you to be my best man."

"Well, hell yeah!" The huge bear hug they exchanged left words unnecessary. Paul, unable to hear what had just transpired, called ahead, "I don't know what's going on here, but people are staring."

"Easy just asked me to be his best man," Nick announced to Paul. Paul smiled and extended a hand.

"Congratulations, but can we finish the state here? I want to know who wins."

"You sneaky bastard, dropping the marriage bomb when I'm putting for the state at fucking Pebble Beach. Do you believe this guy? Unbelievable!" Nick spouted to no one in particular.

Taking ample time lining up his putt, and glancing over occasionally at Easy with mixed emotions, Nick finally decided the putt would break left about fourteen inches. He picked a nearly invisible spot on the green at which to aim and sent the ball on its way. As the putt ran out of gas yet hugged the low side of the cup to sneak in for birdie, and the win, Easy offered Nick his best muted "golf clap." This prompted a smug retort from Nick as he pointed at Easy with his putter. "I think your little plan backfired."

"One may smile, smile, and still be a villain. Nice job, Nick!" Easy graciously offered.

Surprisingly, Easy's birdie bid came nowhere close to going in, as Easy's mind had drifted to other matters. They started to shake hands, as Little League tradition required, when Nick turned the gesture from a handshake into another warm, backslapping hug.

"Congratulations, Will," Nick said sentimentally.

Paul, however, refused to alter his sarcastic tone and sardonically announced, "This is precious. I think I'm gonna cry." His comment, while obviously insensitive, was still amusing to Nick.

"Screw you, Paul. Now dump our shit and meet us inside for some beers." They each shook Paul's hand.

"I'm right behind you!" Paul declared in earnest, admitting he actually enjoyed watching others play golf for a change. Nick would confess later over beers that he really couldn't think of anything but Easy's announcement and that this distraction had probably kept him from choking on his birdie putt.

Seated in The Lodge's famous nineteenth hole, the Tap Room, for a few post-round beverages, Nick turned to Paul, "What's customary for a tip around here? And be honest." Nick asked.

"Whatever you think it was worth is my policy," Paul answered.

"Cut the shit, what do you average?"

"I guess it's around a hundred a bag per loop." Nick pulled three crisp one hundred dollar bills from his pocket. Easy's eyes widened at the sight of Nick with a wad of cash.

"I have three questions," Easy began. "First, are you aware of what a rare sight you've just witnessed? And second, are you interested in joining us for dinner. And third, are you free around ten tomorrow for Spyglass?"

"How about we drive to Nevada. Have you guys played for Nevada yet?" Paul threw a peanut into the air and caught it in his mouth.

Chapter 12

▼

Playing the required fifteen states over the second summer of their bet would prove to be a much greater challenge than either Nick or Easy had expected. Following Pebble Beach, Nick began sensing the new fiancée dynamic when it came to discussing golf plans with Easy, and the feeling left him more and more uncomfortable, almost a third wheel to his own bet and to his best friend.

Adding further concern for Nick was the condition of his golf swing. Nothing felt right. Charlie, looking at Nick from behind a video camera, abruptly popped up from behind the lens and glared straight into the eyes of his young apprentice.

"This feels weird," Nick said in a rather unsettled tone.

"Christ! You hit the ball better in high school. Son, it ain't supposed to be like grabbing a handful of tit. Nick, you gotta rest the club lightly in your fingers, not choke it with your palms."

"Okay, okay, I get it!" Nick said, as he set up again and Charlie re-centered the camera. After hitting a flush iron, Nick smiled at Charlie.

In a departure from his usual stick method, Charlie offered Nick a carrot. "See, that's what I'm talkin' about. Now do it again, and remember, easy, swing easy, tempo is the key!"

"Speaking of Easy, did you hear? He's getting married," Nick announced a touch of excitement in his voice.

"You're fucked," Charlie casually commented, adding a dismissive nod and smirk.

"Naw, we're gonna finish," Nick said, showing genuine confidence.

Charlie suspended the lesson and grabbed the golf club he kept handy as a substitute cane. Deliberately, he hobbled over near where Nick was standing and offered a sad look. Nick reached into his front pocket, pulled out a cigarette, and put a light to it.

"Yeah, and I'm gonna grow a new foot," Charlie offered, a hint of defeat ringing through.

"No, she's pretty cool about it, really."

"You see, Nick," Charlie began with a touch of fatherly consolation, "she's cool now; they're always cool until they get that ring. Then wham, outta nowhere, they turn from cool to frigid. You can't change a woman's nature, Nick. They hate golf, they hate old friends, and most of all they hate old golf friends. It just doesn't agree with their maternal values."

"Normally, I'd agree. But, she's different. I don't know how he does it, but he's even made snagging the perfect girl look easy."

Charlie's lecture continued. "We're the last of a dying breed, Nickie. That's why I don't read books or go to the movies. Real life is just too fucking entertaining. Perfect girls cheating, perfect girls lying, perfect girls getting divorced. It's that Jerry Springer mentality." Charlie swung his cane as he continued pontificating, the smooth motion of his club carrying over to his lecture. "You're better off in the long run anyway, Nick. This eight-iron here won't ever kiss my fuzzy balls at night, but it won't destroy my friendships or break my heart into little pieces either."

"Charlie, with that attitude, you're bound to die alone, like a hobo or somebody's cat," Nick suggested, hoping his future and the view to which Charlie subscribed would share nothing in common.

"You'll see!" Charlie added. "But for now, while she'll still let him play, let's fix that hook so we can at least get one more state under our belt before the little bastard screws us again."

Besides safe delivery of the wedding ring, the best man has but one meaningful task to which he must devote his energy—the time-honored tradition of the bachelor party. Out of genuine respect for Cassie and, for once, not wanting to put the screws to Easy, the obligatory stripper (fun dumpsters as Charlie liked to call them) was not among the scheduled festivities. Instead, a friendly round of golf and a poker game were Nick's activities of choice. With all of the surrounding states having been played, nothing of significance could be wagered, so the round would indeed be friendly, unless you counted Charlie's endless, scotch-induced monologues extolling the virtues of lifelong bachelorhood.

As wedding ceremonies went, this one was small. Neither Cassie nor Easy was from a large family. In this regard, they made a good match. Their future would likely be spared of drunken uncle types, nasty family squabbles, and the prying and interference large families often inject into a new marriage. The last thing Easy wanted was his in-laws complaining about him traveling the country playing golf, leaving Cassie home alone.

With Cassie and Easy cheek-to-cheek for the traditional first dance, Nick and Kendra, in their respective black tuxedo and maroon bridesmaid dress, sat together at a nearby table drinking beer from plastic cups. The Carpenters' *"We've Only Just Begun"* played in the background. Nick felt like vomiting with each passing note of what he described to Kendra as "vile, cheesy wedding music."

"So where's Rachel?" Kendra asked curiously.

"She got called in at the last minute for a flight. What about you and Boob?" Nick jested, recalling the time he first met Bob more than a year and half earlier at Kendra's birthday party.

"We're still seeing each other, off and on," she said, without much excitement.

"Why didn't you bring him?" Nick asked.

"He's showing some of his work at a gallery downtown. Plus, I wanted to have some fun for a change."

"So, I get the first dance, right?" Nick asked.

"Absolutely!" Her delight was apparent as Kendra thought of actually having an opportunity to dance to something other than Bob's usual preference for slam dancing or Euro-trash disco.

Watching his best friend begin what was certain to be an exciting and important new chapter in his life, a chapter that would no doubt change the nature of their lifelong friendship, Nick began to reflect upon his past decisions involving his many failed relationships, and to daydream of what his marital future could hold.

Much to his credit, Nick was quite comfortable sharing these thoughts and vulnerabilities with Kendra. After all, they'd known each other as long as Easy and Nick had known one another.

"I don't think I'll ever get married," he said bluntly.

"Why do you say that?" Kendra asked, surprised by the comment. After all, she figured, if Will got married, Nick couldn't be far behind.

"I like someone, they don't like me. Someone likes me, I don't like them. It just never seems to click," Nick offered, all the while trying to mask the real disappointment underlying his simple assessment.

"What are you looking for in a woman?" Kendra asked, near certain of what the answer was likely to be.

Nick thought for a moment, his eyes searching the ceiling. "How about a girl that goes down faster than my handicap?"

"Cute, Nick. I'll tell you what your problem is. You don't respect women."

Nick, aside from being in no mood for a lecture, was taken a bit by surprise at the harshness of the remark.

"Really?" A blank look and a puff from his cigarette complemented Nick's reply.

Kendra looked Nick in the eyes. "Yeah, and if you don't find respect, you won't find love."

Nick raised an eyebrow. "Jesus, you sound like your brother."

"Yeah, and here we are, sitting alone again," Kendra added, now taking stock of her own choices.

"Hey, want me to give Boob a call?" Nick joked, trying to lighten the mood.

Kendra ignored Nick's comment as they simultaneously gulped a swig of beer and studied Will and Cassie dancing for the first time as husband and wife.

Chapter 13

Brushing past the room service cart pushed against the wall, Easy paused to give the cart a good going-over before plucking the solitary fresh strawberry that remained from their morning breakfast. In one quick motion, he threw the strawberry into his mouth. Before tossing himself into a big wicker chair, he tugged open the brightly flowered curtains to reveal a spectacular view of the Pacific Ocean. With sunshine filling the hotel room, Cassie emerged from the bathroom sporting a sassy, bright yellow bikini. Gliding seductively with an intentional shake and a wiggle, intended to highlight her new swimsuit, she planted herself on Easy's lap and gave him a long, passionate kiss.

"Are you sure you don't want to go along?" Easy asked sincerely.

"Yeah, I'm sure," Cassie said before adding, "The idea of smelly fish and people getting seasick doesn't sound like much fun to me. I'll just hang out at the pool with my good friend Captain Morgan."

"I'll be back around three, four o'clock, so save me some rum," Easy replied, the glow of bright sunshine and a new wife splashed across his face.

Having let Easy continue to dig his grave for the past few minutes, Cassie decided the jig was now up.

"You'll know where to find me when you get back. Oh, and tell Nick I said hi."

As hard as he tried, Easy could not mask his surprise at the fact that he'd just been busted.

"Deep-sea fishing! Yeah right! Don't you and Nick still have to play for Hawaii? There's no way you two were going to pass up this chance. I know better," Cassie said insightfully. She then added, "Besides, I told you it was okay when we planned this. You're the one that said, 'No way, I don't want Nick going on my honeymoon' when I first suggested the idea."

"Are you mad?" Easy asked with a wince, thinking this may well be the first in a long line of post marriage screw-ups.

"At first, yeah, I was a little ticked off, I mean, it is our honeymoon. But I want you two to get this over with so we can have normal vacations like normal people. Besides, I did suggest it in the first place. But don't think that makes it okay to lie. Don't lie to me again, not even a small one. Got it?" she added, punctuating her final words with a stern poke to Easy's chest.

"Are you sure?" Easy asked insistently, hoping that by pushing the issue he might regain some measure of lost credibility and perhaps earn a touch of forgiveness.

"Yes, now go, and don't lose a state on our honeymoon. I don't want you moping around all week."

Cassie promptly gave her man "a kiss for luck" before grabbing a towel for her afternoon by the pool and formally releasing Easy from his honeymoon duties for the afternoon.

"This is why I love you! You're amazing!" Easy said, with genuine wonder served over a healthy dose of kiss-ass.

"I know, and don't ever forget it," Cassie added for good measure as she shut the door behind her.

With the convertible's motor running, Nick waited impatiently at the entrance to Easy's resort, habitually checking his watch and enjoying a cigarette. Easy finally appeared running from the hotel wearing a blue and white flowered shirt, baggy shorts, and the gleam of a man believing he had the world on a string. He jumped into the car without the benefit of opening the door.

"I love doin' that!" Easy said, grinning.

"About fuckin' time."

"We've got plenty of time. This is Hawaii; everybody's laid back, nothing starts on time. And oh yeah, Cassie says hi!"

Nick was immediately dazed and confused. "You told her?"

"I didn't have to, She's not stupid."

"What'd she say? Is she pissed?"

"You're not gonna believe this. She told me not to lose our honeymoon state," he recounted with uncharacteristic, syrupy delight.

"If I weren't a bigger man, I'd tell you your perfect life is really starting to irritate me," Nick said with relief, and a pinch of envy.

"Let's go! I've got a state to win!"

Eager to match Easy's positive spirit of the day, Nick offered his own brand of good news. "You would not believe the girl I met at the bar last night, a cute little Hoosier. We're going on one of those dinner cruises tonight."

"What about Rachel?" Easy asked.

"Its just dinner. Besides, she's already pissed that I didn't bring her along," Nick added, as if this somehow absolved him of any guilt or responsibility for whatever may happen that evening.

Hawaii, they decided, would cap the second summer of their three-year journey. Since Pebble Beach, where Nick had gained a two-state lead, the tables had turned dramatically. Easy had won four straight states on a weeklong road trip throughout the South, bagging easy wins in Florida at the TPC Sawgrass course, in Georgia at a fabulous Tom Fazio-designed course called The Frog, again at a sweet track in Alabama on the Robert Trent Jones Golf Trail, and ending finally with a victory in New Orleans.

It wasn't until Wisconsin, where they played a spectacular course called Whistling Straits, a links-style gem recently unveiled on the shores of Lake Michigan, that Nick won again. This win, however, was offset by Easy immediately taking Michigan. After this last trade of wins, and with Nick still two states behind, they spent a long, tiring week driving through the northern Midwest, playing North and South Dakota, Montana, Wyoming, and Nebraska.

Having split wins in the first four of those states, Wyoming was the swing state of the trip. As had become common practice over the past two years, Nick and Easy had been able to talk their way into getting either coveted times at high profile courses or onto private country club courses by simply explaining their bet to some sympathetic golf nut responsible for policing tee times.

In Wyoming, this led them to the wind-swept Cheyenne County Club, a funky private layout of six par-three's, six par-four's, and six par-five's. A win for Nick in Wyoming would again reduce the difference to a single state. Easy, however, had other ideas. He birdied three of the six par-five's, and won with ease, increasing his lead once again to three states.

Other than a four-day, three-state swing through the Pacific Northwest, where the total driving out-paced the golf by more than twenty hours, and where Nick finally won two of three states, no future plans were made until they were to secretly rendezvous in Hawaii. The wins in Idaho and Oregon, sandwiched around a loss in Seattle, left Nick still two states behind with only the Aloha State to play for the year.

After spending the summer hearing non-stop about tuxedos, reception plans, the house Easy and Cassie were buying, and having played generally horrible golf, the prospect of a long, cold St. Louis winter trailing by three states was not something Nick was looking forward to. And if he didn't capture Hawaii, that's exactly what Nick would be forced to live with until their bet resumed that next spring.

Nick wrestled with an abundance of these thoughts throughout the first part of their round. With this additional, self-imposed pressure to win, relaxed golf was all but impossible. Nick was spraying the ball all over Maui like a whale with a constipated blowhole. So bad was his play, that after just four holes, Nick found himself three strokes down. If not for a long par putt on the second hole, he would have likely trailed by four shots. In contrast, Easy was waltzing around like Freddie Couples, a successful tour pro known for his casual, effortless swing equaled only by his placid, unflappable demeanor.

Unable to find his form, Nick passed on lunch during a brief break after nine holes and decided instead on two beers and a complimentary number of cigarettes. Neither provided much help. In fact, the match was decided well before reaching the final hole, with Easy winning his honeymoon state quite handily, 81-89.

As the boys enjoyed their traditional post-round beer and the spectacular ocean views from the clubhouse patio, Nick stared into his glass as he attempted to find some silver lining in the day's drubbing. "Well, your wife should be happy!"

"Thanks for your help with that Nick. I don't know what I was thinking by trying to sneak this..."

Easy was suddenly interrupted. One puff into a fresh cigarette, Nick immediately launched into a fierce, retching coughing fit. After nearly thirty seconds of increasingly violent coughs and hacks, Nick hurried inside to the restroom, leaving Easy at the table wondering whether he knew how to properly perform the Heimlich maneuver.

In the restroom, Nick, his face flush and red from the episode, struggled to catch a breath. After rubbing his red, watering eyes, he cleared his throat and spit into the sink. Surprised by the bright, rich red of his saliva, he spit again only to find the volume and concentration of blood even heavier. Nick stared, puzzled, as he wiped the corner of his mouth and stared into the blood-soaked paper towel and sink. The blood would not stop flowing. Nearly ten minutes passed before the bleeding would slow enough to allow them to return to Easy's hotel room.

Back in the room, Cassie stood over Nick and examined his neck as he sat on the toilet, Easy watching from the doorway.

"Have you had any vomiting?" Cassie asked in a clinical tone.

"Drunk or sober?" Nick joked. "No, no vomiting," he finally admitted.

Cassie gently probed both sides of his throat and neck. "Any stomach pain?"

"No," Nick answered simply, after his first attempt to make light of the situation was not well received.

"Well, it's probably not an ulcer. How about swallowing, any discomfort?" she asked while running through her mental checklist.

"A little, I've been fighting a cold."

"It sounds like it may be a respiratory problem. We need to get you to a doctor. Anytime there's unexplained bleeding, Nick, you need to see a doctor," Cassie said sternly.

"Now? I've got a date tonight. Besides, it's stopped." Nick pleaded.

"Yeah, Nick, now. This is not something you want to mess around with!"

"I'll go when I get back, first thing," Nick promised.

Cassie shook her head as Easy offered a sly smile, relieved that the bleeding had stopped and that Nick seemed for the moment to be feeling his normal self.

For his part, Nick was not about to put his plans for the little Hoosier girl and a potential Hawaiian romance at risk.

Chapter 14

Twitching nervously as he sat in an outer office, Nick was looking more at the others in the waiting room than at the *Sports Illustrated* in his hand. Suddenly, an ordinary woman, expressionless and as white as the walls, opened one of the three doors to the waiting room. Her voice seemed as sickly to Nick as her complexion. As she called out a name from her clipboard, "Nick Rose," he suddenly felt like her grim equal.

As Nick sat waiting alone in the examination room, still in his street clothes and perched nervously on the end of the examination table, Dr. Baumann returned, clutching an official-looking folder. He slid a chair across to where Nick was sitting and deposited his lean frame into an accompanying chair.

"You were here on Thursday, right?" Dr. Baumann asked rhetorically before finding the exact date of their first examination on his chart. "Have you had any more bleeding since we ran the tests?"

"A little," Nick replied.

"That's almost to be expected," Dr. Baumann answered, while setting the chart on a nearby counter before looking directly up at Nick. "Didn't you tell me you had a history of cancer in the family?" he asked.

Nick instantly sensed an increased seriousness in the doctor's demeanor, and his questions. "Yeah, both my mom and dad had cancer. My mom passed away when I was little and my dad died about twelve years ago. Why, what's going on?" Nick asked, his mind racing.

"Well, Nick, we found a small growth on your windpipe just below your collarbone area." The doctor gently identified the area with a soft brush of his first two fingers over the tumor's location.

Nick, his mind suddenly blank, sat soaking in the news. "Is it serious?" he asked meekly.

"We won't know until it's removed and we can perform a biopsy and examine the surrounding tissue," Dr. Baumann explained in a somber, sterile tone.

Nick sensed an odd, punched-in-the-stomach feeling he hadn't experienced since Little League.

"Is it cancerous? What is it? Is it big?" he asked as a stream of grim and self-sickening thoughts quickly peppered his brain.

"It's not much larger than a pea, and we won't know if it's malignant until we remove it and perform a biopsy. The severe bleeding you experienced resulted from its incursion upon one of the primary veins supplying blood to the outer lining of the lungs. I've contacted a specialist and we have a several options set aside at the end of this week for surgery. I'd like you to schedule one before you leave. We need to get a closer look at what we have as quickly as possible," Dr. Baumann explained.

"Yeah, yeah sure," Nick said, now hypnotized as biopsy, malignant, and incursion poured from Dr. Baumann's lips.

"Check with Molly at the nurse's station as you leave." He reassuredly grabbed his knee and shook it gently. "We'll take care of it, Nick. Everything's going to be fine."

Nick impulsively began probing and rubbing the area pointed out by the doctor as he slid off the examination table. "Yeah, thanks," Nick answered, finding it hard to stand, blink, or breathe.

Chapter 15

▼

Finding a stool at the bar was no major accomplishment, as Arnie's Bar & Grill sat nearly empty most weekday afternoons. Today proved no different. Only a scruffy regular in a faded green windbreaker nursing a beer several stools away and a delivery truck driver digging into a late lunch saved Arnie's from sitting completely empty.

Somehow, Nick always knew this day would come. Although he had long ago developed the ability to trick himself into blocking such thoughts from his mind, he was certain that cancer of some type would ultimately decide his fate. Feeding this notion was a saying he had heard once that in many ways had become his mantra for evaluating difficult choices and rationalizing decisions, both good and bad. This saying now echoed repeatedly in his mind: *You can only choose how you live, not how you die.* As hard as he tried that day, he couldn't shake it from his head. *You can only choose how you live, not how you die.*

Craving the toxic stimulants and carcinogens of a cigarette more than healthy, fresh air, Nick derived no pleasure from the red cocktail straw Nick was gnawing on. But smoking another cigarette was out of the question. As he stared into his glass of milk, growing warmer and more undrinkable by the minute, memories of his mother, father, thoughts of Easy, Rachel, Charlie, the golf tournament, Kendra, work, his legacy, or lack thereof, dominated his odd new inner world, his world with cancer. Only Easy pulling open the front door snapped his mind back to the present.

"A little early to be drinking—milk?" Easy said as he sat on the barstool next to Nick, puzzled by the absence of alcohol.

"I got the test results back. I've got a tumor on my throat, and I'm having surgery on Friday," Nick blurted before Easy had a chance to remove his jacket. "How was your day?"

Easy had prepared for the worst, although he had been praying for good news. "Ah man. What else did he say? Is it cancer? What is it?"

"They won't be able to tell until they do a biopsy."

"Have you told Rachel?" Easy asked.

"No, you're the first. But she's gonna trip."

"We'll get through this, man. You're Magnus Ver Magnusson. No matter what happens, we'll get through it."

"It's freaking me out," Nick admitted. "I've been thinking about what my mom went through, all kinds of weird shit. I mean, people I used to hate, I want to talk to, people I should love I'm pissed at," the pace of his straw chewing gaining momentum with each sentence. "I did some research. Twenty-three percent survival rate for throat cancer and…"

Easy interrupted, "Slow down there. You don't even know if you have cancer!"

Nick was already convinced of the worst. "I know, but, fuck, I've seen this shit. I can't go through it."

"I've known you all my life. This is nothing for you. Besides, we've got fifteen more states to play!"

"If I live that long."

"That's bullshit, Nick, come on." Easy placed a hand to his shoulder.

"Oh yeah? My mom only lasted eight months, and the last two were pretty ugly. Remember that time we walked in when she was getting her bandages changed?" Nick recounted with a touch of panic.

"That was a long time ago, Nick. Things have changed. They can cure this shit nowadays."

"I can guarantee one thing: I ain't gonna end up like she did." Nick paused to take a sip from his milk and seemed to disappear in thought for a moment. He ended the uncomfortable silence between them in a soft, searching tone. "No way…no way I'm going through that shit."

"Nick, the number one thing is to stay positive or you'll drive yourself nuts," Easy offered.

Since he'd left the doctor's office two hours earlier, Nick's mind had moved way beyond such sound thinking. "Easy, bottom line, what do you want to get outta life?"

"What do you mean, what do I want to get?" Easy asked curiously.

"I mean, how do you know if you'll ever be truly happy?" Nick asked, turning away from his milk just long enough to throw a frightened look deep into Easy eyes.

"I don't know," Easy wondered aloud, "except that for me it's always been about feeling safe. When I don't think anyone or anything can hurt me, I think I'll be happy."

"But how will you know when you've got that?"

"Well—actually, I think I've found that with Cassie. Everything seems surreal, calm, kind of settled. I just feel safe, like I'll never have to face anything alone ever again. I can't explain it, but since she came along everything's changed. I just know what to do. What's that saying? When you're a boy, it's okay to play with toys, but when you become a man, it's time to put childish things away. She makes me want to change things, be something."

Looking into the half empty glass of milk, Nick shared his disappointment. "That's not the answer I was looking for."

"That's why you've got to fight this thing, so you can find your own answers, your own happiness," Easy offered, desperate to strike some chord that resonated hope.

"Twenty-three percent, Will, twenty-three percent survival rate," Nick said as he buried his face in his hands and rubbed his forehead with eight tense fingers. Easy could only squeeze Nick's shoulder.

As a source of support and comfort, Rachel was woefully equipped for what lay ahead. Their relationship had, as Cassie predicted, become one big party. They'd spent no more than four or five days a month together, and moving to the same city or making their relationship a more permanent arrangement had never been discussed. In just under a year, Nick and Rachel had spent only one holiday together, the first Thanksgiving after they'd met. Nick had never met her parents, and had spoken with them for perhaps five minutes spread over several phone calls. While concerned, Rachel thought Nick was completely irresponsible for smoking in the first place, and was now overreacting to the entire situation. He had never volunteered details involving his parent's passing, and she had never bothered to ask. It was the Slim Fast of relationships.

While the looming implications of the four-hour surgery scared Nick in an immediate sense, it was not what he feared most. His deepest fear was reserved for the biopsy results. *What if it's spread? What if I only have a few months? What if they have to take out my larynx and I can never talk again or eat a normal meal? Is tomorrow the last day I eat solid food, the last night I get to sleep in my own bed?*

Until that night, Nick had always felt in total control of his body. Now, some creature he could not control or understand was devouring his insides. As a small boy, he'd witnessed this power firsthand. He'd stood eye-to-eye with this creature once before, the night he had sat at his mother's bedside and held her warm hand as she took her final breath. For the first time in many years, Nick cried for the pain she had felt, he cried for one more touch of her hand, he cried for himself.

Chapter 16

▼

For the second time in his life, Easy was forced to wait in a hospital, considering outcomes and events over which he had no control. As he examined the room's pictures for the hundredth time and paced about without purpose, a million thoughts mocked his every effort toward optimism. *What was God thinking when he created the feeling of helplessness? And how high would the helplessness of sitting in the surgical waiting room rank on His list of infinity's most helpless feelings? Would it rate as high as five on the list, perhaps eleven, maybe thirty-two? If God has time to make lists of this type, He should reevaluate his priorities. You'd think He'd be too busy.*

How am I supposed to handle this? How would Kierkegaard handle this? I'm not equipped to handle this. What can I do? What can I offer? Is there some manual somewhere, a real good one? By definition, there is nothing I can do. I guess that's why they call it helpless.

I wish I could just act normal, take a break from this shit. What if important news comes while I'm out having a Coke or munching a Kit Kat bar? I can't watch TV, at least properly. Reading a People Magazine doesn't seem right. How can people read that shit anyway. Forget about any of the G's (golf, gambling, or girls.) That's totally inappropriate. It's disrespectful, I think. That I'm sure of.

Rachel, appearing unconcerned with such cumbersome thoughts, sat casually flipping through her *Glamour* magazine as Kendra, Cassie, and Easy waited nearby, virtually ignoring her. Word of Nick's version of her reaction to his diagnosis had left them feeling a little cold toward her. Rachel, however, knew this wasn't a life threatening surgery and had made the trip from Chicago on short notice, all the while still completely unaware of Nick's family history and its influence on his persistent self-inflicted gloom.

Each time someone in surgical scrubs walked through the door of the waiting room, Pavlovian response ruled and everyone snapped to attention in hope of good news. It was finally their turn as an elderly pale surgeon walked in, tilted his chin toward the floor, and looked beyond his bifocals.

"Are you waiting on Nicholas Rose?" he asked confidently.

Easy spoke first, "Yes," he replied, with unmasked apprehension.

"I'm Doctor Breeze, Mr. Rose's surgeon. Well, the procedure went as planned. We believe we've got the entire tumor. We are concerned about the condition of the surrounding tissue, however. Now I don't want to alarm anyone until we get the biopsy results in a few hours, but, based on what I've seen in past cases, it doesn't look benign. I just want you to be prepared."

"Can you tell if it has spread to the larynx or any other organs?" Cassie asked.

"It's hard to say, although the affected tissue seems localized to the immediate tumor area. Did we get it in time? I hope so. However, if the biopsy comes back positive, and I think it will, I'll recommend he start chemotherapy immediately. It's unusual for someone as young as Mr. Rose to have cancer of this type. That's really all I know at this point," he added.

Rachel was suddenly jolted into their reality, and the blank reaction on her face clearly showed it.

"When can we see him?" Easy asked impatiently.

"In the morning. He'll be in intensive care overnight," answered the surgeon, as he'd responded countless times before.

"Doctor, can I tell him, about the cancer? He really doesn't have any family," Easy offered, his voice quivering, his shoulders slumped at the prospect.

"Sure. Now, if you'll excuse me, I hate to run, but I have another surgery. Let's just hope that's the last I see of young Mr. Rose," he added while taking the hand Easy had offered in appreciation. "And Cassie, if you have any questions, call me," he said before leaving, having been told earlier that a staff nurse was among the waiting family.

The last time Easy had spent an entire night at the hospital was the night Pops had passed away. This thought did not escape him, although he knew Nick's problem was not making it through the night but through the next year, and the year after that. As for his feelings about Pops, in an unexplainable way, he realized that he missed his father most every day, especially today.

Following a quick visit to Cassie's station and downing a huge cup of strong, bitter black coffee from the cafeteria, Easy walked into Nick's room to find him having just awakened. Easy flashed his brightest smile.

"No wonder you can't keep a woman. You should hear yourself sleep," Easy joked. "So, how you doin'?"

Nick slowly scanned the room, studying the equipment monitoring his condition and tubes entering his body, suddenly afraid to move for fear he could disconnect something, end up choking on the tubes in his mouth, or even bleeding to death.

"The nurse said you might be thirsty. Are you thirsty?" Easy asked.

Nick nodded, yes.

Per Cassie's instructions, Easy grabbed a water bottle modified with a spray top and shot a fine mist into Nick's mouth. Nick only blinked a few times.

"You won't be able to talk for a few days until the swelling goes down, so I got you a pad of paper." Cassie had suggested this idea as well.

"And blink once for yes and twice for no. Can you handle that?"

Nick blinked three times.

"At least they didn't remove your sorry-ass sense of humor."

Nick took the pad and started writing. Easy took a long look at the short note before responding. "They got all of the tumor, but you got some chemo ahead of you. The biopsy was positive. But don't get freaked out, Cassie said they often recommend chemo as a precaution, as insurance."

Nick immediately started writing again. Easy quickly read the note.

"Just twice a week for six weeks."

Nick penned another one-line note.

"Then more tests. Hell, Nick, we'll be playing golf again in three months."

Nick scribbled once more.

"I don't want to hear that shit, understand?" Easy waited for a reaction. "Hey, we still have fifteen states to play."

Nick turned his head away and wouldn't look at or acknowledge what his best friend was telling him. Easy searched for something to say or do. Professional counseling immediately jumped to mind.

"I know what you're thinking, Nick, but this is no time to give up. You need to dig deep, buddy. This is not a death sentence, so stop acting like it's one."

Nick did not respond.

Chapter 17

Each time Nick picked up the Pebble Beach cap that had become his constant companion, he thought back to the day when he and Easy had played golf there. Each time, his internal reaction was decidedly different. Sometimes he'd get pissed that he had to use this or any hat to hide his head, as he was quickly becoming bald from the chemotherapy. Other times, the memory of that day inspired him to withstand this nightmare and play golf once again. But his positive thoughts and inspiration were rare and often short-lived. With each day of nausea, retching, and cleaning hair from the bathtub drain, he was certain the worst still lay directly ahead.

Rachel had been to visit only once since Nick started chemo, during which time he finally told her of his mom and dad and how he was all but certain things were going to get worse, breaking into tears almost every time they would talk. Although he would never admit it, Nick was actually trying to sabotage the relationship, so he could at least partially control something in his life, control the unpleasantness of her decision to leave him. He was certain she'd already decided this. He was sure she was only waiting for the right moment.

That day came less than three weeks after surgery, as Nick sat slumped on the couch watching TV. He now hated it when the phone rang. Talking on the phone was not in tune with his desire to be left alone. Apparently, Rachel no longer felt like drawing out events either and after only a few minutes of small talk, Nick heard her underlying message loud and clear.

"Yeah, I understand. Nobody wants a terminal boyfriend," he said sarcastically. "I know things weren't great before the surgery, but…" Rachel's interruption and the comments that followed held true to Nick's dire expectations. "Thanks for your concern. I'll see ya around."

He quickly clicked the off button on the phone and sat for a moment: just seconds later he hurled the phone into the corner against the wall. Staring now at the fresh new dent in the drywall and at the phone now scattered in little pieces on his living room floor, he removed the Pebble Beach cap, placed it on the coffee table, and curled into a ball on the sofa.

Chewing his straw and staring blankly through the coffee shop window, Nick noticed a young couple trying to corral their small son. He couldn't help but become fixated at the sight of the young parents trying to feed their child's wily arm into the fat coat sleeve. He stared without blinking until they walked from view. *I guess that's something I'll never have to deal with,* he thought to himself. *It's good I never got married. No wife and kids to put through this hell. Maybe if I start smoking again I can just get this over with.*

The echo effect of the toilet bowl, the tile walls, the small, confined, general emptiness of the room, all worked in concert to magnify the sound of Nick's vomiting.

As he entered the living room, wiping his mouth with a paper towel, Nick walked over to his computer printer. Sitting neatly in its tray were several freshly printed pages. After punching them with holes, he neatly inserted the pages into a small, red three-ring binder and took a seat behind the keyboard. The screen in front of him read: Guide to Self-Deliverance.

Nick nearly jumped from his chair at the sound of the doorbell ringing. In a mild panic, he shoved the red binder in a drawer and closed the ominous window on his computer.

Standing on the other side of the peephole, Nick squinted to find a bright-eyed Kendra holding a covered food dish of some sort.

"Open the door!" she called out just as Nick turned the handle to let her in. "I brought your favorite, three-cheese lasagna!"

"Hi Kendie, what are you doing here?" he asked with an awkward hug, trying not to bump into the lasagna dish.

"I hadn't heard from you for a few days, so I thought I'd drop by and see how you were doing," she said, never revealing her deep concern for unreturned phone calls and Nick's complete disappearance in recent weeks.

Nick, his place a wreck, scrambled to pick up his sweatshirt and several empty water bottles littering his coffee table. "So, how's the bookstore? How's Boob?"

"Bookstore's fine, and Boob's history," she added matter-of-factly.

"What happened?" Nick asked, having quickly made the place presentable.

"I got tired of paying his rent. I should've done it a long time ago. How you doing?" she asked sincerely.

They each took a seat, Nick on the off-white sofa and Kendra in its matching chair to his right. A little short of breath, Nick offered his grim summary. "Tired of throwing up, tired of watching my drain fill with hair, tired of my mouth being dry, just sick and tired of being sick and tired."

"Has your throat been hurting or anything?"

"I don't notice it much any more," Nick said plainly.

"So, what's it like, the chemo stuff?" she continued, unabashed.

"I don't want to bore you with that shit."

"No, tell me, I'm curious," she said, as she settled into the chair.

"You do lead a dull life," Nick joked, hoping to change the subject.

"I just thought you might want to talk about it."

"It probably wouldn't make much sense. I don't even understand it completely."

Kendra pressed on. "Try me."

Nick looked blankly toward the window as he explained, "Okay. Chemo is really just short for chemical therapy. Basically, they pump some of the deadliest chemicals and toxins known to man into your blood. It's supposed to kill the cancer cells; only it also kills all of your healthy ones too, so you always feel waves of this food sickness-type shit. It takes about five hours or so for three IV bags, but it feels like twenty hours when you're lying there thinking about what's going through your veins."

"I've kind of knew most of that. But does it hurt?" she asked, wincing slightly.

"The first time I felt this stinging sensation in my neck, like it was really working, but I think it was just my imagination. Now I just lay there watching these chemicals drip and drip and drip. I trip out every time I go in there."

"Can I go with you next time?" Kendra offered.

Nick didn't quite know how to answer. "Your boredom knows no boundaries, does it?" he joked, not knowing immediately if he would like her to come along or not.

"What do you think about? I mean, what freaks you out about it?" Kendra asked, refusing to let the subject die with Nick's joke.

Looking into his hat, he thought for a second. "Sometimes I don't think about anything. And sometimes, it's like I just sort of leave my body and float around and look back down at myself watching that fucking drip, like it's not even really me in the chair. And sometimes the floating me tries to figure out how to yank that thing from my arm."

An uncomfortable pause settled over the room before Nick spoke again. "And I wonder if it's working."

Kendra had heard enough of Nick's dire and sad descriptions and decided to change the subject. "Remember when we were little kids, and I don't know why I'm telling you this now, but, I had the biggest crush on you until I was about fifteen years old."

Nick shook his head, "I never have understood your taste in men," he suggested beneath a smile.

"Me either."

"Hey, how about I heat up that lasagna?"

"I was hoping you'd find your manners," Kendra answered, with a smile.

"I'm sorry." Nick said, as he strode toward the kitchen with the lasagna in hand.

"And a glass of wine, if you've got it."

Nick yelled from the kitchen, "So how's Junior doing? I haven't seen him for a few weeks."

"Me either. I guess he's spending all his time with Cassie."

"He's not spending it here."

It was "drip time" once again, as Nick had begun to refer to his chemo treatments. Only recently had he begun to feel increasingly at odds with each visit to the sickly, sterile environment. He hated the smell of the place; it reminded him of the odor found in the cabinet under the kitchen sink. Most of the other patients, he noticed, seemed much older. And although it was common practice for children to also receive chemotherapy, here they would schedule the adults and children at separate times. On the course of his treatments, Nick observation about the other patients had evolved, and on this particular visit, he didn't like what he'd realized. He couldn't seem to recall seeing a single person his age or younger among any of the other adults getting treatment. Immediately he considered it a bad sign. It couldn't be good to be so young and so sick. While studying his drip, a Rubenesque-figured nurse walked in to check on his progress.

"Any problems today?" she asked.

"Just the usual."

"Which treatment is this for you, Nick?"

"Number seven," he said without having to think or count.

Nurse Susie gave him a smile. "Only five more to go!" she added cheerfully.

Nick looked up at her from beneath the bill of his Pebble Beach cap. "Don't remind me."

Nurse Susie gave him a casual pat on the leg and quietly exited the room, leaving Nick alone to stare down the IV bag with contempt for a brief moment. Pulling his cap down over his eyes, Nick took a deep breath. *Only five to go,* he thought, as he drifted off to sleep.

Nurse Susie reappeared in what seemed like only a few seconds, carrying a new, much larger IV bag. As she hung the bag, Nick immediately noticed that the usually transparent fluid was now a muddy black. He immediately glanced at the IV line entering the top of his hand. His hand and arm now shared the same blackish color of the IV bag, the black color, he decided, of death. Panicked, he looked across to a giant mirror just a few feet away to discover a deep blackness covering his entire neck and lower jaw. As he removed his Pebble Beach hat to look more closely at this head, with it slid what remained of his hair. Nurse Susie acknowledged his discovery. "What did you expect?" she asked, smiling. Nick yanked the line from his hand, leaped to his feet and dashed for the door. Nurse Susie slammed the open door and blocked his way. The only other door in the room slammed from behind him. Startled by the slamming door, Nick glanced quickly around the room. Nurse Susie was again coming toward him, smiling as she approached, "I'm sorry. Did I wake you?" she asked, holding a clear bag.

"Damn doorbell," Nick muttered under his breath as he lunged off the sofa, grabbed the red binder from the coffee table, and slid it beneath the sofa cushion before lumbering to the door. Over the past several weeks, Nick's red binder had become fat with page after page of ominous cancer-related research detailing his imminent demise. After a brief detour to grab his hat, he made his way to the door where he was surprised to find Charlie Lawrence and his eight-iron standing behind the peephole. Reluctantly, he let Charlie inside.

"Got a beer in here somewhere?" Charlie asked with a shit-eating grin, as he walked through the door.

"Yeah, same one I've had in there for two months," Nick answered as he returned to the sofa.

"Well get off your ass and fetch it for me, son."

"Can I a take a piss first, or do you expect five-star service?" Nick asked as he slowly rose from the sofa and shuffled toward the kitchen.

"I can wait twenty or thirty seconds."

"How gracious of you," Nick said as he walked away.

"Got any little tramps we can call over?" Charlie called back to Nick, while taking a seat on the sofa.

"To hell with women," Nick yelled back.

Charlie instantly felt something beneath him as he settled on the sofa. Rising to his feet, he instinctively checked beneath the cushion and picked up Nick's red binder. "I hate to say I told you so, Nick," Charlie answered, while opening the binder.

"You're a real ray of sunshine, Charlie. What, did you come over here to gloat?"

"Don't take yourself so damn seriously," he growled back, leafing through the pages.

"Bud or Bud Light?" Nick yelled from the kitchen.

"Bud Light," Charlie replied, as he realized exactly what he was holding.

"Do you want me to make you a friggin' sandwich, too?" As Nick's voice approached, Charlie quickly stuffed the binder beneath the cushion and planted himself on the seat above it.

"So, you missed our lesson last week and you haven't returned my phone calls. What's your problem?" Charlie asked curtly, trying to hide his shaking hands.

"Haven't felt much like golf lately. Besides, in case you didn't know, I've had this little cancer thing going on," Nick said, in a tone normally reserved for Charlie's use.

"I see," he answered. They sat for a moment in icy silence. "So, you're just gonna lock yourself in here and sit around all day thinking the worst?"

"No, I get out. I go to chemo twice a week, and to the grocery store. But I am gettin' kind of tired of sitting here hour after hour fantasizing about being healthy again. I can't live this way, Charlie, if you want to know the truth."

"But it's okay to die this way?" Charlie countered.

"Call it what you like, but I call it acceptance. In fact, acceptance is starting to become my best friend since getting well is not looking like much of a fuckin' option."

Nick's response hit Charlie hard. He hadn't made the trip across town to pussyfoot around and coddle to Nick's self-pity.

"Don't hide what's going on here, Nick. When I lost my foot, I kind of felt that same way. Poor Charlie…" he began.

"I appreciate what you're doing here, Charlie, but we're not talking about my foot," Nick defiantly answered.

Instantly, Charlie's eyes turned sad and his look heavy. "You're absolutely right, Nick. It's what's left of your life we're talking about. Now, if you want to give up, have fuckin' at it. But no one gets out of this life alive, no one. All any of us ever get when we cash out is our legacy. But your legacy, the way you'll be remembered if you keep this shit up, is as a loser, a quitter. I hope you think about that, being a quitter."

Nick sat motionless. Charlie stood and stared at Nick for a few seconds before walking to the door. Just as he was about to leave, Nick finally responded.

"You just don't understand, Charlie."

"You're right, I don't. I've rescheduled your lesson for the day after tomorrow. I expect to see you there."

Nick remained silent as Charlie walked toward the door. Suddenly, Charlie stopped, turned around, and looked hard into Nick's eyes.

"So, I guess Will wins again." He opened the door and walked out, never waiting for Nick's response.

Chapter 18

▼

On the toilet seat, lid down, Nick sat focused like a laser beam on his red binder of death. A soothing jazz cranked on the stereo. Reaching into a paper bag, he carefully removed and examined several items: a painter's mask, a two-foot long clear plastic bag, and a large, fat rubber band. Checking the red binder once more for precise instructions, he placed the painter's mask over his nose and mouth and began blowing into the clear plastic bag, filling it with air and then checking it for leaks. Satisfied with its integrity, he slid the bag over his head. Next, he pulled the rubber band over his head and around his neck. With the fat rubber band sealing the bag airtight around his neck, Nick slid his hands up under the rubber band and inside the bag with his palms against his cheeks allowing air to flow in from underneath.

After sitting still for several seconds, Nick relaxed his arms and let his hands fall. With his hands now hanging at his side, the rubber band formed a tight seal with the bag around his neck. The bag moved as he breathed, with the painter's mask blocking the plastic bag from direct contact with his nose and mouth.

Seemingly out of nowhere, Easy walked into the bathroom and, in a flurried horror, instinctively lunged toward Nick.

Startled, Nick jumped from the toilet and with a racing heart, quickly snatched the bag from his head. The rubber band still squeezing his neck, the painters mask still in place.

"What the fuck are you doing here?" a breathless Nick asked.

Easy was part dumbfounded, amazed, and angry, "Charlie called me. Holy God, Nick, what are you doing?"

"You scared the shit outta me! Don't you knock?" Nick asked as he pulled the painter's mask from his nose and mouth, leaving it hanging just below his chin.

"I did knock, and what in the hell is going on here? This is crazy."

"Testing my deliverance machine," Nick admitted without much emotion.

Nick's cavalier demeanor shocked Easy. "You're insane."

"Relax, Junior, I was not trying to kill myself, not today anyway, 'cause if I were, you'd be late coming to the rescue, and you're obviously not late. And anyway, I was just practicing. Besides, I don't have my tranquilizers yet. That's where you come in."

"Don't just throw stupid shit at me like that!" Easy said.

"Seriously, Will. Tomorrow's D-Day."

"D-Day for what?"

"My tests come back tomorrow, and if it turns out that the cancer has spread and it looks like I'll end up a bed-ridden, ninety-pound piece of shit, I'm checking out, Easy. Fuck it all! Now that's my final decision and it ain't open for discussion. So, if you're my best friend, you'll help me."

"Help you? Who do you think I am, Dr. Kevorkian? You're crazy. That's fucking nuts!" Easy said. Why, he asked himself, hadn't he insisted on counseling? How could Nick have come to this point without him knowing? Had he forgotten that tomorrow was the date? Thank God Charlie had called.

"No, I'm perfectly sane, and you're married to a nurse who can get me the drugs. All I have to do is pop the pills, chug a quart of tequila, and hope the bag or rubber band doesn't break and I end up in a stupid coma. It's all very clean and painless. In less than an hour, I get blotto, pass out, then quietly suffocate," Nick indifferently detailed.

"You've got to be kidding. You can't expect me to help you do this!" Easy answered, astonished at the request.

"You'd rather see me in extreme pain, drugged out of my mind, unable to talk, my face half eaten away, unable to recognize you or anybody else? You'd rather watch me suffer? Thanks, thanks a lot."

"Don't ask me to do this, Nick," Easy pleaded. "I won't do it."

"Look, Will, at that point, I'm already dead. You're doing me a favor.

"You make it sound so simple. Hey Nick, have a happy death. How can I help?"

Nick had predicted this reaction, and although Easy's surprise visit hadn't allowed him to fully prepare his case for pleading, Nick had ample ammunition at his disposal to sell Easy on his decision.

"Put yourself in my shoes. Would you want to be eaten alive from the inside, your tongue black, teeth falling out, dependent on the kindness of others to wipe your ass for you?"

Easy stood silent.

"Imagine being drugged so far out of your fucking mind that you don't notice the pain of your inner flesh burning and rotting away, knowing this was it and you had no chance for recovery. If it you were you, would you want Cassie to see you go through that?"

Easy blinked his eyes as he swallowed.

Nick continued, "No need to answer, Will. I can see the answer in your eyes."

Easy rubbed his forehead. "No, no I probably wouldn't. But this is fucked up. I don't think I could do it if I wanted to."

"Then you'll at least consider it? I can do it without you, you know," Nick added for good measure.

Easy, his facial muscles near frozen in place at the thought, struggled to get his mind around Nick's request. "I don't know. I'll have to think about it. But, we won't have to go that far cause you're gonna be fine.

In fact, I'm taking this creepy shit with me," Easy insisted as he collected Nick's paraphernalia. "And don't bring it up again."

"Take it if you want, but I think I can find another rubber band and plastic bag before you reach the car."

Defeated, Easy threw Nick's suffocating collection of devices to the table, dropping them as if they contained some vile bacteria he was afraid of catching.

Nick put his arm around his friend and whispered, "I'd do the same for you."

Easy was not impressed with Nick's offer. "Get your arm off me, and don't make fun of this shit, Nick."

"I'm not."

Dim light, teeming shadows, and the lacquer-like shine from the over-polished tile floor surrounded Easy as he made his way through the quiet hospital corridor toward where Cassie was working alone at the nurse's station.

"What are you doing here?" Cassie asked. Checking her watch, she was surprised to find it was nearing 2:00 AM.

"I couldn't sleep," Easy offered lamely.

She put her clipboard aside and moved around the chest-high counter Easy was resting his elbows upon.

"Couldn't sleep, huh?" she asked while rubbing his shoulders.

"Nah."

"How's he doing?" she asked.

"I wish I knew. How long until you go on break?"

"I can go in a few minutes. Why?"

"On your break, would you walk me down to the cancer wing?" Easy asked softly.

"Why, what's going on?"

"I had the scariest conversation with Nick today. You've got to swear you'll never say anything 'cause I promised Nick, but...if the tests come back tomorrow and it looks like, like he may be real sick, you know, he wants to kill himself. And he wants me to help him. He wants me to get him some pills."

"What did you say? You told him no, didn't you?"

"I told him I'd have to think about it."

"What's to think about? You can't do that. It's illegal and it's wrong. Besides, he's probably just really scared and you shouldn't support that kind of thinking right now," she insisted flatly, her earlier sympathy giving way to stern advice.

"Yeah, but I remember what his mom was like at the end, and Nick's not gonna let that happen to himself. He'll do it, I know he will."

"That doesn't mean you have to help. It's not the way things are supposed to go. It's unnatural. I can't let you do it."

Easy had been thinking nonstop of nothing else since he'd left Nick earlier that evening. He had said and done everything he could think of over dinner, but Nick's mind was made up. In fact, Nick had been so convincing, Easy was starting to consider Nick's request in a much different light.

"I never thought I'd say this, Cassie, but, is it so unnatural? Is it so wrong? Shouldn't we be able to leave behind pleasant images of ourselves for the people we love? Why should the final impression we leave be so…ugly, if it doesn't have to be? If we're capable, why not take control?"

"Could you even do it?" she asked.

"I don't know," he answered with complete honesty. "I don't know. Can we go for that walk now?"

For Nick, it seemed his whole life had come down to this day. As he passed familiar restaurants and buildings he'd visited on sales calls, and by parks and golf courses he'd played, he felt an odd inner sense of nostalgia. Although Nick and Easy had driven virtually this exact same route many times before to play golf, they had never made the drive without speaking. Nick wondered if he might be seeing these places for the final time. He thought of his mother.

Nick was reluctant to bring "it" up first, and Easy had already decided he wouldn't answer immediately anyway, not until he knew for sure what he might be called upon to do. Besides, in Easy's mind, it was not something that would need to be addressed for several months in any case. Nick, however, was considering an immediate exit. A long battle was not an option. The sooner, he thought, the better.

Nick was first to break the silence. "Why are we driving thirty miles an hour?"

"Sorry," Easy answered.

"So, what did you decide?" Nick asked, unable to wait for Easy to volunteer his services.

"About what?"

"Yeah right. You know what I'm talking about."

"I don't know, Nick. It's not as easy as a simple yes or no."

"Yes it is. You either watch me rot away like a dead squirrel on the pavement, or you let me die with what's left of my dignity," Nick responded, without hesitation.

"I'll let you know later, after the appointment."

"Bullshit, I need to know now."

"Why now, what's so important about now?"

"Because I just need to know now."

"Well fuck it then, Nick. If you can't tell me why, then fuck it. Find someone else."

"You're a dick."

"Yeah, you ask me to help kill you and I'm the dick."

"Look," Nick began, seeking empathy, "I just need to know, either way what my future is going to be. It's the only way I can get through this. I need to know what's ahead. Satisfied?"

"No."

"Please, Will, please. I'm begging here."

Easy pulled the Jeep over to the side of the road and slammed it into park, his hands clinching the steering wheel, his palms sweating.

"I love you like a brother Nick and I'll help you. I'll do whatever you need. But never, ever mention this again. Ever!"

"I won't. I promise. And thanks," Nick said, softly.

Although Easy had his choice of chairs in the reception area, he preferred to stand, to pace, to pretend rapt interest in the fuzzy, non descript oil paintings that adorned the vanilla walls. Nick, having grown marginally accustomed to the dread of the waiting room, preferred to sit, slumped, with his head looking toward the floor, gnawing his red straw as he stared at his sandals. Both of their heads swiveled when the receptionist announced that the doctor was ready to see him. They exchanged one final anxious look as Nick disappeared behind the door.

Nick failed in every desperate attempt to appear composed as Dr. Baumann entered the examination room carrying that same damn folder he carried the day this nightmare began. Nick's face felt hot, his lungs empty, as if someone large and angry were sitting on his chest.

"Well Nick, I won't keep you in suspense. You're perfectly healthy. Nothing of consequence showed up on any of the tests. All blood levels, cell counts, and tissue tests appear normal. One hundred percent clean and clear."

Nick clinched both fists, closed his eyes, and finally exhaled. A shuddering of euphoria overtook his entire body. He swallowed, acutely and physically aware of his saliva as it passed the very point in his throat that just ninety days ago he was certain would kill him. "Thank you, Dr. Baumann, thank you so much!"

Dr. Baumann gave Nick a hearty smile and a stern warning, "But don't even think about smoking again."

"Don't worry about that. I'm a changed man," Nick declared, with near religious conviction.

"We're still gonna need to do some maintenance chemo twice a year for a couple of years and some bloodwork for the next four or five years, but in similar cases, reoccurrence is practically non-existent. If you do experience any return of the symptoms, even a sore throat, get in here immediately, okay?" he added.

Nick was beaming. "Anything you say, and thanks again!"

Nick practically floated from the doctor's inner office to the reception area. Easy knew the news was good the instant he caught a glimpse of Nick's face as he emerged from behind the door. They hugged hard.

"I'm glad I don't have to kill you," Easy said.

Nick was choking back tears. "Next time, don't agree so damn fast, okay?"

Chapter 19

"Look Nick, look at this, see here?" Charlie asked three times in his typically overbearing tone, never allowing time for an answer. "The key is in the left wrist. Don't let the left wrist break down. Always keep the left wrist firm and pointed toward the target."

Nick lined up another putt as Charlie dropped what looked like five hundred golf balls at his feet. "If we're gonna win this thing, you've got to work on your short game until you get your strength back. If little Junior's shooting in the 70's, we've got to have a better short game."

Charlie was pumped. Nick was only three states behind, it was early April, and they had all summer to play the remaining fifteen states.

Nick stopped practicing for a second and threw Charlie a worn, warm puppy dog look. "Thank you, Charlie."

"Hey, I've got money riding on this," Charlie replied, knowing exactly what Nick was referring to but not willing to acknowledge it.

"That's not what I'm talking about, Charlie. I'm talking about the kick in the ass you gave me. I've got a lot of friends, but most of 'em pretty much avoided me. It was even hard for Will to come by, like they didn't know how to act or what to say. And I know I didn't make this easy for everyone, so, I just want you to know I appreciate what you did."

Having discovered Nick's red binder during their last visit, Charlie felt a greater weight to these comments than Nick would ever know. Removing his hat to wipe the sweat from his brow, Charlie waved past the balls littering the practice green and walked to within a few feet of where Nick was standing. Replacing his cap, Charlie held up his hand, gesturing Nick to stop practicing as he nervously twirled his eight-iron. "Nick, I don't have a lot of friends, and the ones I do have, well, let me put it this way, they more or less just put up with me. I know I'm a pain in the ass. But there's something most of them don't know. I'm a proud man and I'm proud of my country. I volunteered to go to Vietnam. Can you believe that? I actually volunteered. This country is about freedom, Nick. How many communist, Russian, or Vietnamese golfers do you know? None! How many famous Chinese doctors can you name? None! Our freedom is what allowed us to cure polio, invent the telephone, save millions of lives, even invent those treatments that saved your life. I didn't lose my foot fighting for your inalienable right to be a pussy. I fought for our right to make choices. Now, back to my bet." He knocked a ball toward Nick's feet. "I also fought so I could live in a country where I could be a cranky bastard and do it without much interference," Charlie added, a rare smile punctuating his salty satisfaction.

For the next several hours, Nick stroked putt after putt, chip after chip. Although exhausted, he didn't want to stop.

All I can say is "Thank you, Jesus!" Thomas offered, with a quick hug. "I prayed for you every night, me and Donna both."

Nick had called him earlier with the good news. By placing Thomas second in the pecking order of those receiving calls following his visit to Dr. Baumann, Nick had hoped to erase what he thought were Thomas's lingering doubts regarding his place among Nick's inner circle.

"Amen, brother," Nick added, although never particularly religious.

"So, what's your maintenance program like?" Thomas asked.

"Chemo twice a year for two years," Nick answered.

"By the way, and you don't have to answer this if you don't want to, but did they have you donate sperm before chemo?"

"Yeah, they did," Nick replied, a curiosity in his tone.

"Did you go to St. Lukes?"

"Yeah, how did you know?"

"Did they make you watch that stupid video?" Thomas asked.

"Okay, you're freaking me out here. How do know about all this shit?"

"That Dr. Sherman's supposed to be the best in the business."

"Thomas, what's up? There's something you're not telling me."

"Don't no one know, Nick, but family." Thomas answered.

"What? Did Donna do in vitro?"

"Not really."

"Then what?"

"Can you keep a secret, cause no one here at work knows, and I'd like to keep it that way."

"Sure."

"Ceramics, Nick, I'm sporting ceramics," Thomas answered.

"I don't follow."

"My maintenance is just the same as yours."

Nick's face turned long and blank as he absorbed the words. "Are you saying you had cancer?"

Thomas tilted his head as he replied, "Got cancer, we are never really cured, Nick."

Nick could hardly believe his ears. "What kind?"

"Testicular, got it about six years ago. Took both my nuts out, put ceramic ones in."

"Holy shit. Why didn't you say something?"

Thomas looked toward the ceiling. "The same reason you didn't talk much about it. It ain't the kind of thing people really understand, unless you been through it. You seemed to want your privacy. I had to respect that."

"But this is different."

"Not really." Then Thomas added, "That's why I changed jobs. Word got out and people started treating me different, like a baby. I hated the reminder, so I came to work here where no one knew."

"I see what you mean. It's kind of bizarre, isn't it?" Nick replied.

"It gets really weird up when people know it's your nuts," Thomas countered.

"How you doin' now? Is everything cool?" Nick asked.

"Not a trace, six years running."

"That's fucking incredible, Thomas."

"Ain't it?"

"I can't believe it," Nick said, his head shaking.

"Life goes on. Speaking of which, I'm glad you're back. My sales days are over. Way too much pressure," Thomas admitted, with a new-found respect for the profession apparent.

Nick laughed. "I thought you liked the coat and tie look."

"Oh no, it's too stressful. And this new project, you're not gonna believe the hoops they want us to jump through. You're gonna be under more stress than Mike Tyson's deodorant."

Nick laughed again, something he'd done more in the last three hours than in the past three months. "I'm actually looking forward to that!"

"Not when you see how we screwed the specs on this," Thomas added.

"Thomas, can I ask you a question?"

"Sure," Thomas answered, "about the cancer?"

"No. We'll talk about that later. There's something else I've always wondered about."

"All the cards are on the table, Nick. Ask me anything."

"Okay. So, why are you busting Mike Tyson's balls all the time? I mean, that's not showing much respect for, shit, I'll just say it, a fellow man of color."

"My wife asked me that same thing. It's simple, Nick. Most of the time Tyson acts like a complete idiot. I don't care what color someone is if they act like a moron. Besides, black people don't always stand up for someone just because they're black. That'd be stupid. Look at O.J. Simpson, not all blacks think he was framed. Besides, some of the stuff Tyson says is just funny to me! Can't help that."

"I can't believe you didn't tell me about your cancer."

Within weeks, Nick's hair and eyebrows had begun to sprout. Indulging a steady diet of cheeseburgers, he'd quickly replaced most of the fifteen pounds lost during chemotherapy, and his energy and psyche had nearly returned to its old form as well. It was time to play golf again, and Nick worked harder on his game than a one-legged Charlie in an ass-kicking contest. He had to. Down three states with only fifteen still to play, he had little margin for error.

Not that it was poor planning—as Nick and Easy had learned quickly that playing all fifty states in less than three summers was nothing short of a logistical nightmare—but the fifteen states that remained were spread out all across the country. Yet the challenge was manageable, nothing they couldn't work out over a pizza and a few frosty beers.

"You'll never believe this shit, Easy," Nick suggested as he turned up a bottle of juice and studied the road atlas. "Thomas told me yesterday he'd had cancer."

"What?"

"Yeah. I couldn't believe it."

"What kind?"

"Testicular, but don't let on that I told you. I promised I wouldn't say anything."

"Wow, that's some serious shit," Easy acknowledged as he chomped from a bag of trail mix sitting between his legs. "How long ago?"

"Six years."

"Is he okay?"

"Says he's doin' great. I just can't believe he never said anything that whole time."

"It's not like you inspired much conversation, Nick."

"I thought I handled it pretty well, considering."

"Considering what? Considering the painter's mask?"

"Considering…let's not talk about that."

As they drove, both decided that the remaining fifteen states of their bet would require five separate trips. One monster trip to the northeast, a slightly more complicated trip through three southwestern states, two short weekend trips, and the grand finale, if needed.

The first jaunt would be a three-day road excursion to Kentucky and West Virginia. It was roughly six hours each way from St. Louis to Charleston, West Virginia, and they knew going in that this leg would not be one of their more glamorous outings.

State number thirty-six, West Virginia, offered a decidedly average golf course, and average golf. In the end, it was one of only a handful of states that didn't seem to offer some unique event or defining moment. In this regard, most every state had a signature, a unique incident that seemed to frame each state: a classic course, some drunken Betty or Divot to rail on, an incredible shot, or someone getting Lanced by a big putt on the final hole.

With Nick watching on from the middle of the fifth fairway, Easy prepared for a shot to the green.

"I was thinking how cool it's gonna be going to Alaska," Nick confessed, then added, "Get it, cool in Alaska?"

"Yeah I get it, but it's not gonna matter if you don't win a few of these states," Easy said dryly, showing everything between them was as near normal as ever.

"You're right, I should have it wrapped up by then. That'd be a shame, wouldn't it?" Nick suggested.

"Can you stop talking just long enough for me to hit this shot?" Easy asked, slightly annoyed at the chatter.

"Can you make a shoe stink?" Nick shot back.

As Easy waggled over his ball, Nick studied the surroundings, surveying the golf course. He immediately decided the course looked like the overgrown grassy area that divides a highway, like it had been abandoned for several weeks, hardly a venue, he thought, worthy of such an important component of their bet.

Meanwhile, Easy lofted his ball weakly into the greenside bunker, then turned to throw Nick an equally weak stare.

"They fucked up a perfectly good forest when they built this place," Nick said, modifying a line he'd heard a professional golfer once use to describe a rather nondescript tour stop.

"What do you expect for bum-fuck West Virginia?" Easy lamented.

"I don't know, maybe, they could…try mowing a little grass or putting some goats or cows out here to keep the weeds down," Nick suggested before adding, "What do you think we'll find in Alaska?"

Easy thought for a moment. "Women that look like caribou? Hell, I don't know."

"If it goes down to the last state, let's make it Alaska," Nick proposed with some excitement.

"That's a good idea, since I never want to go there," Easy said wryly. "It'll give me some extra motivation."

At Charlie's insistence, Nick was looking over a ten-foot putt from every possible angle. It had been the sole focus of an earlier lesson—to check and double-check each putt from all possible perspectives. Finally deciding upon the line, Nick realized if he didn't take a slap at the ball soon, Easy would soon take a slap at him. Finally behind the ball, he quickly stabbed it into motion and stood watching in disgust as the ball ran out of enthusiasm nearly three feet short of the cup.

"Man, I suck," Nick complained, as he picked his ball up and shook Easy's hand. "I putt so bad I could hit it off a table and leave it half way down the fucking leg!"

"You played pretty well for dead man walking. How do you feel?" asked Easy.

"I'm fine, except I suck," Nick answered. "But I've got a question, Easy. Have you been practicing while I was dying?" he asked dryly.

"Nope."

Nick couldn't help but be somewhat skeptical. "Are you sure? Because you hit the ball a little too damn well today," he added as they hopped into their cart and motored toward the clubhouse.

"Positive," Easy answered.

Not that it really mattered if Easy had put in some practice time. It wasn't as if it was against the rules. Nevertheless, Easy did look suspiciously sharp for not having played in almost five months, and the score seemed to support Nick's suspicion, with Easy taking West Virginia in a rout, 78-86.

As they drove to Louisville, the reality that he was now trailing by four states with only fourteen to play had begun to induce a mild panic attack within Nick's fragile psyche. Four states was a lot of ground to make up, especially with Easy playing so well. As Nick analyzed his situation, a steady barrage of ominous thoughts peppered his brain. *Should I postpone the Northeast trip and get more practice? If I get down too many, I could lose the whole thing with five states to play. I've got to win Kentucky! If I win Kentucky I'm back to three down.*

As well as Easy had played in West Virginia, he played just as poorly in Kentucky, with Nick winning, 81-87. In fact, Nick couldn't remember Easy spraying the ball around so much, hooking one drive, slicing the next, chili-dipping around the green. Nick wasn't quick to offer Easy much sympathy either. He had his own problems.

Although still behind three states, Nick's earlier panic was now replaced with thoughts of winning at least six of eight states on their upcoming swing through upper New England. Taking six states would give him the lead once again, he thought to himself, as they drove Interstate 64 back toward St. Louis.

Not much was said between naps and fast food during the three and a half-hour trip home. Although somber by their usual standards, Nick was still happier than a man with a twenty-five handicap breaking 80 to be back on the road and once again in his best friend's company. A lot had happened in five short months, but the bet was now back in full swing, and so was Nick's attention to, and affection for, his prior life.

Rescheduling what was to be a ten-day trip with eight separate tee times in eight different states was not something Easy was looking forward to, but he had no choice. Cassie was dreadfully sick and it was not something that was going to take care of itself any time soon. She was now more than ten weeks pregnant. Easy had been instructed under penalty of death not to mention anything to anyone during the first trimester, since so many times a variety of unforeseen events could derail a pregnancy in the delicate, early stages. Even Easy's pleading for an exemption to tell Nick fell on deaf ears.

"Nick, it's me. Hey look, Cassie is really sick. I'm gonna have to use one of my challenges: we're gonna have to reschedule," Easy said into the phone without taking so much as a breath.

"Is it serious?" Nick asked, knowing Easy wouldn't cancel unless it was something serious.

"She's gonna be fine, but I just can't leave until this clears up."

Nick could sense how badly Easy felt and elected to wait for a more appropriate time to pile on the required grief. "So, I've got you running scared, huh?" Nick said, with manufactured pride.

"Yup, that's it, I'm scared to death. Look Nick, I'll reschedule everything, okay? I'm really sorry!"

"No problem, Junior, let's reschedule for two weeks," Nick offered, matter-of-factly.

"I think I can work that out. And thanks!"

"Yeah, talk to you later," Nick answered, while wondering for more than a brief moment if there wasn't more to the story than Easy was letting on.

Monday morning, no one was more surprised than Thomas Brown to see Nick sitting at his desk, typing away at his laptop, working like an elf.

"What the hell are you doin' here?" he asked.

"Easy had to cancel," Nick answered, his slight disappointment apparent.

"Do you win the states?" Thomas asked.

"No, he used his last challenge," Nick said while typing away without looking up.

"Hey, why don't you come over for dinner tonight? You owe me a dinner," Thomas reminded him.

Nick mentally checked his schedule. "Can I bring a friend?"

"As long as she isn't the kind of girl that requires cash up front," Thomas joked.

"What time are you thinking about?"

"I don't know, let me go check with the warden," Thomas replied and then quickly darted from the office.

Nick grabbed the phone from his desk and dialed. After a few moments, he sat up a bit and delivered a semi-affectionate greeting, "Hey good lookin', I was wondering if you're free tonight?"

Nick paused and looked toward the ceiling, before continuing, "I just got a dinner invitation and I was wondering if you'd like to come along?"

Another pause. "Great, I'll let you know what time. Call you later," he said while hanging up the phone, obviously happy with the outcome.

Armed with the remote control, Thomas sat parked in front of the TV in his throne of a recliner, his only piece of furniture less than ten years old. A beer sweat patiently within arms reach on a nearby table. The sudden arrival of two excited little girls, blocking the TV with their hectic antics, destroyed his moment of TV tranquility.

"You two need to take it to the other room. My show is on," he declared quite ominously. There would be no discussion or appeal; the girls left as quickly as they'd arrived, both giggling.

This return to peacefulness proved short-lived as the doorbell rang several times in rapid succession. Thomas popped from his chair, walked to the door, and squinted through its peephole. Thomas had been waiting all day for this moment. He opened the door and grinned.

"Nick, when did you start dating girls?" he announced in a bellow so loud the words and his intent to embarrass could never be mistaken.

"Sorry pal," Nick answered with a smile, "but we've known each other a long time. Thomas Brown—this is Kendra Easley." The two shook hands.

Thomas was taken aback. "Kendra Easley? Any relation to Will Easley?"

"He's my brother," she said, a smile matching the one Nick was simultaneously flashing.

Thomas's grin widened. "Come on in. What can I get you to drink?" he offered as he left quickly for the kitchen.

"Red wine, if you have it," Kendra called out.

"A beer for me," Nick added.

As Thomas disappeared into the kitchen he could be overheard calling out to his wife, "Donna baby, wait until you hear this shit!"

On the surface, Nick quickly marveled at how Donna and Thomas Brown seemed to make such a perfect pair. Not an ounce of tension could be felt anywhere between them or in their home. Nick thought back to their cancer discussion, to Thomas's admission, and he realized instantly that their chemistry was not accidental. It was born from gratitude for one another, for a second chance to live a life worthy of having a second chance.

When one's regular diet consists of pizza and fast food, a home-cooked meal often tastes better than anything the finest restaurant can offer. Such was Nick's view of the feast Donna had systematically placed before them on the dining room table. Mashed potatoes heavy on the butter, juicy meatloaf with tons of ketchup baked in, and green-bean casserole: it didn't just hit the spot, it hit every spot. And Thomas's two girls, five and seven years old, when not fidgeting and fighting, were the unscheduled entertainment for the evening. The girls served another purpose as well; they kept the dinner table conversation G-Rated, which was driving Thomas completely crazy. He wanted details on this budding relationship and he wanted them immediately.

When the girls asked to be excused so they could resume romping the house in search of more important activities, Thomas was all too happy to comply. "Have you finished your homework?" was his only question.

Following their synchronized "yes," Thomas quickly gave them the green light. "Okay, you're excused. You've got one hour and then it's bath time." Immediately, the girls darted off and Donna and Thomas set about clearing the table.

"Anybody want coffee?" Donna asked.

Thomas, however, had far more pressing questions. "So, what's Will think of you two dating?" he asked, coming out of the blocks quickly.

Nick and Kendra looked at each other. "He doesn't know yet," Nick announced.

"Why the big secret?" Thomas was quick to ask.

"That's what I'd like to know!" Kendra injected with genuine bewilderment.

"I'm just waiting for the right time. He gets funny about shit like that. He doesn't even like to talk about other guys Kendra has dated, and when he does, I can't remember him calling them anything but a dick or a dork," Nick answered.

"And you think it's going to get easier the longer you wait?" Donna asked over the annoying whiz of the coffee bean grinder.

"Listen to the woman, Nick," Kendra echoed.

"He doesn't seem like the type to blow a gasket. Just tell him," Thomas suggested.

"I will, it's just got to be the right time," Nick replied, annoyed that no one seemed to appreciate his perspective.

"Just tell the man!" Donna repeated.

Nick gulped a drink from his beer and slid into his mouth the red straw that he now chewed habitually in place of a cigarette.

"I'll tell him. Don't worry."

Chapter 20

▼

Her morning sickness subsiding, Cassie felt well enough to give Easy the green light for a quick, one-day trip before they rescheduled the big New England swing.

With Nick gamely fighting a road map, Easy steered them along Interstate 35 toward Des Moines, Iowa. While most states in close proximity to St. Louis were checked off the list early, a last-minute business trip had forced Nick to use one of his challenges to reschedule Iowa.

"How much farther?" Easy impatiently asked, bored from nearly four hours behind the wheel.

"By my estimation, one hundred and thirty miles," Nick informed him.

"Well then, in about six hours, you'll be four states behind."

"Yeah, and little pink turtles are gonna fly through giant peanut butter clouds straight up my ass."

"Where did you hear that goofy shit?" Easy asked.

"Charlie said it once. I think it's funny!"

Easy shook his head. "That figures. Hey, I've been meaning to ask you, have you gotten the old sex drive back since chemo?" Easy asked without discretion.

"Yeah, I'm good. But chemo does some weird shit to your brain. I remember watching TV and nothing looked good, from the Baywatch chicks to baby back ribs, nothing. I can see why those dudes use Viagra. Hell, I didn't even look at a Playboy for two months," Nick spewed.

"Have you had him out for a test drive yet?"

Nick ignored the question. "You know what, it's funny looking back. For a while there I really thought I was going to die. And you know what I fear most now? I don't fear death half as much as losing a state."

"It appears to me that a fate worse than death awaits you," Easy said with a smile.

"Someone's feeling pretty cocky."

Miles later, Easy made a right turn past a sign marking the entrance to Waveland Golf Course, one of Iowa's finest. With its 1940's style red brick clubhouse, it felt to both like a more modest version of The Country Club of Saint Louis. But in contrast to The Country Club, Waveland was open to the general, post-Tiger Woods, can't get a decent tee time anymore, golf-crazed public.

Perhaps the most meaningful offshoot of their coast-to-coast excursion was that both would develop a keen interest in golf history, and more specifically, classic, older golf courses. Henry Colt, C.B. McDonald, A.W. Tillinghast, and Donald Ross had become their favorite "golden era" architects, with relative "new guys" Robert Trent Jones, Sr., Jack Nicklaus, Tom Fazio, and Rees Jones (the youngest son of Robert Trent Jones Sr.) as other course designers who ranked highly on their list of favorites.

During Nick's leave from work for chemotherapy, he'd also taken to consuming golf books by the dozens, with writer Dan Jenkins quickly emerging as his favorite. He loved Jenkins' acerbic wit and vivid characterizations in *The Dogged Victims of Inexorable Fate* and *Dead Solid Perfect*. Very little Nick read fell outside his appreciation, from countless biographies, novels, and Irish short stories, to vintage instruction books. If written by or about Bobby Jones, Ben Hogan, or Jack Nicklaus, Nick had read it. Nick's keen interest in golf lore and literature had nearly become an equal to Easy's long-held interest in philosophy.

Over time, they had also agreed that there was no substitute for the purity, restrained elegance, and tradition of an older, classic course. With very few exceptions, the new, high profile, sausage-link developments of recent years simply failed to measure up to the old chestnuts. The newbies, in most cases, were designed as nothing more than a real estate sales gimmick or an outright attempt to steal a golf lover's IRA. Easy once said after playing a modern "experience" course that the entire day "was like a $200 lap dance with a buddy's mother."

Much to their liking, Waveland Golf Course was definitely not a "lap dance" course. It was as old school as they came, very hilly with wide fairways woven between titanic old oak trees. A fun and tense walk in the park lay ahead, with fair greens that lacked modern gimmicks.

Walking together in silence, Nick and Easy arrived at Waveland's first tee box, where Easy methodically threw a tee into the air. He also threw a wry smile at Nick, who had been named, at least according to the little wooden stick, the chosen one.

"I believe I'm up. Let's go to war!" Nick declared.

Easy, as if having prepared for this very moment, offered his own battle cry. "This is more than war, Nick, for war is only capitalism with the gloves off."

"Yeah, well I have a little saying for you," Nick countered.

Easy looked curiously at Nick, given this really hadn't historically been an area where Nick had tread. "Oh yeah, what's that?"

Nick searched his mind for a brief second before lamely pulling a saying from out of the blue. "You can no more win a war than win a thunderstorm," he sheepishly declared, somewhat satisfied he'd thought of anything.

"That's a real nice saying, Nick, but I don't see how it applies here," Easy replied, in his most condescending tone.

"Once I kick your ass, it'll make sense," Nick countered, aware of the sophomoric nature of their posturing and completely unconcerned with trying to keep it in check. After blasting a mammoth drive into the heart of the fairway, Nick grinned toward Easy to add, "Better trade those gloves for a raincoat, 'cause that ball's bringing thunder."

Easy was not the least bit intimidated; they'd done this far too often. Easy laced a solid drive just short of Nick's blast. "I'd stick to golf quotes if I were you," he said, as his ball came to rest within a stride of Nick's.

After four holes, the match sat tied. As Nick watched from the fairway, Easy nailed his approach shot to less than fifteen feet from the flag. Nick countered with a short wedge that landed just left of the stick, only eight to ten feet from the hole. Punch—counter punch.

Easy's birdie putt came up short, giving Nick a real chance at grabbing the first lead of the day. Nick gamely started his putt rolling toward the cup, but after watching it cover only half of its intended trip, he began walking after it: the ball was drifting off-line. After wasting a great shot at birdie, Nick hurriedly picked up the "gimmie" and promptly threw the ball into the greenside lake.

Easy could not ignore the opportunity. "If only you threw the ball that well in Little League."

Nick glared. "Hitting was my problem in Little League, not throwing."

Not much later, Nick's par drew first blood as Easy three-putt a short par-three for bogey. But Nick's immediate double-bogey, followed by yet another bogey, quickly returned the lead to Easy. As the lead bounced back and forth with each hole, so too bounced Nick's emotions. He groaned and cussed or grinned and fist-pumped with each spike and valley the day produced. Both boys, however, were playing the best round of golf relative to par that their tournament had seen thus far. They arrived at the eighteenth dead even, both certain to shoot in the 70's together for the first time.

Standing in front of a sign marking the par-five, eighteenth tee box, Nick studied the scorecard as Easy teed his ball.

"All tied," Nick announced.

"How about a side bet?" Easy proffered, thinking an added little dose of pressure might force Nick into a mistake.

"What do you have in mind?" Nick asked gamely, keenly aware of the tactic Easy was attempting, yet eager to show he was not going to let the strategy bother him.

"Not only will I win the state, but I'll win by two shots," Easy claimed calmly.

"What's the stakes?"

"Loser buys both plane tickets to New York," Easy suggested.

Without a breath of hesitation, Nick stepped up, adding, "You're a fool and I accept. Now hit the damn ball."

Without hesitation, Easy split the fairway with his best shot of the day. Nick's mind churned, immediately wishing he could have hit first and perhaps turned the tables in his favor by giving Easy something to shoot at, something to think about. Distracted by these thoughts, Nick aggressively over-swung and pull-hooked his ball down the left side of the fairway.

"Oh, that looks like trouble," Easy mused matter-of-factly. His assessment proved deftly accurate once they arrived at Nick's ball.

Although the hook provided some extra distance, Nick was in serious trouble. Not only was he caught in the deep grass on the left side of the fairway, a large grove of sycamore trees blocked any direct shot to the green.

Easy, with the shorter of the two tee shots, had already hit his second and was looking at a short third shot into the green. As Easy looked on from the middle of the fairway, Nick took a perfect half-swing with his three-iron and punched the ball low, rocket-hot under the trees. After several big hops, kicks and bounces, the ball chased pin high as it settled in a deep greenside bunker some twenty yards left of the flag.

Easy clapped softly at Nick's heroic escape from the trees before turning his attention to his own shot. Following a moment of stern concentration, he swept his club through smoothly and watched as the ball sailed onto the front of the elevated green. While some thirty to forty feet short, he was still on safely in three.

With Easy on the green, Nick studied a difficult third shot from the deep bunker. Poking his head up and down repeatedly from nearly eight feet below the green, and having finally gotten a solid mental picture for the location of the blind shot, Nick dug his feet into the sand and put a full swing on the ball, kicking a cloud of sand into the air as the ball exploded from the bunker. Easy's eyes began to bug as the ball tracked straight for the cup. Nick raised his arms and, leaping from the bunker, let out a yell, "Go in, baby!" while Easy watched in disbelief.

If not for hitting the flagstick, it might have gone in. Instead, it kicked off to the right, its final resting spot just four feet from the hole.

"You Lanced me, you lucky bastard," Easy muttered. Nick nearly floated from the bunker, the implications of his potential birdie showing in his grin.

Although Easy was near certain he had lost the side bet and was on the hook for a plane ticket to New York, he could still make birdie with his upcoming putt. With birdie, he'd still win Iowa if Nick missed. Should both two-putt, Easy would stay four states ahead. Digesting all the various permutations, Easy lined his putt up and quickly sent it on its way. With less than six feet left to the hole, Easy believed he still had a chance. Nick, his eyes glued to the ball, let out a small sigh as Easy's ball crawled to the hole and died a mere two inches short. Easy shook his head.

All Nick had left was to drop his four-footer, a putt he'd made a thousand times before. Just as he settled in behind the ball for his birdie and a claim to Iowa, Easy called over to Nick.

"Nick, did I tell you Cassie's pregnant?"

Nick stopped his pre-shot routine, looked directly at Easy and in his best deadpan tone, answered Easy's strategically placed question with a question of his own. "Congratulations. Did I mention I was dating your sister?" Nick immediately dropped his head and quickly hit his putt. It rolled squarely into the center of the hole.

Easy watched in disbelief. "Nice putt, and you better be joking."

"Nope," Nick said quickly as he walked to the hole and triumphantly plucked his ball from the bottom of the cup.

"Let me summarize. That'll be match, plane ticket, Iowa, and Kendra."

"Game's over Nick, quit fucking around."

"I'm not kidding, Kendra and I have been going out for a couple of months."

The ride home was cut with such tension, Nick felt as though he were standing over his final birdie putt to win the final state. Despite repeated prodding, Easy offered hardly a word for most of two hundred miles. Nick tried to initiate some sort of dialogue, to break Easy's brooding silence, but Easy would only stare square-jawed at the road ahead.

"I thought you'd be happy, for both of us!"

Easy replied with nothing more than another empty stare over the steering wheel.

"What's the big deal, you little friggin' baby?" Nick goaded.

"Okay! You want to talk, let's talk! How long…how long have you been buddy-fucking behind my back?" came Easy's first comment in hours.

"Buddy-fucking? You're kidding, right? Jesus, dude, this isn't high school."

"No, I'm not kidding. This is worse than buddy-fucking, Nick. Kendra isn't some Waffle House waitress or cart girl. She's my sister!"

"I know that. But while you were off living the American Dream, she was there for me. Kendra came by all the time when I was sick. Where were you? You hardly ever came by!"

"Nick, you were being too much of an asshole. You didn't want anyone around. Besides, that has nothing to do with this. Things finally start working out for me, and you don't like it, so you get back at me by dating my sister? That's what this is about."

"Look, I'm sorry, you know what I mean," Nick tried to explain without success.

"No I don't, Nick. I don't know what you mean," Easy insisted, the anger rising in his voice.

"Just listen for a minute," Nick pleaded. "When I was sick, I realized a lot of things. And one thing I realized was...I didn't date women I respected."

"No shit." Easy's mind flashed back to the women who had come and gone in Nick's life and wondered why this revelation had suddenly taken form. As sure as a pirate stole treasures, Nick had been taking and breaking hearts since he was old enough to buy soda, and Easy had always been there supporting whatever choice Nick would rationalize. It always fell on Easy to console Nick's never-ending stream of women d' jour. "He's really sorry. He cared about you a lot. He just wasn't ready." How many messes had Easy cleaned up over the years on Nick's behalf? How many women had Nick failed to respect enough to break up with them properly? Easy shook his head.

"Let me finish. So, Kendra and I were talking at your wedding and she called me out on it, told me that until I learned respect I'd never find happiness. Well, there's no woman on earth I respect more than your sister."

"Well, I don't like it. She's my only family and I'm not gonna let you fuck her over," Easy declared in an unmistakably serious tone.

"Will, I'm telling you, I would never do that."

Easy, however, had more than two hundred miles to think this through. "You're not gonna have to worry about that cause you're not gonna date her."

"You're nuts! You've lost it! You can't tell me who to date!" Nick said, half-believing this was some sort of a ruse on Easy's behalf to gain advantage for their next match.

"In this case, yes I can. And you're gonna be very nice about it. You're gonna tell her you don't think it's a good idea, give her some shit about ruining the friendship, and you're not gonna see her anymore. Understand?" Easy detailed in no uncertain terms.

"You're nuts, completely nuts!" Nick said, punctuating the remark by rotating his index finger around his temple in a tight circle.

"Keep seeing her and you'll see how nuts I am," Easy stated, steadily fixated on the Interstate's dotted white lines. Nick shook his head as he stared out the side window.

Checking his options, Easy settled on a juice bottle from the refrigerator as Cassie walked in to welcome him home and to get details on his day. Easy went toward the cabinet for a glass.

"So who won?" Cassie asked, leaning in to kiss her husband on the cheek.

"The Goofy bastard," Easy said, staring into the cabinet.

"Okay, what happened?"

"Did you know Nick has been seeing Kendra?" Easy shut the cabinet door hard.

"Really! I think that's great!"

"Well, I don't."

Cassie could sense from Easy's demeanor, his lack of inquiry into how she was feeling, and his generally surly attitude that Easy was excessively worked up.

"What's wrong with it? I think they're perfect for each other. Actually, I wish I'd of thought of it," she stated matter-of-factly.

"You don't know Nick like I do. Nick just uses women. How would you like it if we had a daughter and she ended up with a hound like Nick?"

Cassie was astonished. "It's hard to tell you two are best friends. Give it a chance before you go jumping to conclusions."

"I just don't like it," he said, filling his glass with juice.

"Slow down, Honey! Sheesh. What did Nick say about it?"

"Who cares what that goofy bastard thinks!"

This particular remark ignited Cassie's fuse. "Am I talking to Will, Jr., or Will, Sr., here?" Cassie said, before adding, "And yes, I feel fine, thanks for asking." Her final comment and immediate exit from the room was now the focus of his complete attention.

Across town, Kendra was lying on the couch enjoying a book profiling prominent women of the Civil War, when Nick walked through the front door.

"So, who won?" she asked, almost identical to Cassie, knowing that Nick would not answer directly but instead relate events of the day in the form of a "suspenseful story" before arriving at the actual outcome of the match. Nick's circumspection was an aspect of his character she loved in exact proportion to how much it drove her crazy, though she noticed that she awaited his stories, as well as his arrival home, with a good deal of giddiness.

"Not your psycho brother." Nick's choice of words sent up a huge red flag.

Setting her book on the coffee table, Kendra sat up. "Okay, what happened?" she asked, almost afraid of the answer.

"I'll tell you what happened. He told me I should tell you, in a nice way, that our friendship is too important and that I'm not going to see you anymore. It's not allowed," Nick explained, omitting a considerable portion of their confrontation, while still providing enough detail to spin his point.

"Let me make sure I got this straight. He told you that you couldn't see me anymore?"

"Yup, and that was all he said for the next two hundred miles."

Deep down, Kendra had always taken considerable, albeit, unspoken comfort in the fact that her big brother was looking out for her, but this was crossing the line. Especially since it was Nick they were talking about and not Boob or some other questionable sort.

"Really? We'll just see about that," she thought aloud.

Kendra scanned the apartment until she spotted the cordless phone sitting on the kitchen table. With an angry determination she grabbed the phone and dialed.

Nick considered this course of action. "No, don't call him. He'll cool off."

Kendra raised her hand in a wait-a-minute gesture. "It's okay, really! It's okay."

Kendra waited, pacing the room with the phone against her ear, smiling at Nick. Ten long seconds passed before she spoke. "Will?" she said calmly, confirming her brother's presence on the other end. Then, without forewarning, she screamed near the top of her lungs, "Stay the fuck out of my life!" Hitting the off button, she took a deep breath and placed the phone back on the table. "I've been waiting a long time to do that."

"Well that was diplomatic," Nick said, as he wondered what Easy must have now been thinking.

Chapter 21

It didn't take long for Cassie and Kendra to begin plotting covert operations. The first point of business on their reconciliation checklist was to arrange a meeting between the warring factions. Nick, they decided during their two-hour strategy lunch, would not be an obstacle. He was eager to put the entire episode behind them. Kendra, for her part, had already forgiven her brother and again found her brother's protective nature far more sweet than meddlesome when given time to think about it. The second part of the plan was sit Easy down and reassure him that Nick had been nothing less than a complete and total gentleman. Over and above this reassurance, Cassie spent the next two days giving Easy the silent treatment or referring to him as Pops when she did speak. Soon enough, they decided, Easy would fold.

Arnie's Bar & Grill was to play the role of Switzerland. Nick and Kendra sat waiting in a booth when Cassie walked through the door with Easy in tow. After a brief hug between the girls, the four took their seat.

Kendra took the stack of menus from the end of the table and began divvying them. "How you feeling, Cassie? And congratulations, Nick told me I'm gonna be an aunt! I'm so happy for you!"

Cassie rubbed her stomach and smiled. "Thanks, Kendra. You know, I would've never guessed a year ago that I was going to be a mom."

"It's amazing how things change, isn't it?" Kendra said, glancing sidelong at Easy.

"Yes it is," Cassie said, nodding vigorously.

"Don't you think it's amazing, Nick?" Kendra kicked Nick gently under the table.

"Uh, yeah…I mean, yes, Kendra, it's amazing."

"All right, all right, I get it," Easy said, grinning. "Now let me get this over with. I'm sorry. I was acting like a jerk. As long as you two are happy, I'm happy." Easy extended his hand across the table.

Nick took his hand without hesitation. "Thanks, Will," Nick said. Kendra followed their gesture by sliding from the table and hugging her brother.

"Thank Cassie. She put things in perspective," Easy confessed.

Kendra, given her multiple discussions with Cassie over the past few days and all too aware of her "Pops" strategy, decided it only appropriate that her brother squirm just a bit longer.

"Really?" she asked, playing dumb.

"Yeah, she told me to stop acting like Pops. Oh yeah, one other thing. Nick, we'd like you to be the baby's godfather," Easy added, extending another olive branch.

"I'd be honored. But, I thought you didn't believe in God."

"I don't. But I figured that 'universal-collective-unconscious-unrelated-cosmic-zeitgeist-father' was too long to say. Besides, what do you care?"

"I don't. I just don't want to screw up again. I know you're very specific when it comes to weirdness." Under the table, Nick reached for Kendra's hand.

Easy looked down at the menu. "I'm so sick of burgers. Arnie needs to put an eggplant sandwich on the menu."

"Sounds like a hell of a day," Charlie said, unwilling to mask his winsome grin. Next to a kick-in birdie or a fine single malt scotch, nothing seemed to make Charlie quite as happy as something or someone getting under Easy's skin.

"I'd have loved to have seen his face on that last putt. It reminds me of that credit card commercial. Round of golf, $50; plane ticket, $500; humping your best friend's sister, priceless!" Charlie laughed aloud. "Looks like you're in peak form, son. When do you leave for New York?"

"Next weekend," Nick answered, adding, "and don't talk about me boning his sister. That's my girlfriend you're talking about."

"Jesus Christ, son, don't be such a marshmallow. And start hitting some of those balls. You haven't forgot what balls are, have you?"

Near the midpoint of the New England swing, the level of golf had been quite average by past standards, and the matches between them less than dramatic. Nick won New Jersey by three, 81-84, to draw within two states. Easy countered by claiming New York, 79-82, to return his lead to three states. In Connecticut, although the score was close with Nick's double-bogey on the last hole, lacked any genuine excitement as Nick coasted to a two-shot win, 81-83. With three states behind them, Nick had only closed the gap to two states. It wasn't until Rhode Island that the drama they'd come to expect would reemerge.

Coming to the seventeenth hole, Easy had managed a slim one-stroke lead. It was amazing that the match had been so close. Even more remarkable in Nick's mind, was that Easy was ahead, as Easy readily admitted that his hangover that day had peaked way past Pinehurst on the nausea meter and was by any measure of comparison the worst he'd ever had.

In downtown Newport, the night before they were to play for Rhode Island, Easy had been set up. While the entire ruse was Charlie's idea, Nick could not resist a little payback for the whole Kendra debacle. As Charlie explained it, Easy's pride, ego, and intellect were not only his strongest traits, but also his major vulnerabilities. "Challenge Easy to a mind bender," Charlie explained, "and there's no way he'll resist the chance to prove he's the smartest damn kid in class." Of course, Charlie just happened to have the perfect game already in mind.

The scheme involved ten cocktail straws. Charlie showed Nick how to configure the straws into three connecting squares. After a few beers, Nick would then bait Easy into the challenge, asking him to move two straws, but only two, while reconfiguring the three connecting squares into three different connecting squares of a new configuration. Easy would get a sixty-second head start before he would have to take his first tequila shot. After that, with the clock running, it was another shot every thirty seconds for the next five minutes or until he correctly rearranged the straws. Nick calculated that this worked out to the possibility of nine tequila shots and the virtual guarantee of a hung-over, club-weary partner and a victory in Rhode Island.

"There's no way he'll be able to solve it," Charlie assured Nick. "He'll wake up with the worst hangover he's had in years, and the state will be yours. It's a lock."

"I don't know about this," Nick responded. "Its borderline evil."

"It's not evil, son. Its plan B." Charlie said.

"What's he get?" Nick asked.

"Offer the little bastard two a side."

"I'm not giving him four strokes. That's crazy."

"Trust me Nick, I've seen this fifty times. No one gets it in an hour, much less five minutes. Hell, you played with the damn thing for forty minutes and never got close."

Easy had immediately laughed at the challenge. "Four strokes, right?"

"That's right."

"There's no way I won't be standing on the first tee in the morning without a four-shot lead in hand," Easy began, "but if this is some bullshit trick that can't be done, I'm taking the four shots anyway. Deal?"

"Deal." Nick answered.

Several minutes later, nine shots of tequila were ordered and delivered to the table by a confused but impressed waiter. To Nick's considerable amusement and to Easy's credit, he'd managed to get seven shots down in four minutes before vomiting in the hallway leading to the restroom.

Just as Charlie had seen many times before from others foolish enough to attempt the challenge, Easy never came close to solving the straw puzzle.

His night ended with a drunken phone call to Cassie, who immediately declared him "sloppy drunk," to which Easy responded by announcing that "he'd married Albert Fucking Einstein."

Watching Easy stagger to the first tee at eight o' clock the next morning, Nick reveled at how well Charlie's plan had worked. What he hadn't planned for was the fact that his head was splitting, too, turning their morning in Rhode Island into a potpourri of Gatorade, wild tee shots, missed putts, and hanging heads.

At the par-three, seventeenth, Easy, near puking and afraid he might actually faint, briefly considered conceding the state. He was first off the tee. A dead pull into a greenside pond was met with only a weak thump of his six-iron and a case of dry heaves. Nick faded his own six-iron safely on the green.

With double-bogey and a par, Nick was now up one shot going to the eighteenth tee, a fair test of a par-four at 438 yards with a dogleg elbowing left. While both Nick and Easy hit the fairway, they still had more than 180 yards left to the green. Easy again pull-hooked the ball and sent it sailing well into the trees that protected the left side of the green. Nick left his second shot short, but safe. Another double-bogey for Easy to Nick's chip and two-putt bogey, and Rhode Island belonged to Nick. It didn't matter that it was their worst round thus far, 91-93: Nick now trailed by only a single state.

There was no drinking that night. They instead spent a quiet evening in the musty confines of room 161 at the Montpelier, Vermont, Comfort Inn, eating pizza, watching TV, and lounging around with less zest than two old men after a full day of gardening and checkers.

Watching Easy pick the mushrooms off his pizza, Nick resolved that he would never again descend to any plan B, no matter how desperate he got. He wasn't sure how he would do it, but he would win this thing without tricks, fair and square.

With Vermont in the morning, followed by New Hampshire, Maine, and Massachusetts in the next four days, the boys decided that their version of tournament golf was probably more demanding than that of the pampered PGA pros. This inflated assessment lead to another interesting discussion.

"How much do you think we've spent so far?" Nick asked, a number bouncing in his head.

Easy began his mental calculation. "I'm guessing about twenty grand by the time we finish. That would put it at around four hundred bucks per state. Yeah, that sounds about right."

"That's pretty good math for a guy who can't figure out how to work ten straws," Nick joked.

"That's a lot of money on a bar bet, if you could call it that," Easy concluded, suddenly forced to consider expenditures like diapers, braces, and college funds for the first time.

"Don't you think it's kind of ironic that we both used inheritance from two militant tight-ass fathers, that we didn't really get along with, to pay for something they both would ridicule as frivolous?" Nick said, surprised by the flash of insight.

"Ironic, no; poetic justice, yes. Hey, flip it over to the weather channel," Easy requested indifferently, not wanting to dwell on the dads, but instead more interested in whether or not the rain forecasted for the morning might interfere with their golf plans.

Easy's weather concerns proved justified. Vermont was more Amazon rain forest than midsummer New England, and umbrellas were required by both golfers on the first tee.

Canceling the round, however, was not an option. Waiting another day would make shambles of their tight itinerary, and rescheduling for a later date would leave a lone state sitting as far away from St. Louis as a state could get. Besides, playing in a steady rain was far more agreeable than playing under the conditions they faced just the day before, with hangovers that would make Elvis cringe.

Forty-two down, eight states to go. Nick was trailing by only one, or Easy was ahead by one—the answer depended entirely upon who was asked the question. What they were inclined to agree upon, however, was how important each remaining state had become. Nick was on a mini-roll, and Easy was aware that if he didn't get his shit together, Nick could possibly take the lead by the end of the trip.

Nick's mental torture had him thinking at both ends of the spectrum. Scenarios that had Easy trailing were obviously preferable, but he couldn't ignore his own potentially ominous tally where being down two, three, maybe four states with only four remaining was also quite possible.

Their nonstop, worsening penchant for outcomes and calculations, combined with the lingering brain damage from the night before, made the mood and the golf in Vermont suddenly quite serious. Easy, only one over par after twelve holes would have normally expected to lead by more than just two shots, but Nick's game was also dialed in. Were it not for a lost ball on a narrow, tricky par-four, where he eased up trying to get a little too smooth with a three-wood and pushed the ball into the trees, Nick would have stood at one, or perhaps even two over par.

The margin stayed at two strokes over the next three holes with both collecting three straight pars. After fifteen holes, Easy, his focus unflappable, remained only one over par. Nick, still at three over, felt his chances slipping away. As they walked to the sixteenth tee box, Nick scarcely had time to think before the words slipped from his mouth. If ever there were time to play the Charlie card, this was it, Nick thought as they walked to the sixteenth tee box.

"Hey Junior, I still can't believe you fell for that shit the other night."

"What shit?" Easy asked, planting his ball in the ground.

"Charlie said you wouldn't be able to lay off a bet like that and damn if he wasn't right! Said you couldn't resist proving you're the smartest kid in school."

"That was a Charlie stunt?" Easy asked, glaring, his question postponing his setup behind the ball. "That's pathetic, Nick. You can't even do this on your own. How sad."

This was not the response Nick had hoped for or expected. And neither was Easy's next shot, a solid drive laced straight down the middle. Easy promptly walked from the tee without waiting to watch Nick's shot and instead took his seat in the golf cart.

For the rest of the round, Easy played in silence, letting his golf do the talking. Pars on the final three holes left him at one over 73 for the round and the win. Despite finishing with a respectable 77, Nick had much work left to do. He now faced five hours of fence mending and apologies on the drive to Dixville Notch, New Hampshire.

As the two men settled into the drive, Nick tried to think of ways to explain away his vulnerability to Charlie's rogue influence. But before he could begin his monologue of apologies, Easy spoke. "Nick, sorry about bringing up the 'can't do anything on your own' crap on the sixteenth," Easy offered with genuine regret.

"I never did get what you meant by that," Nick confessed.

"You're kidding, right?" Easy asked.

"Nope," shrugged Nick.

"I was talking about the pills, you know, the painter's mask, the plastic bag, how you wanted help…" Easy stopped speaking, suddenly sorry he'd said a word.

"Well that's just plain fucking mean," Nick snarled, suddenly understanding. He then looked at his friend. "Guess I deserved it though, huh?"

For most admitted golf junkies, securing the first tee time of the day often meant little more than an early finish to the round or an opportunity to play at one's own pace, undisturbed by slower golfers. Cancer had changed that for Nick. Cancer had not only deepened realizations of his mortality, it had also changed his awareness of both the people in his life, and as importantly in his mind, for the world that surrounded him. He'd discovered an almost spiritual aura engrained in once-overlooked moments of quiet purity. Simple words now failed to adequately explain the nourishment fed to his soul from something so simple as the tranquil solitude of a silent golf course waking to the morning's orange sunrise.

The connection between his second chance and the sweet smell of freshly cut grass was now impossible to ignore. To leave behind the day's first footprints on a dew-soaked fairway was no longer simply a privilege of the early bird; it was a small wonder. Watching the horizon come to life with a heavy sunrise full of rich, streaking colorful clouds was now a big event.

For Nick, it was as if the start of each new day, and every round offered both golfers and survivors the same notion. The notion of a fresh beginning, the rebirth of an eternal optimism that finally, this new day was the one they had been waiting for. That it was now time to unleash the day's unfulfilled potential upon friend and foe alike. Or as Easy had once explained it, perhaps it really did embody the search for that mystical moment you find true center and everything finally makes some sense. Until his recovery, he'd always played as if winning was all that mattered, but now Nick realized that the deeper gift was in simply being there.

All of this and more greeted Nick and Easy that particularly amazing New Hampshire morning: the first tee time, a crisp early breeze, and a classic 1912 Donald Ross design called *Panorama*, aptly named for it's lofty perch atop a granite mountain high above the stately Balsams Resort.

Despite such a grand setting, Nick was ever mindful that he was now two states down, with all that remained of their longest trip to date being the morning's round at *Panorama*, then Maine, and then Massachusetts.

It started routinely enough. Just the two of them and a wide open golf course. Coming off yesterday's rounds in the 70's—despite a steady rain—had left Nick and Easy optimistic that an even better score could be shot under such perfect conditions. Emerging equal to that belief, both were only one over par after five holes.

Having played a lot of golf, both boys knew that some of the most frustrating rounds were those that followed some of the best. It was golf's way of saying, "Sorry, big boy, but I'm not that easy!" It was her less-than-subtle way of bringing back to earth those delusional and terminally confused souls who thought they'd figured it all out.

By the time they reached the signature twelfth hole, a 387-yard, par-four requiring a precision tee shot into a blind landing area, then an uphill approach shot to a green built into a mountainside, Nick held a slight lead at five over, compared to Easy's six over par. The greens, typical Donald Ross, large, steep, lightning fast and rolling, had been the main culprit in their less-than-stellar display of scoring. Three-putts were piling up on both scorecards faster than third-world debt.

But their mediocre play became an instant memory when, out of nowhere, an old ghost appeared. Nick, as he bent down to tee his ball, suddenly began a violent coughing fit as traumatic as any brought on by his tumor. Between a brutal gasp for air and a deep retching hack, Nick's watering eyes bulged as he looked helplessly toward Easy.

"What can I do, Nick? What should I do?" Easy pleaded, having bolted to Nick's side, now desperately whacking him on the back.

With a gnarly final hacking hew, seemingly near ten seconds long, Nick unfolded from the waist and staggered to one side, as would a semi-conscious boxer rising from the canvas after being caught flush with an uppercut.

So many thoughts emerged from behind the looks they exchanged that neither knew what to say next. Nick felt that his hands were wet and slowly lifted them toward his face, fully expecting to find them covered with blood. To their shared relief, only snot, saliva, a white golf tee, and other goo filled his palms and fingers.

"That was fucked up!" Nick offered, still a bit unnerved but slowly catching his breath.

"What the hell happened?" Easy asked, a ghostly white paining his face.

"I was just chewing this golf tee when I bent over to tee my ball. I guess I hit it with the handle of my driver and accidentally jammed it into my mouth. I must have been swallowing 'cause the tee got caught a little sideways in my throat," Nick explained.

"Are you kidding me?"

"No! That's what happened," Nick shrugged innocently.

"Fuck, I thought you were having another tumor attack."

"No, I'm fine, I guess. Wow. Let's play golf," Nick immediately suggested, trying to act as if nothing major had happened.

"That scared me half-to-fucking-death!" Easy confessed, still frozen in his tracks, his mind finally returning from its sudden and unexpected trip back to the oncology ward.

Spooked by the sheer magnitude of the incident, Easy proved incapable of making a charge, allowing Nick to close out New Hampshire 80-83. At the end of the day, each man quietly obsessed about the implications of his standing: Easy was one state ahead or Nick one behind, depending on whom you asked.

The drive from the Balsams in New Hampshire to Sugarloaf Resort in northern Maine offered the same eerily similar look and feel as the one made just a day earlier from Vermont to New Hampshire. Exploring the country's most beautiful scenery was on some level quickly and quite sadly bordering on monotonous, following a cycle of seven straight days consisting of five hours of golf, five hours of driving, eating, showering, sleeping, and repeating.

With Nick behind the wheel, Easy daydreamed from the passenger window. "I'm starting to get that Bill Murray *Groundhog Day* feeling with all this driving."

"Not me. I feel great," Nick replied, sitting tall behind the wheel.

"I've seen all those pill bottles the past few days. Are you taking some kind of super vitamin?" Easy asked.

"Just the regular shit the doctor's got me on."

"Any of them steroids?"

"Yeah, why?"

"Seriously?"

"Yeah, they always give you steroids with chemo to help rebuild the immune system and replace lost muscle mass."

"Christ, I guess we're going to need a drug testing program for the last six states."

"Yeah, cancer's a big advantage for me. That was my plan all along."

"Don't you think it's border line cheating, being all juiced up?"

"What I think is that you're getting more like Pops every day."

"Seriously, I'm not trying to be a prick about it."

"No, but you are getting senile," Nick suggested. "I think it's about time to put you in a home."

When they arrived early that afternoon at Sugarloaf Golf Club, a Robert Trent Jones, Jr., design at the foot of Sugarloaf Ski Resort, it looked better to Nick's first glance than advertised on the website. Sugarloaf Golf Club presented the feel of Rocky Mountain golf meeting Pinehurst. With a roller coaster of elevation changes, pine tree lined fairways, and big fast greens, its unspoiled presence was as striking to the eye as any course they'd played.

Not since Mississippi two summers before had a round finished with a tie. And although spectacular, Sugarloaf would not prove particularly sweet for either golfer.

Easy held a slim lead after nine holes, 39-41. But Nick, thanks in part to a couple birdies offset by two double-bogeys, won the back nine, 41-43. Their first tie in over two years left Nick still one state behind as they hit the road for another long haul south to Cape Cod and their final round of the trip.

The plan was to leave Massachusetts for last, hoping against hope that they could weasel their way onto The County Club in Brookline. As their bet had progressed, so had their intent not just to play in every state, but to experience the very best each state had to offer, to make each state a mini-pilgrimage. Ultra exclusive, The Country Club in Brookline fit this calling. Consistently ranked among the Top 10 courses in America, the course had hosted four U.S. Opens, with the 1913 Open the most significant of all. An unknown American, Francis Quimet, defeated British legend Harry Vardon in what golf history viewed as one of the greatest underdog stories of all time, and the moment responsible for popularizing in America what was a Scottish dominated sport in that day. Not only was the course on America's Top 10, it was also on Nick's Top Ten.

But Old Dickey from Arkansas, despite claims of being well connected, was no help in securing access to this prestigious club. Charlie's contacts at St. Louis's high profile clubs proved equally worthless, as did every other angle they tried, including a desperate plea to the Assistant Head Pro at The Country Club itself.

Much like other mega-elite courses of Pine Valley, Cypress Point, and Augusta National, The Country Club was simply beyond their reach. And nothing irritated Nick and Easy more than being considered second-class golfers without sufficient stature to play many of the country's finest courses.

In reading so many books and stories of golf abroad, both knew that many of the great courses in Scotland and Ireland, including most private clubs, allowed at least some public play. The Old Course in St. Andrews actually set aside several tee times each day and conducted a daily lottery to ensure public access to at least a few coveted slots. The fact that most of the premier courses in the states would not be as accommodating as their foreign counterparts annoyed Nick and Easy to no end. Furthermore, they concluded early on that The Country Club in Brookline, Augusta National, Seminole, Pine Valley, and the like were simply the trophies and playgrounds of elitist snobs, uninterested in accommodating true golf enthusiasts. Many of the members of these clubs, they would learn, were aging, crusty, and tired and could no longer walk without assistance from the restroom to the first tee if their grandchild required rescue from a rogue alligator. The most disturbing rumor the boys had heard throughout their travels was that many of the super elite courses could often see an entire day pass with hardly a dozen members on-hand to enjoy them. It seemed like such a waste.

Sadly enough, Massachusetts proved typical of just such elitism, as only one of the ten highest rated courses in the state was open to public play. Adding further to the disgrace was this particular seaside resort's ridiculous requirement of a five-day stay at the hotel to gain golf privileges.

Thus, Nick had been forced to find a less than stellar alternative in North Falmouth as a last-minute substitute. Set atop the highest point on Cape Cod, Ballymeade Country Club and Estates was well groomed and designed along classic lines. If the course played as advertised, it would offer a more than fair challenge.

Having made the required phone calls to St. Louis to update the girls on who'd won what, to confirm arrival times for the following day, and to see how everyone was doing, it was time to play golf.

During warm-up for the final round, both struggled to find their form.

"Tired at all?" Nick asked Easy, noticing more standing around than ball striking.

"No," Easy replied. "I boosted some of your pills this morning."

"Yeah right. Seriously, Junior, you look like shit. And judging by yesterday's mustard incident, you didn't even bother to change pants."

As Easy laced a final bullet to the end of the range, he turned to Nick. "How is packing more clothes than a trust fund debutante going to win any states for you?"

"Look good, feel good, play good," Nick answered.

"You looked great when I kicked your ass in Vermont."

"Want to know the truth?"

"What's the truth, Nick?"

"Truth is, when you look back on this day thirty years from now, you'll know you lost to a man who played the game with style, whereas all I'll remember is thrashing some hobo with hot dog stains."

Easy chuckled at the thought. "Game over style, Nick. That's what I'll remember."

"Enough bullshit, mustard boy. Let's do this."

Gathering their bags, they left the driving range and made their way some one hundred yards down a steep hill to the first tee. Easy was bringing up the rear by a substantial distance.

Waiting to greet them on the first tee box were Bill and Judy Brown, their thirty-something partners for the day. This wasn't the first time they had been paired with "a couple," and they had learned early on to reserve judgment until critiquing at least one swing. Nick and Easy were, however, instantly forced to add a new category to their list of personalities prior to seeing that first ball struck. Bill and Judy Brown, bordering on albino, were officially crowned "Sun Pussies."

Covered from head to toe in thick, pasty white, two million SPF-rated sunscreen, even Bill realized that he'd gone a little overboard and suggested they forgo the customary handshake until he could get the goo completely worked in. Nick gladly accepted his offer when he noticed more sunscreen between the webs of Bill's fingers than he'd have used to cover his entire body if standing buck-naked directly on the equator.

And Judy, not to be outdone, stood insulated from all of nature's elements with knee-high socks, long shorts, and a hat—make that a bonnet—more appropriate for the Kentucky Derby than the golf course. She also had enough SPF-gunk resting in either ear to cover the entire foursome.

Standing behind their cart as they dug through their golf bags for the day's supply of tees, Easy decided he could no longer withhold judgment.

"This is gonna suck," he muttered in Nick's ear.

But to their astonishment, Bill had a serviceable, compact swing and hit the ball a respectable distance straight down the middle. Judy, meanwhile, apparently quite experienced and comfortable from the ladies' tees, chopped a nice three-wood 130 yards just off the fairway. Both Nick and Easy considered the effort quite amazing since neither looked as if they had ever been outside before.

On the out nine holes, the match played tight, with neither gaining more than a two-stroke lead or proving able to hold it. And despite initial appearances, Bill and Judy proved a refreshing surprise. While still "Sun Pussies," both were easy going, mildly entertaining, and quick to pick up their balls when the wheels fell off.

By contrast, Nick and Easy were locked in a tense battle. It had also grown increasingly quiet, not only from tee to green, but also in the cart. Having known one another for so long, each knew when to needle and when to keep quiet, and this was one of those times to keep quiet.

Making their way to the eighteenth tee, a 581-yard par-five, Nick was in a mild panic. Trailing by one shot, he was all too aware that a loss would leave him two states behind with only four to play. With Easy having the honors, he'd have a chance to see how Easy's shot turned out before deciding how aggressive his play would need to be. Easy, seemingly unaffected by the close score and appearing ever calm, put his typically smooth swing to the ball and laid out a precision fade, cutting most of the distance from the right dogleg. Although he was playing down wind, any hole measuring 581 yards long was almost out of Nick's range, even with two near perfect shots. And this particular layout was virtually impossible for him to reach in two. Water, actually a small lake, guarded the entire front of the green. With Easy in position for a routine par, Nick knew he needed to reach the green with his second shot.

Charlie once told him during their many hours of practice that when you needed a big shot, "think long, but swing easy." As Charlie explained it, most people thought hard and swung hard, then overcooked the shot. By thinking long and swinging easy, you could trick yourself into applying just the right amount of extra swing speed.

Employing Charlie's advice, Nick hit it a ton, but sent it hooking just enough to catch the leading edge of a forty-yard long fairway bunker guarding the left corner of the dogleg. Rather than ride in the cart, Nick walked to his ball. Easy drove ahead and waited, with Nick about forty yards behind him.

Needing to choose a club that would clear the lip of the bunker yet still chew some yardage, Nick calculated a four-iron as the right stick. If he caught it just right, he'd have but a mid-iron to the green, leaving birdie in play if he pulled off both shots.

It was a well thought plan indeed, only he caught way too much sand coming through the ball. Floundering lamely for only thirty or so yards before catching the steep lip of the trap, Nick's ball rolled weakly back into the sand. A quick glance toward Easy to gauge his reaction found him looking blankly at the ground.

Nick's jaw tightened as he snapped the four-iron in half over his knee in a single motion. Easy looked up briefly, recognizing the sound, then looked back to the ground.

"Yeah, all right, I snapped that bastard in half. So what?"

Nick briefly considered getting another club from the cart, but he was too frustrated at the thought. Instead, he decided in his rage to use the now smaller version of his four-iron for his third shot from 283 yards, all but certain the match was lost. Stooped over his ball, he clutched the wounded mini-iron and gouged a short pop-shot that finally found grass. Still more than 250 yards from the green, and without another club to either hit or break, he leaned over his fourth shot with the broken four-iron and promptly stabbed a low flyer that, to his surprise, darted from the deep grass, skipped across the fairway, and seemed destined to scoot into the lake. Were it not for more deep grass at the edge of the fairway fronting the lake, Nick's ball would've become, as Big Dickey liked to say, a "Jacques Cousteau."

It was finally Easy's turn, and only one option was seriously considered, a five-wood. Hitting it flush would be a bonus, but even a bad shot would leave a third shot of only 160 yards to the green. As it played out, his effort left only 142 yards to a flag cut in the front right corner of the green, some twenty-yards over the lake's edge. With Nick having walked some fifty yards ahead to his ball, Easy grabbed an eight-iron and focused his attention away from the flag, safely toward the center of the green. Realizing a routine iron and two putts would take the state, Easy put his typically smooth swing to the ball.

"Holy shit!" flew from his mouth nearly as fast as the huge clump of grass he took flew down the fairway. He'd hit it fat and was now forced to watch in shattered disbelief as his ball tracked perfectly toward the center of the lake. Plunk. Dead in the water.

"Fuck!"

This sudden turn of events set Nick's brain working overtime. He was back in the match. After calculating more than eight potential outcomes, he decided that Easy would likely get double-bogey. If Nick could hit close and one-putt, he would win Massachusetts and end this trip all square.

With a pitching wedge from the rough, Nick knew the ball wouldn't stick on the green from that lie, so he planned to land it just off the front of the green and hope for a good bounce and roll.

As soon as the ball clicked off the clubface, Nick knew he'd striped it and tracked its perfect flight toward the flag. He felt a slight rush of adrenaline. Landing with one big hop before settling into a steady roll, his ball looked for a brief second as if it might actually catch the hole before slowing to a stop a few feet past the cup.

"Magnus, baby, yeah!" Nick yelled, his teeth and fist clinched, now certain of carding an unlikely bogey.

Had Nick not knocked it stiff, Easy would have safely played for the heart of the green and taken his chances with a two-putt double-bogey. But if he two-putted, the state was history. From his drop on the fairway side of the lake just inside seventy yards, Easy took a sand wedge from his bag and dead aim for the flag.

"Be the right one!" Easy yelled at the ball in mid-flight, looking up at the ball then down quickly at the flag, and then back to the ball.

Without saying a word, Easy threw a wry smile from across the fairway toward Nick, now on his tiptoes, stretching to get a look. Easy quickly had his best Freddie Couples walk working again, twirling the club as he calmly strolled toward the cart.

It was hard to tell which ball was closer once they reached the green. One thing was certain, however; neither lay more than eighteen inches from the cup, and certainly not far enough away that either golfer could miss.

Easy surveyed both balls as they reached the flagstick, his being a bit farther away. Calmly, he looked over at Nick and conceded the putt. "That's good, Nick, pick it up."

"Yours is good too," Nick allowed in an exchange of sportsmanship appropriate for putts of such length. They shook hands.

"Two ties in a row. This is a habit we need to break right now," Nick suggested.

Easy shook his head, "Like a four-iron?"

"That club betrayed me. It had it coming."

Their New England excursion had totaled more than 1,700 miles, 144 holes of golf, nine nights in nine different hotels, and more than eight states added to their tally.

"They'll think we're lying about two ties in a row, you know. The girls, like we're trying to drag this out," Easy suggested.

"I am trying to drag it out," Nick confessed. "I'm behind."

Chapter 22

Easy was only one state up, or Nick only one down, depending on whom you asked. Just four states remained: New Mexico, Arizona, Texas, and, if needed, Alaska.

Easy set aside his book and looked out the window of the airplane as they flew across the rugged desert landscape toward Phoenix. Not a single tree visible for as far as the eye could see. He silently wondered about the golf courses they would play, how anything could grow in such harsh conditions. He thought of his decision to drop out of law school. He thought of becoming a father.

As the plane descended upon Arizona, Nick's mind was mulling a similar blend of his domestic self and his golf self. Early on in the flight, he'd obsessed over the decision he and Kendra had made about moving in together. So much was changing. But as touchdown approached, golf thoughts overtook all others, and these thoughts did not allow concern for trees or vegetation or domestic bliss, for that matter. "Do you realize how boring our bets are going to be once we finish this thing?" Nick asked from his aisle seat, the reality hitting home that this could well be the final trip of their bet.

"Nick, boredom is nothing more than a desire for desires. Besides, have you no imagination? We'll find plenty to bet on," Easy said as he reopened his read for the flight, *Golf is Not a Game of Perfect*, by Tour guru and noted sports psychologist, Dr. Bob Rotella.

"I guess you're right, but you know how women go through depression after having a kid. I'm already starting to develop a serious case of post-bet depression," Nick half-seriously admitted.

"We're gonna need to get you a really good therapist when I kick your ass this weekend!" Easy said, starting the gamesmanship before the plane had touched ground.

The itinerary began with a five-plus hour drive from Phoenix to Las Cruces, New Mexico. They'd decided upon the New Mexico State University Golf Course in Las Cruces, as one golf magazine had recently ranked it as the second best public course in the state. At only $25 bucks for over 7,040 yards, it was an outstanding value: slightly less than a third of a penny per yard. (Easy, esoteric as ever, had recently started calculating cost per yard as a component of measuring course value.)

Mundane valuations aside, the course appeared to be a well-kept, interesting layout. Charlie, Nick decided, would have simply loved the place. And not for the cheap green fees, stark desert setting, or the jagged mountain overshadowing one side of the course with a giant "A" painted in the hillside for New Mexico State's Aggies, but mainly because there seemed to be a pro shop Mafia at work controlling tee times. Twice that morning, the staff had bumped the boys scheduled tee time, nearly forty minutes in all, and inserted their cronies without tee times ahead of the boys. This sort of thing happened all the time back in St. Louis, but Nick and Easy had always been benefactors of the practice, with Charlie playing Mafia Don. They knew the score, but as outsiders they also knew they had no course for appeal.

Anticipating a six-hour round, by day's end it looked to be a nineteen-hour roundtrip, including golf and drive time. Neither, however, was going to openly complain about a long day, or accept it as a distraction. Their impending journey from Las Cruces to Phoenix would put an end to three years of interstates and long, grueling days, since travel from Phoenix to Houston was by plane, and they certainly wouldn't be driving to Alaska.

As the cushion of remaining states dwindled, when a match grew tight, the tone would turn decidedly somber and serious. And play during state number forty-seven started both pensive and close through the first thirteen holes. Neither had carded a birdie, with only pars and bogeys thus far. There was one exception; Nick's solitary double-bogey on the tenth hole. With Easy nursing a one-stroke lead on the 204-yard par-three, fourteenth hole, he arrived at the tee box smelling a win. And true to form of that day, his crisp three-iron delivered, leaving just fifteen feet for an uphill run at birdie.

"Nice shot," Nick acknowledged, feeling the momentum shift, while silently begging his brain to rise to the occasion and match Easy's effort. He did not fare well, however, finding the steepest of greenside bunkers—a horrible, semi-buried lie—and very little green to work with. Decelerating on his bunker shot in an effort to float it high and land it softly, Nick promptly chunked his sand wedge and watched in disbelief as the ball floundered into the face of the bunker before rolling to a stop within inches of his feet. Finally finding the putting surface on his third shot, Nick quickly two-putt for his second double-bogey of the day, prompting four "fucks" and one "son-of-a-fucking-bitch" in rapid succession.

Making matters worse, Easy ran his birdie putt into the heart of the cup, and in one hole had increased his lead to four strokes.

"Good putt," offered Nick as they walked in silence to the fifteenth tee.

At a par of five, the scorecard suggested that the 512-yard fifteenth hole was one of the easiest on the course. Nick knew he not only needed birdie at this point, he needed help from Easy along the way: he needed a mistake. Yet Easy once again mustered a solid drive safely to the right-center of the fairway. Although Nick matched Easy's drive, he had only three holes left and four shots to trim from Easy's lead. With 240 yards left to the hole, Nick unleashed an atomic three-wood that tracked smartly toward the green before leaking at the very end. Despite taking a weird kick to the right, his ball settled just off the green's edge. He was pin-high, leaving a short chip for eagle, and at worse, a chip and putt for birdie. Nick regained a sliver of hope.

Easy was all business as he stepped up and nailed his own three-wood just off the front fringe of the green. Just that quickly, Nick had lost what little advantage he'd earned only moments before.

To make matters worse, Nick misread the green on his chip and watched in disgust as his ball curled short below the hole, a good twelve feet from birdie. Experiencing a minor meltdown, Nick repeatedly slammed the toe of his wedge deep into the greenside turf.

Ignoring Nick's tantrum as best he could, Easy sent his chip on a perfect line toward the cup. "Go in!" he shouted, unconcerned with the ball's inability to actually accept instruction.

"Magnus, Magnus, Magnus!" Easy shouted, his arms raised above his head as the ball sat in the bottom of the cup. Between the two archrivals, it had taken 47 states and exactly 1,688 holes of golf before the first eagle was penciled on a scorecard. From Easy's perspective, that first eagle could not have come at a more perfect time. For Nick, it was the final nail in his New Mexico coffin.

"Christ, good chip."

"Thanks."

Easy rode his eagle to a 78-84 win and had increased his lead to two states, with just three to play.

Nick's post-round depression was quickly transforming into a near breakdown, as he considered his sudden, harsh reality. He needed two straight to tie, all three in a row to win. He needed a drink. Convincing Easy to stop at a local tavern across the street before starting the long drive to Phoenix proved no problem. As much as Nick felt like drowning his sorrow, Easy felt like celebrating.

Yet with four pints of beer chugged in rapid succession, Nick's mood had not improved. He quickly ordered a fifth pint. "Will, want another one?" Nick asked, with plans for a solid binge firmly set in his mind.

"Naw, I got to drive," Easy answered, before adding, "I gotta take a dump, but if you insist on drowning your sorrows, let's grab a twelve pack for the road."

"Sure, go take your dump. I'll settle up the tab and meet you out front," Nick offered.

"Sounds good," Easy said, with a slap on the back as he hopped from the barstool and headed toward the restroom.

"Hey bartender, can you put another beer on the tab and close it out? And put a shot of Cuervo Gold on there too."

What the fuck happened? Nick asked himself as he downed the tequila and chased it with a slug of beer. He began counting in his head: five beers and a shot in the past hour, at least four beers on the course, and three states left. Only three states left.

Glancing around the bar, he wondered what in Hell's name he was really doing there, five hours from nowhere in a shit-hole bar, pissing away a small fortune playing out a stupid bet he had secretly never expected to win.

Two stools away, a heavy-set fellow Nick suspected was a regular customer based on his rapport with the bartender, sat enjoying a cigarette, a Marlboro Light, his old brand. "What the hell," Nick murmured to himself as he slid from his stool and walked toward the older gentleman.

"Excuse me, can I bum a cigarette?" he asked politely.

"Yeah, no problem."

Nick took the cigarette and slowly rolled it between his fingers. "Thanks," he said as he returned to his stool, grabbed a book of matches from the bar and, without a second thought, snapped a flame and lit up.

Following a quick puff to expel the match sulfur, he sucked back a deep long draw, held the smoke in his lungs for a second, then sent a thick cloud of smoke toward the ceiling.

Ahhhh, said Nick's inner voice as he settled in for another toasty puff. As he lifted the cigarette toward his lips for a second taste of twisted comfort, a blur of a paw flashed before his face, snatched the lit cigarette from his hand, and crushed the burning tube right before his eyes. Nick's eyes widened to unnatural dimensions as Easy grabbed him by his shirt collar, pulled him to his feet, and stuck his nose within a half-inch of Nick's face.

"Don't ever do that again, especially as long as you're dating my sister. If you do, not only will I beat you to a such a bloody fucking pulp they'll need photos to rebuild your face, but I swear to God I'll never speak to you again. Now let's go, before I change my mind." Clint Eastwood couldn't have delivered a scarier admonishment. Easy neatly released Nick's shirt and, with an icy final stare, walked away.

More than an hour would pass before Nick felt it safe to talk. Deep down, he knew he couldn't start smoking again. It was simply not an option.

"Look, Easy…" Nick began.

"Nick, I've said all I have to say. I don't know what you were thinking and I don't care. But if you have any fucking sense whatsoever, you won't do it again, end of story. Now, what time do we tee off in the morning?"

Nick wheeled around to the back seat to grab the folder containing their golf and travel arrangements.

"I don't know for sure. Let me check." Nick grabbed his folder, settled back into his seat, and studied Easy's expression. "Don't worry, I'm not gonna start smoking again, I swear on my mother's soul!"

"Good, 'cause if you do you won't need to bother with surgery again. 'Cause I'll personally rip your fucking throat out."

"Nine-thirty-five," Nick said, regarding tomorrow's tee time. "And don't think for a minute that I'm going down without a fight," he added.

"I know," Easy countered, "I wouldn't expect anything less."

Nick just wished he, too, truly believed his own bravado.

Unlike Easy, Nick had a difficult time falling asleep that night. His false bravado of earlier had steadily given way to more dire thoughts, and they peppered his restless mind without mercy. Would Easy tell Kendra of the smoking incident? When combined with visions of how losing tomorrow's round would put a cold and sudden end to their odyssey, and after recycling what had happened that afternoon with Easy's eagle, Nick resigned himself to the harsh facts. Part one of his life as defined by his Little League failure was about to be roundly trumped by yet another monumental humiliation at Easy's hands. He thought of the two-year losing streak, of his hatred for anything Neil Diamond since the *Mutter Mill Café*, of how composed Easy had played every state, especially that very day in Las Cruces when so much was on the line. It was fast approaching three in the morning, and Nick's brain had yet to allow a single yawn.

Bored of channel surfing and tempted to kill the lights in one final attempt to talk himself to sleep, Nick noticed Dr. Bob's book of golf psychology sitting on the nightstand. Desperate for anything to numb his brain and induce sleep, Nick realized his magic sleeping pill sat within arm's reach.

Although he'd read books covering most every subject on the game of golf, psychobabble of this sort, whether golf related or not, still held zero interest for him. After a disinterested glance at the table of contents he flipped through several pages with no specific purpose in mind, until a random passage jumped from an equally random page. It spoke about focusing on the shot rather than about winning or losing, birdie or bogey. It waxed about playing golf while foregoing any thought of the future. Further, it went on to describe the most pervasive element of poor performance, attaching too much importance to the outcome of a shot or hole, rather than properly focusing oneself on the only element over which a golfer has control, the shot process itself. Nothing else really mattered outside the simple moment of the golf swing at hand. Nothing else mattered.

Giving the book's premise immediate consideration, Nick thought back on the day's events. It didn't take long to realize that visions of woe and fear of falling further behind were what he thought about most often when standing over the ball. *Got to get a birdie: got to make up one, two, three shots* were his dominant thoughts that day. Whether it was losing that afternoon or the dread of losing at Troon North in less than six hours, he realized that the negative outcomes and dire visions of the bet nearing its end had in fact ruled and controlled most every pre-shot consideration.

That morning found Easy engaged in an unusual and mighty struggle to get Nick out of bed. No matter what Easy's pleading—a fire, ten minutes until their tee time, Kendra on the phone—every bogus declaration and less than friendly nudge was greeted with the same request for "ten more minutes of sleep." At first, Easy found the irony of the spikes being on the other foot mildly amusing, as it was normally Nick pushing Easy toward the shower twenty minutes behind schedule.

With their actual tee time less than fifty minutes away, Easy quickly found he was forced to drastic measures and was soon at the bathroom sink soaking a white bath towel in ice-cold water. With his final warning ignored, Easy hung the icy towel over Nick's head and gave it a rigorous wring, drenching the pillow, bed, and one side of Nick's face. Not quite satisfied, Easy ripped the covers from the bed and snapped the frigid towel several times at Nick's mid-section, near his boxers.

"Okay, okay, okay!" Nick shouted, his bed now soggy and uninhabitable. "I'm up, okay," Nick groaned as he lumbered from the bed toward the shower.

"Hurry your ass up. You've got five minutes," Easy shouted.

Their pursuit of each state's best course had them scheduled for Troon North Golf Course in the Phoenix suburb of Scottsdale—more specifically, Troon's Monument Course. One golf magazine had ranked the Monument course among the Top 10 open to public play and among the top 50 of any courses in the country.

Built over rolling, rocky terrain, the lush green, carpet-like fairways drew a dramatic, almost out-of-place contrast to the rugged, rusty desert. Rocks and cacti were so large and abundant they seemed nearly fake, as if strategically planted to enhance the experience. The course was also pricey, with its $240 green fees ranking it third behind Pebble Beach and Pinehurst as the most expensive course they would play. Or, as Easy had calculated, almost three and a half cents per each of its 6,636 yards, a substantial increase from the one-third of a cent per stroke paid just a day earlier.

With the possibility of their cross-country sojourn ending this day in the desert, Easy stepped forward with an unusual gesture, He offered Nick a handshake as they stood on the first tee, cleared by the starter to "hit away."

Then, quite sincerely, Easy leaned toward Nick and said, "No matter who wins, I wouldn't trade the last three years for anything in the world."

Nick, while touched by the sentiment, was keenly aware that winning two in a row was not out of the question. He'd done it many times before.

"I appreciate that Will, but it's only over if you win. So let's save the speeches until we're done, okay?"

Nick and Easy watched in earnest as Nick threw a tee into the air.

"Throw it up again," Easy suggested, unsatisfied that it had landed pointing decisively toward either man.

"What? Afraid to go first?" Nick asked sarcastically.

"No, I was giving you another chance."

"I don't want another chance. Go ahead and hit," Nick insisted.

"Then close your eyes, 'cause this might hurt a little," Easy deadpanned, a confident bounce in his step.

"Just hit the damn ball!"

Easy, without benefit of a practice swing, teed his ball into the ground, stared down his target for a moment, setup, and launched a dart straight down the center of the lavish, green opening fairway.

"Nice shot, Will!" Nick offered, while taking several slow practice swings.

As Nick stood behind his ball and prepared to hit, he stared off in the distance at nothing. Approaching his ball, Nick forced all thoughts of winning or losing from his mind and instead recited three specific thoughts repeatedly in his mind: *This is the only shot that matters, give it your best swing, and accept the outcome.*

Unbeknownst to Easy, Nick had been up well past six o'clock that morning reading Dr. Bob's book. In his all-consuming desperation, he'd decided to try a technique suggested in the book to clear his mind of all negative and consequence-related thoughts. Regardless of the situation, he would repeat his new mantra religiously throughout the day. No matter what happened or why, he would not fret over bad shots or unfortunate bounces. He would not worry about his score, or allow thoughts of their bet to enter his mind. Knowing that dark clouds and bad thoughts would inevitability attempt to storm his brain, Nick swore to himself that whenever they appeared he would simply and immediately recite his silent new chant and force them away.

Whether directly influenced by Dr. Bob or simply the result of a nice swing, Nick's first shot of the day sailed long and straight, passing Easy's ball on the fly.

A "Linda Ronstadt," he would tell Easy as they returned to their cart.

Through five holes, Easy was but two over par with Nick earning a slight lead at one under. A birdie on the par-five, 544-yard third hole sandwiched between a pair of pars, and with his mantra echoing in his head, Nick was now doing his own version of the Freddie Couples walk.

This is the only shot that matters, give it your best swing, and accept the outcome.

Closing out the first nine with a stop at the snack bar, Nick sat one over par, leading 37-40. Easy was impressed, but undaunted.

"Nice front! Think you can keep it going?" he taunted.

"I don't know, we'll just have to see," Nick replied.

Another birdie on the 170-yard, par-three thirteenth hole had Nick at even par for the round and five shots ahead.

"Damn Nick, you've got a career round going!" Easy asserted, hoping to plant a few seeds of anxiety and doubt in Nick's head.

"We'll see what happens," was Nick's matter-of-fact reply.

This is the only shot that matters, give it your best swing and accept the outcome, Nick silently chanted, trying desperately to block out Easy's compliment and thoughts of tomorrow's round in Houston.

By the time they arrived at the eighteenth tee, only a catastrophic meltdown stood between Nick and victory as he sat two over par sporting a comfortable five-shot lead. Both had played fabulous golf, considering they had never before seen the course and the stakes between them were so high.

As Nick studied his target line on the final tee, now, more than any other moment during the round, he experienced trouble staying focused. He must have murmured his new mantra a thousand times during the past four hours, but now he could almost taste victory, and thoughts of Houston overwhelmed his mantra's ability to drive them away. For his final swing, he abandoned all thoughts but one: *Accept the outcome; accept the outcome; accept the outcome.*

Nick closed with par and a personal best of 74 to Easy's 78. He was only one state behind with two to play, although the "new" Nick wouldn't allow himself to consider this proposition for more than a few fleeting moments.

Chapter 23

For state forty-nine, Charlie was their unlikely hero. An old army buddy of his, a top-ranking executive at one of Houston's largest oil and gas companies, was a member of River Oaks, one of Texas's most revered and prestigious country clubs. Until now, Charlie had not directly injected himself into their wager, but with River Oaks, he intended to leave a lasting footprint.

Much to their astonishment, Nick and Easy discovered shortly after meeting their host for the day, Jack Butler (guest play required a member be present), that Charlie had pre-paid for everything, including caddies, tips, and all drinks.

As they weaved through the ritzy neighborhood surrounding the grounds, past the twisted trunks of hundred year-old oak trees and up the circular drive approaching the regal facility, both stared wide-eyed from the window of the car. Houston's premier playground for the wealthy felt almost foreign to their middle-class, municipally trained sensibilities. As they breezed past several elegant dining rooms and a maze of mysterious offices and corridors and entered the men's locker room, featuring twenty-foot ceilings, cozy round tables, and complete bar service, Nick wondered aloud what it would be like to be rich. He couldn't imagine having access to such a place on a daily basis. "I could just stay in here all day," he told Easy with boyish awe.

The course itself was an extraordinary, classically designed Donald Ross layout measuring 6,865 yards from the tips. The greens were signature Ross: scheming, rolling, and fast. The fairways were framed with huge oak, magnolia, and dogwood trees accented with numerous beds of azaleas and other colorful flora. And unlike most modern sausage-link country club developments, no homes cluttered the course, although many magnificent mansions sat tucked among the trees along the course's boundaries.

After meeting their caddies on the first tee, Jack Butler paced impatiently, constantly glancing around for the arrival of the final guest invited to complete their foursome. Not more than a minute or so of small talk about the drizzle beginning to fall passed before a sturdy black fellow sporting a brown wicker hat and fat cigar strode up to the tee box and handed his large, white leather golf bag to a waiting caddie.

"Gentlemen, I'd like you to meet a good friend of mine. This is Walter Morgan," Jack announced.

Holy Christ, Nick thought to himself as the name sunk in.

Easy, having immediately made the connection, was already shaking hands with Mr. Morgan, a.k.a., The Sarge. Nick quickly did the same as he and Easy exchanged a knowing look, each appreciating the irony and privilege of playing with an actual touring professional, and almost as importantly, with such a prominent link to Charlie's ten-toed golfing past.

"Jack tells me you two have a small wager going," The Sarge said, managing the fat cigar jutting from his mouth as if he'd never spoken without one. "Where do we stand?" he asked, in a deep, cheerful tone.

"I'm one state up with two left," Easy replied, assuming the background necessary to understand their wager had already been covered in sufficient detail.

"That's some bet, boys. I've heard of some doozies in my day, but nothing quite like this. Let's rip it up and see how this turns out," Walter suggested.

Nick pulled a tee from his pocket and threw it into the air. "I hope you don't mind," he said to Mr. Morgan and their host, "but we always start this way."

"You boys do what you got to do. I'm just here to visit Jack, play some golf, and enjoy the festivities."

The tee fell pointing toward Easy. "Here we go, Nick. Play well."

"Yeah, good luck."

After a long, deep breath, Easy slid in behind his ball, eyed his target, and knocked a solid, lazy fade 250 yards down the fairway. The Sarge offered an approving nod in his direction.

"Magnus shot, Will," Nick said, while pulling a new ball from his pocket. *This is the only shot that matters, give it your best swing, and accept the outcome.*

As his newfound Rotella-inspired confidence echoed between his ears, Nick blasted a heroic draw nearly 290 yards down the left-center of the fairway. Both Jack Butler and The Sarge offered a polite clap as Nick held back a grin. After Jack and Walter launched equally impressive drives, the foursome ambled alongside one another down the first fairway, with four caddies not far behind.

"So how's that cranky old bastard Charlie doin'?" Walter asked.

"You know Charlie," Nick replied.

"Oh yeah, I know Charlie damn well," Walter added with a hearty laugh. "He's some piece of work! Remind me to tell you all when we finish about the time Charlie and me had a run in with the Hell's Angels in a bar outside Fort Ord. I thought Charlie was gonna get us both killed."

"Why doesn't that surprise me?" Easy laughed.

"And have you ever seen that fool eat eggs?" added The Sarge, with a puzzled shake of his head.

Grey clouds and light rain shadowed the group as they approached the sixth tee, a 183-yard par-three that, according to their caddies, played a club longer than it looked. Both Nick and Easy stood three over par after five holes, having arrived at that number through different means—Nick with a double-bogey, bogey, and three pars, and Easy by collecting a full house: three bogeys over a pair of pars.

Yet Easy couldn't help but notice how carefree and composed the normally emotional Nick had carried himself these past two days. As they waited for the green to clear in front of them, Easy walked over and positioned himself directly to Nick's right.

"I've never seen you play twenty-five holes of golf this well. You're starting to get me a little rattled," Easy joked half-seriously.

"It's a little something Dr. Bob and I worked out the other night," Nick offered, warily.

"Dr. Bob? You mean Dr. Bob Rotella from my book?"

"Yup, but I can't talk about it. It's top secret," Nick mused, twirling his five-iron.

"I'll be damned, do we have a convert?" Easy quipped. "Never thought I'd see the day."

This is the only shot that matters, give it your best swing, and accept the outcome. Nick chanted over and over again, forcing the entire exchange with Easy to the back of his mind.

As they made the turn after nine holes, Easy took advantage of a fresh dry towel, while Nick waited at the concession counter for their order. The young girl behind the window slid two hotdogs and four beers toward Nick. Rain continued to fall, steady if not slightly harder than at any time so far that day.

"Hey, Easy, got ten bucks for a tip?" Nick called out.

"Remember that twenty thousand we talked about? I'd like to change mine to twenty-one thousand. You're the only guy I know who travels the entire country with twenty bucks in his pocket," Easy proclaimed with mild and mock disgust as he reached for the wallet in his back pocket.

"Ever wondered why I never carry much cash?" Nick asked.

"'Cause you're a dip-shit?"

"No, because you, my friend, are always late. Let me put it in terms you'll appreciate. Consider it a literal late fee. Payback is a bitch."

"Are you saying you've avoided ATM's to annoy me for annoying you?" Easy asked as he withheld the twenty-dollar bill he'd intended to give Nick.

"Brilliant, huh?"

"Nick, I'm impressed," Easy admitted, grabbing one of the hotdogs and two of the beers from Nick's hands.

After nine holes, Easy was only one stroke ahead, 40-41, as they made their way to the tenth tee, a fair par-five of 522 yards. Jack and The Sarge, having already played their tee shots, were waiting off to the side when Nick and Easy arrived. As they gnawed their lunch, Nick and Easy commented that both gentlemen had been almost too polite and respectful thus far in their effort to stay clear of the gypsy twosome and their wager. Nick and Easy quickly added their balls to the others resting in the fairway and proceeded to make par.

Other than a few tense four and five foot putts, until now, neither had found much trouble on the back nine, and both had played solidly enough to keep the match close. As they arrived at the seventeenth hole, a relatively short, 377-yard par-four, Easy felt relieved that the score was in his favor.

Indeed, Easy needed all the help he could get, as he'd pushed his drive to the right and faced a tricky shot under several trees to a well-bunkered green. Trying to keep his ball low, still eat some yardage, yet leave it short of the greenside bunker, Easy punched a firm three-iron that under normal conditions would have been a perfectly played shot. But with the steady rain, the ball came out ultra-hot, skipped atop the wet grass, and rolled to the sand trap. Stopping just short of a steep lip protecting the edge of the bunker, Easy faced a troublesome shot. With the pin cut in the front portion of the green no less than eight steps from where Easy's ball sat against the bunker's edge, just getting the ball out and safely on the green would be an accomplishment: getting it close would require a minor miracle.

Easy surveyed his situation with more than mild despair as Nick sent his own ball flying to the green. It settled some twenty-five feet left of the flag.

Hard as he tried, a miracle was not in the offing. Easy blasted his sand wedge against the leading lip of the bunker and then watched in disbelief as his Titleist ricocheted straight backward, coming to rest a club length from where it had started. Without wasting a thought, Easy again stepped behind the ball and quickly smacked his sand wedge a second time. Although a much less difficult shot, his second effort easily cleared the sand but flew completely over the green. Nick stared at the ground without expression as Easy's fourth shot settled on the green, leaving him with a longish, bending ten-foot putt for bogey. If Nick and Easy both two-putted, it would mean a two shot swing and Nick would take the lead by one going to eighteen.

Nick calmly lagged his first putt within inches and tapped in for a par. Studying his bogey putt as if going for the Guinness record for slow play, Easy finally felt confident with his line. He quickly set up and sent his ball rolling toward the hole. Nick watched from under his umbrella as the ten-footer curled toward the hole while slowing slightly from the rain. As the ball hit the back of the hole, both thought it would fall in. Easy's putt instead hopped straight into the air, then landed on the ground a mere inch behind the cup. Easy glanced at Nick, who threw back a "hell of a nice putt" expression. Frustrated, tired, and wet, Easy pinched the bridge of his nose and squinted into his fingers.

As they walked the short distance to the eighteenth tee box, damp from head to toe, all four players were silent. With so much on the line, Nick decided it was a good idea to confirm the score.

"I've got me one up, is that what you've got?"

"Yup," came Easy's reply.

Measuring 428 yards, the closing hole at River Oaks Country Club was by all standards a classic finishing hole. It was long, guarded, and a challenge demanding two consecutive well-played shots.

As they stood on opposite sides of the tee box, Nick silently chanted as Easy confirmed yardage with his caddie. Nick had honors. After a deep breath, while not allowing himself too much time to think, Nick put a solid move on the ball that had it flying high, and fading fast. As he leaned sideways and to the right, jockeying to follow its flight, Nick briefly lost sight of the ball behind a giant tree only to see it reappear, just as quickly, near the ground with a big kick left. With yet a second huge bounce, Nick's ball settled near the right edge of the fairway, prompting a huge sigh.

Easy produced no such drama as he deftly drew his ball down the left-center of the fairway well past Nick's shot. He rewarded himself with a subtle clinch of the fist. If Easy was thinking about being one stroke down or his double-bogey the hole before, he didn't show it.

First to play from just under 185 yards, Nick picked a four-iron, believing it to be better long than short and thinking clearly enough to consider that the heavy air and a lack of roll would call for a little extra club. As he approached his ball sitting nicely in the well-groomed rough, no less than ten different thoughts and emotions began competing for his attention.

Determined to set aside thoughts of Alaska, Easy's upcoming shot, the greenside bunker, hitting it thin, clubbing it fat, and several other typically dire thoughts, Nick took an extra second to close his eyes and refocus. In a final effort to drown out his inner demons, Nick muttered aloud the new mantra that had served him so well those past 36 holes. "This is the only shot that matters, give it your best swing, and accept the outcome."

Without further delay, Nick marched behind his ball, glanced once more at his target, and launched a crisp, towering shot toward the green. Although it faded toward the end, he was nonetheless relieved to see it land safely on the green, twenty-feet, he thought, from the cup. Par was all but in the bag.

After walking nearly halfway to the green to survey the pin position, Easy returned to his ball, took a light practice swing, and stared down the shot before him. With a steady, steely final glance, Easy laid his six-iron to the ball and stood frozen, tracking its flight and mentally projecting its trajectory.

Four heads were now pointing toward the sky and slowly working down, following the ball as it descended upon the green. It stopped no more than eight feet from the hole. Easy pumped his fist. "Magnus."

As they walked to the green, The Sarge whispered in Nick's ear. Nick began to sense that Mr. Morgan was probably more in his corner at this particular moment. It wasn't that he didn't like Easy, but more that he and Nick had established a rapport reminiscing about Charlie, and because, as The Sarge mentioned, "You two came this far together; it's only right that it go down to the last hole."

Unless Easy converted what appeared to be a very makeable birdie, the outcome would not be decided until playing the final territory that would also become their last state.

Both Nick and Easy placed a coin on the green and tossed their balls to the caddies to be inspected, rubbed clean, and dried.

Jack Butler putted first, quickly picked up his ball, and moved to the side of the green. Although Nick should have played next, The Sarge, in a display of true professionalism, insisted that he putt-out and let the two boys have the run of the green without distraction.

With only two balls remaining, Nick surveyed his putt from every angle, rain dripping from his blue and white umbrella as he paced about. Easy was also busy double-checking his line. Finally, Nick handed the umbrella to his caddie and deliberately made his way behind the ball. Feeling his heart beating through his chest, he took three final, nervous peeks at the hole and struck the ball. Water spun from the top as his ball rolled toward the hole, fueling a mild rush of adrenaline in Nick as it closed in on the cup. As suddenly as it had started, the rush stopped, and so had his ball, a quarter turn from the hole.

"Damn."

"Nice putt," Easy offered blandly, as he moved behind his ball for one final look. Nick was still staring at the hole and his ball in disbelief. "I thought I had it," he said to no one in particular as he tapped in and stepped away.

Easy gingerly bent over and placed his ball in front of his dime, stuffed the coin in his right pocket, and intently examined his line. Moving behind the ball, he stared sternly toward the cup. If he made it, they would tie the round, ending their three-year cross-country tournament. Miss and they would head to Alaska, tied, for one last round.

With a lingering final look, he slowly drew back his putter, delicately sending the ball toward the hole. Frozen, they both stared, each experiencing two completely different sets of emotion as the ball begin its brief, eight-foot trek toward decision. In a journey lasting no more than three seconds, the match would be decided. Losing speed as the ball closed in on the cup and with only enough momentum for perhaps another half turn, Easy's ball curled and died to the right, stopping precariously near the edge.

Nick let out a yell, "North, to Alaska!"

With a finger pointed to the northern sky (actually, as Jack jokingly pointed out later over drinks, he'd pointed south) Nick approached Easy and echoed Walter Morgan's earlier comment. "I guess it's only fitting that we go down to the last state."

Following a heavy sigh, Easy admitted during their handshake, "I've never been so nervous over a putt in my life."

Easy retrieved his ball and joined The Sarge, Jack Butler, and Nick in a brief informal handshake in the center of the green.

In the end, exact scores of that day were unimportant to Nick and Easy, other than that The Sarge easily shot the low round of the day.

"Drinks are on me," Jack declared as they exited the green toward the clubhouse and to the men's locker room, where cushy chairs, full bar service, and colorful stories of Charlie's past awaited them.

Chapter 24

▼

Following nearly a three-year suspension of routine summer activities, life had slowly begun returning to near normal back in sweltering St. Louis—normal, but for the fact that one last state and a conclusion to the ultimate bet was less than a week away.

Nick had returned to work, focused on a new sales effort with Jack Butler's energy company thanks to the relationship they had forged at River Oaks, and Easy had started a new school year and was now neck-deep in middle-school melodrama with his students. Having law school out of the picture seemed to further amplify his already easygoing demeanor.

With the four-day Alaskan trip and the culmination of their three-year adventure scheduled for later that week, future plans and discussions, once dominated almost exclusively by their wager, had now turned to more mundane domestic interests.

No better example would illustrate their pending lifestyle transition than Cassie sitting at the kitchen table, feet propped up on a neighboring chair, watching Easy wash dishes as she methodically dipped her tea bag in a steaming cup of water.

"I know a name we haven't thought of yet," Easy began.

"I'm not naming my son after a town or a president. No Austin, no Camden, and no Grant or Clinton. And anything even remotely related to 'The Simpsons' is out of the question."

"How about Freean?" Easy asked.

"Freean Easley. Have you been smoking crack?" she asked, adding, "What do you think about Quentin?"

"It's a prison name."

"I'm going to bed," Cassie announced as she grabbed her teacup.

"Be there in a minute," Easy called out while stacking plates in the kitchen cabinet.

At Nick's apartment, Kendra, now an official co-habitant having moved most of her belongings to Nick's while they were in Texas, was lying in bed having just made love to a normal, regular guy. Her thoughts on normal and regular were a direct compliment considering Nick was not an artist or a musician, or worse yet, an unemployed artist or musician.

"You don't mind, do you?" Nick asked sheepishly, while kicking his feet from under the covers.

"I'd rather you didn't, but go ahead," Kendra answered.

Nick reached for the nightstand and opened the drawer. After fumbling for a second, he pulled a red straw from the drawer and promptly stuck it in his mouth. Old habits die hard.

"Am I wrong or did you get two that time?" Nick asked smugly, fishing for confirmation of his sexual prowess.

"Who said I got one?" Kendra said, as she rolled from her back to her side and threw an arm over Nick's chest.

"You didn't have one?" Nick asked, genuinely surprised. "That's not possible," he added, recalling a specific moment just minutes before.

"No," Kendra answered, following a long pause. "Three. I had three, but I was kind of embarrassed on the first one. Besides, the first one wasn't that good. But the other two were great," she added, immensely enjoying her mildly treacherous ability to recognize and push Nick's buttons.

"Kendra, there is no such thing as a bad orgasm. And if you don't believe me, let's try for four!" Nick suggested, as he threw his straw to the floor and his arms around Kendra planting his lips to her neck.

The two girls were first to dart from the minivan and run for the front door; Thomas and Donna Brown followed closely behind and, in a hectic exercise mastered over time, corralled the bouncing kids. Struggling to appear organized as Donna rapped on the front door, Thomas gathered his youngest daughter in one hand and held a thin manila folder in the other.

Easy, answered their knock with a genuine "welcome" and waved the gang inside.

Thomas released his daughter from his hand and watched as both girls sprinted from view. "Won't be long until you'll be chasing your little one round the house, Will," Thomas said with a sigh. "They grow up so fast. It's scary."

"I can't wait," Easy answered, as he guided his guests to the backyard, where a large computer-generated banner demanding notice hung above the patio. It proclaimed: "THE BEST DAMN GOLFER FOR ETERNITY GRAND FINALE BBQ."

As Charlie stood on the patio working over both a massive Margarita and Nick's diminishing attention as he explained his latest theory on gun control, Cassie and Kendra had formed an effective two-girl scramble intent on overstocking the picnic table with more salads, condiments, and goodies than could be consumed by a gathering twice the size.

Thomas, meanwhile, quickly turned a sincere and emerging concern toward the main course and was eagerly offering what he deemed considerable expertise with the BBQ to anyone he hoped had authority to anoint him grill master.

Easy immediately recognized and granted his wish, but with one caveat: "Thomas, you can have the grill under one condition. Can you throw a little spit on Charlie's cheeseburger?" Easy then added, "I'm just kidding of course. Dropping it on the patio would be fine."

Later, with the burgers and chicken digesting nicely, a fresh pitcher of margaritas on the table, and Thomas's girls insisting they be allowed to watch the latest Disney video, Thomas returned from the family room waving his manila folder. With an air of urgency and excitement, he called for everyone's attention.

"Okay, everybody. Now I know you got that leather book from Pinehurst for your trophy, but I've been tracking this thing from day one and I put together this log sheet with all the results. It's got every score from every course on it so no one can rewrite history some night when you're all drunk or something. I even put this color-coded map together. I guess you could frame it or something," he said, shrugging.

Donna shook her head in bewilderment. "I don't know what this man is going to do to keep himself entertained when this is over."

Thomas was forced to talk above the considerable laughter his wife's comment drew. "Actually, I've got two maps, one with Nick winning Alaska and one with Will winning Alaska."

"Thanks for the vote of confidence," Nick announced, with a wave of his Margarita glass toward Thomas.

"I've got something too. Just a second," Cassie remembered, as she slid from the picnic table and escaped through the back door.

"Here's what I want to know," Charlie barked, a slight, tequila sponsored slur emerging. "Kendra, Will's your brother, but you're humping Nick here, so my question is this: Who do you want to win this damn thing? And be honest."

"Yeah," Thomas asked.

"Be careful," Donna added.

"Yeah, Sis?"

"Yeah, babe, who?"

Cassie returned, holding a small box. "What'd I miss?" she asked.

Charlie eagerly accepted the opportunity to explain, having missed the opportunity to shock Cassie the first time around. "I was asking

Kendra who she was pulling for, since she has this sexual conflict of interest with Nick," he recounted.

"There could be consequences," Nick warned.

Kendra paused to sip from her Margarita. "Well, he is my brother, but I am in love with Nick, so the answer is, neither. I don't care who wins."

"That's bullshit!" Charlie shouted, with a controlled slam of his open hand on the table. "The whole fucking family's a bunch of marshmallows."

"Take it easy, Charlie," Nick said.

Charlie waved his hand. "Marshmallows, all of them."

"What do you have there, Babe? Is that for me?" Easy asked, like a child on Christmas morning upon noticing the package in Cassie's hand.

"As a matter of fact, it is!" she admitted, as she handed her husband a small box. Easy ripped into the box without regard for the wrapping paper.

"Can you fit a new swing in a box that small?" Nick asked.

"Only if it's yours!" Easy fired back.

"Do they act like little children or what?" Kendra quipped.

Easy separated the top from the box to reveal a shiny gold keychain with a small, round medal hanging from the end. He showed it to the group.

"There's a message on the back," Cassie said, smiling.

Easy read the inscription aloud. "It says, 'Think of Us, Whenever, Wherever, Forever. Love, Cassie and _____.'"

"I'm gonna add our son's name if we ever decide on one," Cassie said. She leaned over to give Easy a hug and a kiss, the latter of which, had it gone on much longer, would have left the guests either blushing or vomiting.

"How about Charles? That's a good name," Charlie chimed in to everyone's surprise. Nick grinned more than the others at the suggestion.

"Charlie," Easy began, "never in my life did I ever think there would come an occasion where I should quote something you've said, but little pink turtles are gonna fly through giant peanut butter clouds straight up my ass before I'll name my son Charlie."

Nick could no longer contain his laughter. Even Charlie, betrayed by the smile on his face, found the comment funny.

"Hey, I've got an idea!" Thomas shouted above the laughter. "Will, do you have a golf tee handy?"

"Yeah, inside."

"Go get it!"

Easy quickly left the patio for the kitchen and made his way toward one of the kitchen counter's many drawers. After shuffling through an assortment of old batteries, rubber bands, pens, lip balm, and the like, he finally found a golf tee. As he delivered the tee to Thomas' waiting hand, Easy smiled and said, "I think I see where this is going."

Thomas held the tee chest high and began explaining to the group what Easy had already figured out. "I want to know who is going to hit first!" Thomas declared.

"We need to find you a hobby!" his wife announced.

"I'm serious. Come on, let's see who is going to hit first," Thomas pleaded.

"Fine with me what do you think, Will?"

"Sure."

Thomas gathered everyone into a semicircle on the patio, with Nick and Easy directly across from one another. As Thomas threw the tee into the air, seven heads followed its path up and then down again until it hit the concrete patio floor. After three or four quick, random bounces, it came to rest pointing in Nick's direction. "There you go," Nick said, simply.

"Day after tomorrow, about three o'clock St. Louis time, we'll be hitting the first tee," Easy announced.

"Are you packed and ready to go?" Nick asked Easy.

"He started packing three days ago," Cassie answered.

"She's exaggerating!"

"Your bags may be ready, but is your game ready, counselor? That's the real question!" Charlie asked, his salty slur even more pronounced.

"Charlie, I've got good news and bad news. The good news is I've quit law school. I'm just a plain old history teacher now," Easy said proudly.

"Well, that should cut down on the cheating!" Charlie snapped back.

"Now Charlie, here's the bad news. Every good history teacher must first know his history and second, have a daily lesson. And the history is this: Nick never has beaten me and he never will. And on Tuesday, I intend to teach him a lesson. So sorry, Charlie! How 'bout that, Nick, you ready for school?"

Nick thought for a moment. "To be honest, I'm just happy to be here."

Chapter 25

Despite having packed the night before, Easy found himself running late. Waiting at what seemed like an especially long stoplight, he thought back to the barbeque and how it had been decided that Nick would hit first off the tee. He wondered what Alaska would feel like. He thought of leaving Cassie alone, and felt relieved that this would be his last trip for the foreseeable future. As he impatiently thumped his steering wheel waiting for the light to turn, another thought hit his brain. Immediately, he checked his pockets. After checking each pocket twice more, he began searching around the Jeep console.

When the light turned green, Easy motored through the intersection, made a quick U-turn, and furiously drove the four or five miles back to his house. He whipped into his driveway. Without bothering to close the Jeep's door, he bolted quickly into the house, darted through two doors, and made a beeline for the kitchen. Sitting on the countertop was the keychain Cassie had given him the night before. He stuffed it into his pocket and scurried back out the door.

Gate 32 at Lambert Airport was the designated rendezvous point, and Easy, truer to form than ever, was nearly forty minutes late. Nick could do nothing but pace about the gate area, scanning each approaching male from a distance. After several long minutes, he made his way to a bank of pay phones in view of their gate. Stuffing two quarters into a phone, he dialed and waited for an answer.

"Where in the hell are you?" Nick demanded.

Easy, his cell phone to his ear, avoided looking at the speedometer to see how egregiously he was breaking the law. "I'm ten minutes away. I forgot the keychain Cassie gave me and had to go back."

"Well, hurry up. Old ladies and children are starting to board," Nick shouted from the pay phone.

Easy recklessly weaved in and out among the rush-hour traffic crowding the interstate, finally relaxing a bit as the airport exit sign came into view.

Nick returned to the gate agent. The boarding area was near empty. "Is this flight leaving on time?"

"Yes sir, we expect an on-time departure."

"Great, you guys are never on time."

Following a quick glance at the dashboard clock, Easy aggressively zipped past several cars. He glanced again at the Jeep's clock, drawn to the flash of the minute changing as it offered a new number. Instantly he realized traffic was at a dead stop within the lane he'd just swerved into.

At first, he thought of swerving back, but it was too late to change or stop. With a frantic cat-quick move to avoid a line of cars stopped ahead, Easy jerked hard to the right and, without forethought or intention, crossed all lines defining the Interstate. Hitting the soft shoulder, his Jeep slid sideways. Another quick jerk of the wheel and he was airborne. Easy braced against the steering wheel as the Jeep sailed nose first down a steep hill along the edge of the service lane. Having lost total control, Easy closed his eyes as the Jeep slammed suddenly and violently into the concrete base of a light pole.

Nick walked quickly from the ticket counter and back to the phone. He fed it another quarter, dialed, and waited for an answer.

"Fuck!"

As it lay on its side, an eerie silence settled over Easy's mangled Jeep. A small beeping sound began to punctuate the silence in two-second intervals. Witnesses stopped their cars and ran to the aid of the unknown young driver inside. Easy, his face splattered with blood, sat twisted, half-slumped, and completely motionless. Sirens grew louder in the background as his phone echoed from the floor.

Nick stood puzzled, stared at Gate 32 boarding area, and listening to the ringing phone.

In a far corner of the emergency room lobby, Cassie sat motionless while she cradled her stomach. Nick was numb. Trying to comfort both Cassie and Kendra with a steady look and stern expression of hope as they collectively fought back tears, Nick thought of the keychain.

"He'll be all right, he's gonna be fine," Nick assured them.

Staring at everyone who walked by in surgical clothing, yet focused on nothing, Cassie began thinking out loud, talking to neither Kendra, or Nick directly. "He called me before he left. He had plenty of time, why was he in such a hurry?" Cassie then looked to Nick for answers and shook her head, dazed and in disbelief.

"Maybe it was someone else's fault, and he was trying to get out of the way or something," Nick lied, his gut churning.

From around the corner, a doctor in blue scrubs walked into the trauma lobby, recognized Cassie, and approached quickly. All tried in vain to read his expression.

When Cassie tried to stand, the doctor placed a firm hand on her shoulder and squatted down before her. With his hand now resting on her knee, he softly delivered the news they had waited nearly an hour to hear. "Cassie, this was an extremely bad accident. The trauma to the head Will experienced was quite severe. He's unable to breathe on his own, so we've put him on a respirator. I hate to tell you this, Cassie, but his brain is not registering any life signs. There's no measurable neurological activity at all. The respirator is the only thing keeping him going."

Cassie immediately wrapped one arm around her stomach and covered her face with her other hand, as his words sucked all air of hope instantly from her body. The doctor tried to steady her in the chair, but she slid to the hard tile floor moaning. She could not acknowledge the doctor's offer for help as he held her by the shoulder and, without letting go, took the seat next to her.

Kendra collapsed screaming in Nick's arms.

Nick struggled to breathe. "You've got to help him, you've got to do something," he pleaded.

"Other than pray, there's not much we can do. I'm so sorry, but we've done all we can. I have to step away for a few moments," the doctor continued, "but I'll be back as soon as I can and we can discuss your options, okay?"

Cassie tried to nod her head "yes" but could not move.

"I'm very sorry, Cassie."

As the doctor walked away, Nick and Kendra encircled Cassie, slumped on the floor. They could manage no more than to cling to one another.

Not far from the hospital sat a nine-hole golf course and driving range where Easy, after visiting Cassie when they had first started dating, would sneak off to practice in secrecy. He never wanted Nick to know his smooth, effortless swing wasn't "natural" and that he actually worked quite hard at his game. For some reason, he'd always believed it was an advantage to maintain this illusion.

Cassie and Nick walked somberly together along a paved path normally reserved for golf carts. As the sun began to set, they had made their way from the first hole to the fourth hole without speaking.

The course was strangely still, except for the presence of a patient father and his eager young son approaching them from behind. Despite gamely trying to manage a golf bag nearly his equal in size, the youngster was nonetheless losing his battle to keep pace with his father. Cassie and Nick stopped and stared at the twosome 200 yards away.

Nick spoke first. "This is fucked up. Why do you think I wanted Will to help me? 'Cause I'm a coward, Cassie. That's why."

"He was right for agreeing to help you. I didn't think so at the time, Nick, but both of you were right. And since I know you won't take this the wrong way, I'll tell you something. I don't even want to see him. I never thought I'd say it, but I don't want that vision of him lying there like that to ever enter my brain."

"But I don't think I can do it," Nick admitted between deep, heavy, sobbing breaths.

"Remember the night we met at the hospital, when Pops had his stroke?" Cassie asked.

"Yeah, sure."

"Well, he was reading Nietzsche that first night; that was my first impression of him—smart, well read, gorgeous," Cassie recalled warmly. "And here's what's ironic. Every great philosopher is known for one or two famous sayings. Nietzsche, the very same guy Will was reading that night, is known for having said, 'One should die proudly when it is no longer possible to live proudly.' Because of what happened to you, I know now that Will believed that. You have to do it, Nick, for both of us," Cassie said, taking his hand.

"Christ, I always hated it when he quoted that shit," Nick said as he wrapped his arms around Cassie, tears trailing down his weary face.

"Nick, he told me about the red binder. If anyone knows what he's feeling, it's you. Please help us."

Cassie, her warm blue eyes puffy and smeared with mascara, was trying with all her will to gather herself, to show resolve, and to offer strength, yet she could hardly stand without Kendra's help.

Nick fought for composure, fought to get the words echoing in his head to somehow reach his lips. "He won't be alone, Cassie. I'll be with him," Nick finally managed to mumble just as the doctor walked toward him, stopped, and firmly placed a hand on his shoulder.

"Whenever you're ready, Nick," the doctor said.

"Can...you give us a minute?" Nick asked between heavy sobs.

"Take as long as you like, Nick, I'll be right down the hall," he offered, as he turned away and walked steadily from view.

"Cassie, I know he would want us to do this. It's the right thing to do," Nick reassured her.

Cassie somehow managed a faint "I know" nod.

"I want you to know something else," Nick continued, after stopping to wipe his nose and clear the lump from his throat. "When I was sick, one day we were talking about happiness. I asked him what he thought it took to be happy and, well, he admitted that day that he'd never really found himself or found happiness until you came along. You gave him something no one else could have ever given him. He was blessed by you and always will be, and he knew that."

As Nick slowly moved away, he paused to place a tender kiss upon her tear-soaked cheek. Kendra and Cassie fell into each other's arms.

Nick slowly walked toward Easy's room, feeling a peculiar, upholding sense of duty piercing through his overwhelming sadness. The doctor noticed him approaching and met him at Easy's door. He again placed a comforting hand on Nick's shoulder.

"Are you sure you're okay with this?" the doctor asked.

Without looking up, Nick took a deep breath and tried without hope to compose himself. "I don't know. I really don't. But I want you to show me how to do it. If I can."

"Sure, Nick, I can do that."

Once in the room, the doctor pointed specifically at two of the many switches and dials on a panel above Easy's bed. Nick's nodding head dislodged a tear from the corner of his eye. As he pulled a chair over to the side of the bed and took Easy's hand, the doctor walked as far as the door before stopping. "Are you sure you're okay?"

Nick nodded.

"I'll be right outside if you need anything."

Nick nodded once more as the doctor quietly exited.

The combination of seeing Easy's lifeless body resting peacefully beneath a crisp white sheet and the task that lay ahead created an avalanche of memories that left Nick numb, beleaguered, nearly nauseous.

He couldn't help but think back to Arnie's and the day of his own cancer diagnosis, of the moment Easy found him in the bathroom, and of the request that day he had made of his friend. Nick sat silent and stiff, watching Easy, staring at his swollen, bandaged head, begging in his heart for the slightest movement. He sat for quite some time, unaware of time, as he reflected upon their life.

"Hey Junior," Nick asked, feeling empty deep within his gut, his pain soaring, "is this it? Is this that life-defining moment you were talking about?"

Nick stared toward the ceiling and paused in thought for several seconds, searching for air, searching his mind for the right words. "After all that philosophy shit you've been throwing around, you finally got one right."

Despite a deep breath, little air would fill his chest. His hands began to shake uncontrollably as he lost his will to fight back the flood of confusion overtaking his spirit and body.

"You were my real family, Will, my only true family. I love you…and I want you to know that I'll take care of Kendra, Cassie, and…your son."

It took Nick three quick gasps to begin breathing again, followed by another deep exhale. Slowly, he took Easy's hand and closed his own eyes, forcing them to empty down his face.

"Get us a good course picked out, okay?"

As he clinched Will's hand tighter and tighter, tears poured down his cheeks. Slowly, Nick's head fell forward, coming to rest against the white sheet covering his life-long friend. The bed sheets muffled his uncontrolled sobs.

Chapter 26

▼

The sea of black worn by those gathered at Easy's ceremony offered an odd, stark contrast, in Nick's mind, to the rich green grass of the cemetery and the thick full leaves that calmly flickered among its many giant old trees. Until now, Nick had always associated grass so green, so kept, and so alive with a golf course, with his friend, and of late, with the journey they had taken. Today, however, it represented only his unspeakable sadness.

Nick, his heart and eyes overflowing in unison, walked to the head of the flower-draped casket and knelt. In his hand was a leather folder. He stared for a moment at the front cover: Pinehurst—Since 1895.

Gently leaning forward and softly touching the casket, he removed a white tee from the pocket of his black blazer and slid it inside the leather Pinehurst binder. Slowly, he placed their coveted trophy on the exact spot where he had just placed his hand. With a slight lean forward toward the casket, Nick whispered softly, "Don't lose this. We've got one more round to play."

Kendra joined Nick's side and gently placed a flower and a kiss upon the casket. After several moments, Nick helped her to her feet and held her as tightly as both could manage.

With the minister providing assistance, Cassie kneeled alone at the foot of Easy's casket. Surprisingly composed, she leaned forward, and kissed the smooth, shiny dark wood.

"Don't worry, honey. We'll be okay, both of us," Cassie whispered between tears. "You will always live…will always live within my soul…and within the soul of our son." Cassie crossed her chest to close her final silent blessing and spoke to Will Edmund Easley, Jr., for the last time. "I love you."

Slowly she placed both hands upon the casket, leaned forward, and delivered one final, lingering kiss. The minister helped her to her feet, allowing the three to stand huddled together, clutching each other tightly as Easy's casket was delicately lowered to its final place of rest.

Chapter 27

▼

Burnt orange, dingy red, and heavy yellow leaves littered the narrow, tree-lined street where Nick and Will grew up. An overcast sky added a cover of gray to the aging, well-kept homes lining their old neighborhood.

As they drove along in relative silence, Kendra, her dark hair much shorter, turned toward the back seat and attempted to pacify their fidgeting four-year-old as Dad chimed in with some stern advice.

"Look son, you need to chill out!"

Nick, Jr., reminiscent of a day nearly thirty years before, began mocking his father. "I'm chilling out!" he said, his voice high and sassy.

"It's scary how much alike you two are," Kendra said, shaking her head. A slight grin hit the corners of Nick's mouth as he looked into the rear view mirror at their son. Without fail, such moments took Nick back in time, back to the countless trips he and Easy had made in the rear seat of Pops' car.

The routine over the years had become a comfortable, familiar one, as Nick and Kendra pulled into Cassie's driveway on a fall Sunday afternoon. After exiting the car, Nick opened the back door and leaned inside. Hardly a moment later, he emerged holding Nick, Jr., under the armpits. Within a second of being planted on the ground, young Nick darted toward the front door. Father and Kendra followed.

Cassie stood waiting with the front door open. She let out a loud yell toward the kitchen. "Will, little Nick's here!"

As Nick, Kendra, and Nick, Jr., entered the house, five-year old Will Easley III ran into the living room carrying a red plastic golf club and an oversized white plastic golf ball.

"Nickie, Do you want to play golf with me? I made a whole golf course in the backyard. Come look!"

The two boys ran from the room and out the back door in seconds, leaving Kendra, Cassie, and Nick shaking their heads and smiling. All three were having a similar, if not the exact same, sentimental thought.

Little Will and young Nick set about kicking up leaves and digging divots of grass as they took turns beating the big plastic golf ball toward several coffee cans planted in the yard. Nick stared from the patio. He was happy, and most importantly, healthy.

Alone in his family room later that night, Nick sat typing on his computer, nursing a cup of coffee. He slowly let go a deep breath and cleared a tear from the corner of his eye as he stopped to read what he'd typed out.

Page 217 read:

More than five years have passed since I last saw Easy. I think about him almost every day. I think about our bet and what it was really all about. I miss playing golf with him. I miss hearing his half-baked philosophies and his unique perspective on what people find important in life and why. I even miss his obscure quotes. But most of all, I miss his friendship. Maybe someday I'll find some hidden meaning in all of this that will help me understand everything that happened.

But most of all, I wonder what he would have said about our strange twist of fate and how our destinies were switched that year. I'm sure he would have had some clever, profound quote handy, something like, "Nick, we must act out our passions before we can feel them or begin to understand them." Or maybe he would have said we were just finding our feminine side.

Still, I have no doubt we'll finish this bet. Although I'd never have dreamed it would end in the most esoteric state of all, eternity. Yet that seems only fitting where my friend Easy is concerned.

The End